THE C
A POST-APOCALYPTIC EMP SURVIVAL SERIES

3: ONE IN THE HAND

Tom Abrahams

A PITON PRESS BOOK

One in the Hand

The Crusader Post-Apocalyptic EMP Survival Series
© 2022 by Tom Abrahams
All Rights Reserved

Cover Design by Hristo Kovatliev
Edited by Felicia A. Sullivan and Sabrina Jean
Proofread by Pauline Nolet
Interior design by Stef McDaid at WriteIntoPrint.com

FREE PREFERRED READERS CLUB: Sign up
for information on discounts, events and release dates:

eepurl.com/bWCRQ5

PITON PRESS

For Courtney, Sam, and Luke

To the ends of the Earth…

WORKS BY TOM ABRAHAMS

THE ALT APOCALYPSE SURVIVAL SERIES
ASH

LIT

TORRENT

AFFLICTION

POX

THE WATCHERS SERIES
THE BAR AT THE END OF THE WORLD

THE BAR AT THE EDGE OF THE SEA

THE BAR IN THE MIDDLE OF NOWHERE

THE SCOURGE SERIES
UNPREPARED

ADRIFT

GROUNDED

THE TRAVELER
POST APOCALYPTIC/DYSTOPIAN SERIES
HOME

CANYON

WALL

RISING

BATTLE

LEGACY

HERO

HARBOR

CHAPTER 1

D-DAY + 4 YEARS, 6 MONTHS, 19 DAYS
HOPKINSVILLE, KENTUCKY

Regina squinted against the light. It was dim, but after spending countless hours or days in a dark, windowless room, any light at all was harsh and blinding.

A thin figure stood in the doorway. The light hid his features, but she recognized him. He stepped over the threshold, and she reflexively flinched.

Violence was never as bad as the constant threat of it. Pain never did as much damage as its promise. Regina's understanding of this was acute. Nausea welled in her empty stomach, and she tasted the sting of bile in her throat.

Perhaps sensing her fear, he chuckled. "Stage fright's perfectly normal, chickadee. Happens to the best of them. Did you know Adele suffered from it? Woman with the voice of an angel, adored the world over, gets scared before stepping into the spotlight. Same for Andrea Bocelli. He's more my taste anyhow. But true enough, he suffers from what the experts refer to as performance anxiety."

He took another step, his dark frame filling the doorway and blocking most of the light. Regina's eyes adjusted, and his features clarified.

Leo. The man who had taken them hostage two weeks

1

earlier was back. Regina had prayed he was dead. But being a woman of wavering faith, she never gave much stock to her own prayers. Others seemed to have more luck.

But even Rebecca and Lucy, her post-apocalyptic traveling companions, failed to summon a deus ex machina or any sort of miracle as they wasted away in the dank, fetid room somewhere in Hopkinsville.

Leo crouched in front of her. He squatted like a baseball catcher and rested his elbows on his knees. He wrung his hands together. "Look up at me," he said.

She kept her gaze at his midsection, not wanting to give in to the demand. Regina didn't like demands.

He reached out; she flinched. He chuckled and gently lifted her chin until her eyes met his.

Blood streaked his face. It was brown and crusted, long dried in a quasi-Rorschach pattern that gave him a macabre mask around his nose and underneath one eye. It reminded her of the tattoo the former boxer Mike Tyson had sported after his glory days passed.

He grinned, and it stretched the stain like a funhouse mirror. How were his teeth so white?

"No need for the stage fright right now," he said. "You're not the one I want. I want her." He jutted his chin toward Lucy.

Regina said nothing, but a shudder ran through her weakened body.

Regina and Lucy weren't really friends. Not in the traditional sense. They were at best tolerant companions since Lucy's adopted family had tried to rob Regina, and Regina had helped kill all of them except for Lucy. Regardless, they were in this mess together. Regina ascribed to the ancient proverb *"The enemy of my enemy is my friend."* Apparently, Lucy agreed.

Regina bristled, and he rubbed his calloused thumb against her chin. If she weren't bound at the wrists and ankles, she would've mustered what little strength she had to attack him like a feral cat.

Leo studied her expression, and his eyes widened with recognition. Or was it surprise? He laughed and shook his head. "Oh no, pretty. I'm not interested in *that*. What do you take me for? An animal? Hardly. A woman's love must be earned, not taken. What kind of gentleman would I be if I allowed such thuggery in my kingdom?"

Still nursing an injured ankle and foot, Rebecca laughed. It was sharp and barbed with the young woman's trademark sarcasm. Even in the dark, Regina saw Rebecca roll her eyes and smirk.

"You like to hear yourself talk more than anyone I've ever met. If this is how it's going to be, just put a bullet in me now. I'd rather die than listen to you drone on like a self-satisfied narcissist."

Leo shrugged. "That could be arranged. But I'd rather see you heal up and die valiantly in the arena."

He snapped his fingers, and a young man came into the room. He was slender but muscular and carried with him a rag. He moved quickly and offered the rag to Leo, stealing a glance at Regina. Her gaze met his for a split second before he averted his eyes.

"Anything else, sir?" the young man asked.

Leo looked at him. He wiped blood from his cheeks. "Who are you?"

"Casca, sir. I'm one of the young soldiers who—"

"A grunt? A go-fer?"

"Yes, sir."

Leo snorted and tossed the rag at the young go-fer. "Why are you here?"

"I was with you at Churchill Downs, and I knew you—"

"Leave us."

Casca nodded in deference, but as he turned, he locked eyes with Regina again. It was unsettling. As if the grunt had something to say to her. She watched him leave and shifted her weight. Her left leg was almost numb, and her foot tingled.

"What's the arena?" she asked.

Leo smiled again. "Yes. Arena."

Regina narrowed her gaze, unsure of what he meant. None of the women spoke.

"Technically, it's not an arena," Leo elaborated. "It's the old high school football field. They called it the Stadium of Champions, which, as an old history professor and lover of the Roman Empire, I completely appreciate. Did you know the word champion comes from the Latin word *campionem*? Pretty appropriate for our cause, am I right? It's kismet. Meant to be and all that."

Regina was incredulous. "Wait. You're a history teacher?"

Leo stood and brushed himself off. "I was a history *professor.*"

Rebecca laughed again. "Right. And I'm God Almighty and the Light within."

Leo clasped his hands behind his back. He leaned forward on the toes of his boots and rocked. He clicked his tongue against the roof of his mouth. His expression tightened as if straining to think or see. Then it relaxed, and his gaze fell on Rebecca.

"This is awkward, then," he said. "Because I really was a history professor. Hopkinsville Community College. I taught sections of world civilizations one and two and every so often a history of Europe through the mid-seventeenth century. I always had a love for the Romans and their approach to entertainment."

"Are you talking about gladiators?" Regina asked.

Leo quirked a brow. "A student of history, too?"

"Everyone knows what a gladiator is."

"What's a gladiator?" Rebecca asked.

"A fighter," Regina said. "Someone who fights to the death for the entertainment of others."

Rebecca's expression flattened.

Leo unclasped his hands and pointed at Lucy. "We'll get you fed, washed up, let you choose your weapon. Then it's showtime."

Regina shook her head. "No. I'll do it."

Leo's eyes widened. He folded his arms across his chest. "Interesting. I have to admit, I did *not* see that coming."

"You don't have to do that," Lucy said. "I'll fight."

Regina shook her head more forcefully. "No. You're here because of me. I'll do it."

Lucy studied Regina, then faced Leo. "We're all going to fight, right? All three of us?"

Leo nodded. "That's the plan."

"Then I'd just as soon get it over with," Lucy said. "Thanks, Regina, but I'll do what he wants."

Regina's posture sank. She leaned back against the wall behind her. It wasn't worth the effort. If they all had to fight, her noble offer was useless.

Leo scanned the women. "So it's settled?"

Lucy nodded. "It's settled."

"Good. Because I want to watch you die. One at a time. Painfully, slowly, at the hands of my champions. I'll have somebody here in a few minutes to get you ready."

He spun on his boot heel and started to leave. Before he reached the door, Regina called out to him.

"Where is John Beck? What did you do to him?"

Without turning around, Leo answered, "John Beck is dead. Hanged for his crimes."

Regina's chest tightened. "I don't believe you. You're lying. He's alive, and you're—"

Leo turned back and marched with purpose toward them. His expression drew tight; anger swelled. He stopped inches from Regina and looked down on her with fiery eyes. He jabbed his finger at her face. "He is *dead*. I took him to the Sheriff. They put a hood over his head and carried him to the gallows. I saw it with my own eyes."

The tightness in her chest hurt. A knot grew in her throat. Still, disbelief remained. She couldn't admit the truth as Leo told it.

Regina motioned at his face. "What's with the blood, then?"

Leo frowned and touched his face. He looked at his fingers, rubbed his thumb across their tips. No blood was there.

"It's dried. On your face."

His expression still tight with anger, Leo said, "The Sheriff didn't want us hanging around. We protested. They got off potshots that killed two of my people."

"You ran?"

Leo's hands balled into fists, and he lowered them to his sides. His jaw flexed as he gnashed his teeth. His nostrils flared. "We were outnumbered. Better to retreat and fight again than die and never have the chance."

"So you don't know if Beck is dead, then?" Rebecca asked.

"He's dead."

"Did you see it?" Rebecca pressed. "Like, did you see them put the rope around his neck and drop him? Or however they do it?"

"He's dead."

The knot shrank in Regina's throat, and she swallowed past it. The ache in her chest subsided. Leo didn't know the truth. Not for certain. She grinned. "You don't know. You think he's dead, but you can't be sure. You didn't see it, so you're guessing."

Leo crouched and brought his face to within an inch of Regina's. Saliva spattered her cheeks and forehead as he yelled at her. "John Beck is dead! He's in the ground, and you'll join him! No guessing. That's what is happening."

Regina didn't blink. She absorbed the tirade. "You're the one who's dead. Beck will come for us. He *will* kill you. You'll wish you'd taken the chance to end him."

Leo's right eye twitched. He grunted, stood, turned. The door slammed behind him and left the women in total darkness. But unlike the days or weeks before he'd entered their dungeon, they had hope.

Regina smiled. All in all, this was a good day. They just had to survive the arena.

CHAPTER 2

D-DAY + 4 YEARS, 6 MONTHS, 19 DAYS
LOUISVILLE, KENTUCKY

John Beck finished the bottled water and wiped the excess from his chin with his sleeve. He handed the bottle to his daughter and thanked her.

"I'm ready," he said. "We need to go. It's been a week, right? They could be hurt. Or worse."

Millie stood at his bedside. She held the bottle in one hand and adjusted her Stetson with the other. It was a nervous habit. A tic. She ran her thumb along the underside of the brim and tugged the hat up and down, adjusting it to the same position at which it already lay on her head.

"Dad," she said, "I'm not sure you're ready. I understand your desperation, but you're no good to anybody if you're not one hundred percent. Remember, you nearly died. It's amazing you're alive, really."

Beck pulled the sheets back and swung his legs to the floor. He sat up, and the motion made his head swim. His vision blurred for an instant before he focused and the momentary fog cleared.

"Take it easy, Dad," Millie warned. "The last time you tried this without help, you fell and hit the back of your head."

Beck glanced at his daughter. Her concerned expression, the tightness around her mouth, gave him pause. He pushed ahead regardless. People counted on him. He had to prove he was ready.

He urged himself forward and, using his momentum, got to his feet. He wobbled and braced himself against the bed. Then he stood and took several unassisted steps across the room. He touched the wall on the opposite side of the space and crossed back again.

"See?" he said. "I'm good to go. We should load for bear and hit the road in the morning. Even at good speed, with the horses, it could take us four days to get to them. Maybe longer. Let's do this, Millie."

She planted her hands on her hips and sighed. It was a frustrated exhale; a parent worn from an insistent child who refuses to take no for an answer. "You haven't been eating your food, Dad. You'll never get your strength back if you don't. I know it's not the best food in the world, but it's energy."

It was not lost on Beck that since their reunion, it seemed their roles were reversed. She was the adult, the leader making the rules he, as the follower, had to abide.

Neither were quite comfortable with their new relationship. It showed on their faces, in their voices, in the way they interacted.

"We could go without you, Dad," said Millie. "I get that you're worried about them. You're impatient. That's fine. But I can't risk losing you again. You stay here, and I'll send a party to get them. I've got very skilled people who do as I ask. This isn't our first run-in with the militia. We're already dealing with them."

Beck's heart raced. He was tired from the short demonstration and took the opportunity to sit on the edge of the bed. He tried to play it off as though he were thinking, listening to her. "What does that mean?"

"Don't worry about it, Dad. Suffice it to say that Leo, the guy in charge down there, isn't content with his little kingdom, no matter what he says. He wants our territory too. He wants me dead, even though he thinks the Sheriff is a guy."

"He wants you dead?"

"Not me specifically. The Sheriff. He thinks if he can kill off the Sheriff, he can absorb our territory and resources. What he really wants is our big farm."

"Farm? Where—"

She raised her hand. "Dad, don't worry about it. There's plenty of time to talk about this. What I'm saying is that the militia is bad news. We know about them. We've kept them at bay for more than two years, and we have a plan to take them out."

"Take them out?"

"In a manner of speaking. It's complicated. All I'm saying is that we can handle getting your friends. You don't need to go. I can tell they're incredibly important to you. Otherwise, why would you be obsessing over them? We'll handle it."

"I'm not obsessing."

She sat next to him, put her hand on his knee. The sentiment, intended to persuade him of her idea, made him feel old. Millie was no longer the girl he'd chased across the country trying to rescue. She was an adult woman now, trying to save him. From himself. He also didn't like the *obsessive* comment. Was she upset with him? Was there a problem? Before he could ask her about it, she patted his knee.

"You give me as much information as you can about the three of them," she said. "I'm sure my people can find them. They can get them out and bring them back here. We've done this sort of thing before."

Beck looked at her. "What sort of thing?"

"Rescued people. Dad, you weren't the only *hero* out there doing good work. I mean, I'd like to think I didn't fall too far from the tree, you know?"

Beck's cheeks flushed. He felt the heat on his face, on his neck. He shook his head and looked away from Millie to his feet on the floor. Even his toes looked old. Then he wondered if she was being serious or making fun of him. Was there an edge to the way she said *hero*?

"I wasn't a hero. I never was a hero."

"Of course you are. You saved people, gave them hope. I read all about it in those books, and I heard the stories. So you must be a hero. Heck, you're a legend."

"The Loch Ness Monster is a legend, too," Beck said. "Doesn't make it real."

"So you didn't help people? You didn't protect the sheep from the wolves?"

"I did. But not like you think."

"How so?"

"It wasn't benevolent. I didn't do it to be…what's the word?" He paused. "Altruistic."

Beck snapped his fingers to accentuate his word choice. Gabe would be proud. Altruistic was straight out of the dictionary.

Millie repeated her question. "How so?"

"I only helped people to get closer to you," Beck said. "It was always a trade. Information for assistance. I wanted to find you, and I figured I'd have more luck getting a bead on you if I helped people along the way."

She shook her head. "I don't believe that. I mean, here you are, just having reconnected with me, and you're thinking of your friends. You want to save them. I think you wanted to help all good people. I remember before D-Day, that's what you call it, right? D-Day?"

"Yeah, D-Day."

"Well, I remember you talking with Mom. You told her how you wanted to do right by us. You wanted to make up for your mistakes and prove to us you were worthy of us. You told her you were going to volunteer at a soup kitchen. You were going to coach my soccer team."

Tears glazed his eyes. "You heard that?"

"Mom had you on speakerphone. She was cooking."

"I didn't mean for you to hear that. You shouldn't have heard that."

"Why? I wasn't stupid, Dad. I was well aware of the good and the bad. I actually hoped you would do those things. I believed you would. I wanted you and Mom back together as much as you did. I never wanted to move to Tuscaloosa."

"I know. You told me."

"All I'm saying is that I did learn good things from you. And regardless of what Mom used to say, I always wanted to be like you when I grew up. Before D-Day and after."

"Regardless, huh?"

"You helped those people because you felt guilty, Dad. You were trying to make up for the wrongs. Right? It wasn't just because of me."

"Okay," he said. "A little. Probably."

"How many people you figure you've helped since D-Day?"

Beck knuckled the tears from his eyes and cleared his throat. "Almost as many as I killed, I figure."

Millie chuckled. It was her mother's laugh, and it made Beck happy and sad in the same moment. Loving someone was never easy. Still, there was an unspoken tension between them. He sensed it, even if she wouldn't directly address it.

"I'm going to guess it's the other way around," Millie said. "Point is, you helped a lot of people who might not be alive if it weren't for you and your de—"

She stopped herself and pressed her mouth closed. Her eyes flitted to the floor, and she thumbed the brim of her hat.

"My what?" Beck prodded.

"Nothing."

"Say it, Millie."

She faced him and blinked. Her jaw flexed before she spoke. She inhaled. Exhaled. "Your demons."

He nodded and smiled. That seemed to ease the tension. "Yeah, my demons. They're always a part of the equation."

"Well, I'm part of the equation now. I'm another one of your demons. A heaven-sent demon, and I'm here to help. So let me do it, Dad. Let me send my people to save your friends."

Beck sighed. She was formidable. Strong-willed as ever, and smart as a whip. While he saw the little girl in her eyes, she was undoubtedly a grown woman.

He reached for her hat. He wanted to see her without it shading her face. She wrapped her fingers around his wrist.

"Don't, Dad."

"Don't what? I just want to see your face."

"Please."

Beck lowered his hand. "Okay."

Her expression hardened. She readjusted the hat and stood, planted her hands on her hips, and jutted her chin at him. All hints of his little girl evaporated with the movements. Her back straightened. Her stance broadened. She was the Sheriff now. Even Millie's voice took on a different tenor.

"Chow's about ready. I'll have someone bring you a plate. I'll stop by before shut-eye, and we can ferret out a strategy

13

for my team."

Beck started to protest, then apologize. He'd clearly ruined their moment. Despite being unsure about what he'd done, he wanted to make it right. She was already out the door before he could say anything.

Beck sat on the edge of his bed. Alone. People talked in low murmurs outside his door. The conversations were among several people but otherwise indecipherable. Boots clacked on the hard floors. The conversations softened until only silence surrounded him. He picked up his feet and pivoted back into the bed. Despite the days on a mattress, however thin, he still had not grown comfortable with something soft underneath him.

Standing on his own, he marched back and forth across the room. From one side to the other and back again. Beck counted the laps and tried to regulate his breathing even as sweat bloomed at his temples and the back of his neck.

While he had no clue as to what bothered his daughter such that she flipped a switch and left him alone in his room, Beck was sure of three things as he paced.

One, he would eat whatever they put in front of him for dinner. Two, he would pace back and forth until he couldn't stand; then he would do it more. Three, there was no way in hell he wasn't going to rescue his friends.

CHAPTER 3

The football stadium was in disrepair. The field, likely once green and lined with the markings of a gridiron, was dirt. Occasional, persistent weeds clustered in patches at what might have been the end zones. Only one of the goalposts stood. The other was on its side, snapped at the crossbar. The stadium seats were rusted, and the concrete steps crumbled in the stands.

Leo sat at the center of the boisterous crowd as would an emperor on a throne. Back straight, hands on thighs, he beamed with pride as the conscripted gladiators fought barehanded on the field.

Regina sat next to Leo. Her ankles were free but her hands bound behind her back. She was between him and Rebecca, who was identically restrained.

Both were afforded a small meal, grubs and greens, and an opportunity to wash themselves in a basin. Neither did much to make them feel whole, but it was better than nothing. So were the ill-fitting but relatively clean clothes they now wore.

On the field, the two men grappled. One was bigger than the other, but the smaller man was quick. Agile. He escaped the larger man's grip and fought valiantly.

Leo leaned his shoulder against Regina. "I truly enjoy these matches. They're brilliant for morale, too. I ask so much of these soldiers that giving them some joy is the least I can do as thanks."

Regina watched the small man escape the big one again. The larger fighter was relentless in his pursuit. He was packed with muscles that made his movement slow, somewhat ambling, but he was in perpetual motion.

She turned her attention to the crowd, especially the people sitting closest to them. While they appeared engrossed in the bloodbath below, there was something off. She sensed apprehension and unease among those in the audience. It seemed to her, the longer she sat amongst them, that they were play actors. It wasn't that they enjoyed these games, but rather pretended to enjoy them.

"How did a teacher become the leader of an army?" she asked. "How did you become king?"

Leo's attention stayed on the fighters as he shrugged. "Cult of personality, I guess? Some of the first soldiers were students of mine. Much younger. They were afraid when the power went out, didn't know what to do, where to go. After a week, they sought my counsel. I obliged."

"Obliged?"

"I took them in," he said. "Not permanently, mind you, but I gave them shelter on my farm outside town. I was self-sufficient there. So when they needed food or soap, I helped them out. They told two friends, and they told two friends. Before I knew it, I had two hundred young men, most with some military experience, spending time at my farm. We traded."

"Traded what?"

On the field, the smaller fighter tripped the larger one and climbed onto his back. He pulled his hair and yanked his ears.

16

The larger man struggled but reversed the leverage and freed himself from underneath the scrappier fighter.

"My skill set for their loyalty. See, knowledge of history can be as valuable as the ability to mill soap or craft candles. If one understands what has happened before, he or she can have an almost prophetic understanding of what will come next. You know we're not the first civilization to crumble in on itself."

"Like Rome?"

He stole a glance at Regina before returning his eyes to the field. He cheered the larger man. He had the smaller one in a headlock. The smaller man flailed and kicked. It was pointless. Unless the larger man released his grip, the smaller one would fall unconscious in seconds. The big man arched his back and let out a grunt. The small man's eyes fluttered. The color leaked from his face. His lips purpled.

"Not at all like Rome," said Leo. "Rome did not fail because the civilization crumbled in on itself. It failed because it spread itself too thin. At the dawn of the second century, under Trajan, it was some two million square miles. You might argue, 'Leo, that's half the size of what used to be the United States. It's not that big.' I would counter and say to you that back then, one in every five people on the planet lived within the confines of the Roman Empire."

Regina watched the little man's fight leak from his body. The larger man arched his back and tightened his hold. The sharp movement produced a crack, and the smaller fighter went limp.

The crowd roared. They stood and applauded the larger fighter, who unceremoniously dropped the dead man to the dirt and stood over his body. He flexed and cried out in celebration. Leo cheered and offered his own standing ovation.

Two men hustled to the field and dragged the body away. The winner took a victory lap around the running track that encircled the field. He kept his hands over his head and pumped his fists. The crowd's cheer became a chant. Although it was clear they were shouting the man's name as they clapped their hands in unison, Regina couldn't decipher what it was.

Leo sat and slapped his hands on his thighs. "That was a good one. I thought for a moment the little man might hold out longer. But Brutus never loses. He's patient. That's what it takes to win, to build an empire. Patience."

"His name is Brutus? Isn't that a little on the nose?"

"It's not his real name. But he's so huge, I thought it was either that or Kong. I like Brutus better."

"Brutus betrayed the king," Regina said.

Leo smiled and wagged a finger at Regina. "You know just enough history to be dangerous. I like that. I'll be sad when you die. But let's get back to your theory about Rome. I've learned from the Caesars' mistakes. They wanted to rule everything. I want to rule what's mine. No need for expansion. Why would I want to rule land I cannot see? It's pointless."

Leo laced his fingers together and held his hands in front of him. He shook them for effect.

"Proximity. Tight control. The ability to put maximum force into the smallest possible space. That's how I'll survive. That's how I'll avoid the mistakes of empires past. It's how I've grown my army without expanding my territory too much. Just a nibble here or there."

"Kings are never satisfied with what they have, are they?" Regina asked. "They always want more. Complacency breeds weakness, doesn't it?"

Leo shifted in his seat so he could better look at her. He

studied her for a long moment. Below them, on the field, the next fight was about to begin. It was two women. Both of them were about the same size, though one appeared much older than the other. The younger one appeared stronger but more anxious. She paced back and forth, stalking her opponent like an apex predator about to pounce.

"You're fascinating," Leo said to Regina. "You're clearly intelligent, but you're not as smart as you think you are. It's like you have a Wikipedia knowledge of everything. Do you remember that website, Wikipedia? It was the bane of a college professor's existence. Nothing of what was written in that open-source site was trustworthy. None of it. I would tell my students that while it might be a good jumping-off point, a place to find reliable sources, its text could not be taken at face value. Ever. They never listened. You seem like that type of student, Regina. Fascinating. Disappointing, but fascinating."

Both women on the field carried long sticks carved into something like spears. They stood twenty yards apart and balanced the spears' weight in their hands. Neither appeared entirely comfortable with the weapons.

"Why are you talking to him?" Rebecca whispered to Regina. "Why do you care what he has to say?"

Regina scanned her surroundings, soaking in every detail, from the ruts in the oval track to the holes in the fencing that encircled the property. She inhaled odors and listened to the chatter. This was real-time intelligence. Sitting in the stands gave her the opportunity to observe, ingest, calculate, and plan. She kept studying the people around her. No doubt they were playing a part. Leo's hold on his kingdom might not have been as secure as he would lead her to believe. There was an undercurrent of revolt. She sensed it. It was there, bubbling under the surface. One strong act of rebellion might unleash the fury of the oppressed.

Rebecca nudged her. Regina dipped her head and whispered, "I have a plan."

Leo scooted his hip against Regina's and leaned across her. "Whispering is a weapon of conspiracy."

The women exchanged a glance.

"It's also the tool of discretion," Regina said. "What are you afraid of, Leo? You have us bound and under your control."

Leo stared at her for a moment, then eyed the field and the fighters below. He stood and applauded. The sycophants around them took their cue and joined in the standing ovation.

Leo sat and pointed to the older woman. "I used to date her."

Regina must have looked dumbstruck, because Leo grinned and slapped his hand on her leg. Then he shook his head as he chortled.

"Before the power went out," he said. "Years ago. Her name is June. She was a librarian at the community college. We went out once or twice. No sparks, though. None of that lightning that has to happen for a relationship to work."

"So you're putting her in the arena to get rid of her? All these years later?"

June held the stick with both hands in front of her. She stood her ground as the other woman attacked. June winced and closed her eyes as she blocked a stabbing thrust.

"No," he said, "I'm not like that. I didn't even know she was among our champions today. I don't usually make those decisions. Only in special circumstances like yours would I put someone into the arena. I have lieutenants who pick the players."

"What did she do?"

June was on her heels, but she fended off a flurry of attacks. With a quick outward whip of the stick that found a gap between attempted blows, she hit her opponent on her hip and slowed her. June regained her footing and advanced. Confidence lifted her shoulders. It tightened her focus.

Leo kept his eyes on her. "Who? June?"

"Yes. June."

"She hid an interloper."

"What does that mean?"

"It means she gave refuge to an outsider. I don't...*we* don't...allow that. Not here. It breeds discontent."

"How so?"

Leo furrowed his brow and gestured to the field. "I'm trying to watch the champions. We'll have plenty of time for a philosophical discussion. For now, enjoy the festivities."

With a flourish of his hand, he again gestured to the combatants and then exhaled with exasperation. He shot Regina a glance before refocusing his attention on the fight.

June proved a worthy opponent for the stronger woman. While she lacked the brute strength, like the smaller man who'd fought before her, she was quick and agile. It was surprising, given her relative age.

It was nearly impossible to guess someone's true age more than four years after the power went out. Anyone who survived this long had aged exponentially. Only very young children looked their ages. Even then, it was hard to tell a preteen from a pre-D-Day twenty-something. There was something about the hard living, the perpetual stress, and the constant beat of the sun, wind, and rain that weathered all survivors.

Regina couldn't recall the last time she'd looked at herself in a mirror or any reflective surface. It had been a long time. But she could tell her face bore the wrinkles of time and worry. The backs of her hands and her forearms bore sunspots, discolorations from outdoor exposure. The strands of her hair were sometimes gray when they plucked loose in her fingers.

She could only imagine the wear on her organs. How she had abused them through dehydration or starvation. A day was like a week. A week, a month. A month, a year. The world spun faster without power, without law. It seemed to Regina it might accelerate to the point where it came loose from its axis altogether.

June took a swipe across her triceps. It drew blood, a wince, and renewed determination. She ducked and dodged before a fast lunge drove the tip of the whittled spear into her opponent's thigh. The woman wailed. She threw her head back, and like a banshee, the pitch of her cry grew into a shriek.

Goosebumps ran along Regina's arms and her spine. She couldn't look away, though, as June twisted the staff before yanking it from the wound. The movement sucked another howl from the younger woman as her body twisted, and she dropped to the dirt. Her hand-hewn spear lay out of reach.

June advanced. Dark red blood dripped from the spear. She raised it, drawing back to deliver another powerful stab.

The crowd gasped. Held its collective breath in anticipation of the final blow. But the younger woman was too quick.

She rolled to one side and reached her spear. She lifted it at a sharp angle as June bore down with unwavering determination and swept her leg. The movement tripped June, and she plunged down and onto the stick's whittled tip. She gasped, and her eyes bugged wide from the shock of the unexpected injury. She staggered, held up only by the stick itself, and her weapon buried itself deep into her opponent's side. Both women had skewered each other. Mutual winners and losers at the same time.

Only their ragged, futile gasps for air punctured the stunned silence of the arena. Then the stick supporting June's weight lost its purchase, and she fell forward. Regina watched her eyes flutter and the fishlike movement of her mouth slow.

Blood drained from their bodies and pooled underneath them. It leached across the dirt, a macabre encore to the intense violence of the main act.

Leo whispered aloud, "Oh my." Then his voice rose. "That's magnificent. That! Is! Magnificent!"

He shouted, "Am I right?!"

The shocked murmur around him rose into a crescendo of applause and hoots. Men and women whistled their approval at the quick reversal and unexpected ending of the fight.

Leo cupped his hands at either side of his mouth and hollered his approval. He arched his back, tilted back his head, and called like a wild hound. Others around him mimicked the lupine adoration until he stopped and motioned for the grounds crew to clear the field of its dead champions.

He clapped his hands together, puffed his cheeks, and dropped back into his seat with an astonished grin. His shoulder touched Regina's, and he nudged her.

"That was as wonderful a finish as I've seen. Neither woman saw that coming, am I right? It will be hard for your little friend to top that. Hard to top it."

Regina's body tensed. "Lucy's next?"

"She is. The grand finale. At least for today. I mean, it will be hard to beat that last one, no doubt. That's the fight everyone will be talking about for days. Weeks. Months, maybe. You just don't see something as spectacular as that, am I right?"

Regina tried to see the field from her seat. People stood up in front of her and obscured her view. She couldn't see clearly enough to spot Lucy or her opponent. Were they even on the field yet?

"Who is she fighting?" Rebecca asked.

Leo didn't answer. He withdrew what was likely once a white cloth from his pocket, now stained with dirt and blood in a kaleidoscope of browns. He swiped it across his sweaty forehead, dabbed it on the back of his neck.

Before he spoke, the answer marched into the arena. A large man with a classic prison physique. Large, broad shoulders supported a neck as thick as a rain barrel. They framed cartoonish arms, which boasted ropey triceps and bulbous, tattooed biceps. His torso narrowed to a tiny waist and legs better suited for a ballerina than a nightclub bouncer.

His head, angular and with a protruding jawline, appeared disproportionately small atop the neck. He wore what little remained of his hair tight against his scalp. It was either blond or white and appeared translucent in the bright sunlight, which beat down on the dirt arena.

Regina stood to get a better look at him. She was not alone. He was enormous by any measure and drew the collective awe of the audience. Leo chuckled. He didn't stand. Clearly, he had seen the beast before.

"He makes Brutus look small," said Leo. "Am I right?"

Regina was transfixed. The man carried long claw hammers in both hands. He swiped them in front of his body in some sort of practiced warm-up routine. After swinging them down, he twirled the long wooden handles in his hands and then shot his arms skyward, arcing the hammers in a looping maneuver that looked deadly even without a target.

"His name is Horace. He's a foreigner who was training with American troops when the power went out. He stayed,

---

trapped here by circumstance. Suffice it to say, he's not a fan of his predicament and enjoys taking out his frustration on whomever we put in front of him. He is the champion of all champions."

Rebecca shook her head. The color drained from her face, and she swallowed before asking a question whose answer she already knew. "You're having Lucy fight *him*?"

Leo nodded and shrugged. He crossed one leg over the other and pretended to pick lint from his pants. The nonchalance maddened Regina. She drove her shoulder into him and knocked him sideways. He fell into an unsuspecting audience member next to him, who appeared mortified, as if it were his fault the exalted leader had bumped him.

Leo apologized to his seatmate. He patted the frightened man on the shoulder and told him not to worry. Then he faced Regina. His jaw flexed with renewed vigor, and behind his eyes, the machinations of a madman ground and whirred.

Regina stiffened. Her muscles tensed as she braced for physical retaliation. Instead, Leo ran his tongue along his teeth and chuckled again.

"I admire your pluck," he said. "It's admirable. Really. I applaud you. I might've been disappointed if you sat there and did nothing. But I can promise you both reactions…" He paused for effect and lifted his hands palms up as if weighing objects in both. "They have the same result. So I suggest you moderate your blood pressure and relax. Really, Regina, relax. I'm not going to tolerate an outburst like that a second time. Okay?"

Regina stewed silently. She dug her fingernails into her palms, trying to direct all of her anger into her tightened fists.

"You know," Rebecca said, "this is so cliché. You're a meme."

On the field, the giant Horace continued his warm-up. He

bounced on his toes, light as a feather on those ballerina legs, and backhanded the claw hammers with such speed their cut through the humid air made whooshing sounds loud enough for Regina to hear them over the crowd.

Leo raised an eyebrow. "A meme? How so?"

"Everything you do is like something I might've read in a bad novel. You're like the bad guy in a cartoon. Or comic book or…"

"Graphic novel?" Leo asked. "You're saying I'm the antagonist in a graphic novel?"

"At best," Rebecca said. "I feel like I've read your story, listened to your self-indulgent soliloquies, smelled your funk, a thousand times."

"Those are big words for such a little girl."

Rebecca rolled her eyes. "*So* predictable. Did Malcom Gladwell write a book about being evil I don't know about?"

"Malcom Gladwell?"

"Someone had his book in my village. A mix of cultural observation and self-help. I read it a couple of times. It was called *Outliers*. You're like the opposite of everything in it, like a caricature. It's amazing to me any of these people listen to you. Cult of personality, my butt."

"I know of whom you speak," he said. "It just surprised me that you do too. Do you play chess?"

"What?"

"Chess. The game. Do you play it?"

"Not in a long time."

"But you know the rules?"

She shrugged. "Sure."

"Good to know. Now, as for the graphic novel comment, I am actually quite—"

A sudden rise in the chatter from the audience stopped Leo mid-sentence. On the field, Lucy appeared. She wore yoga pants and a tight-fitting tank top. It was a stark contrast to the baggy layers of clothing Lucy normally preferred. For the first time, Regina saw how womanly Lucy really was. Her impressive physique offered hope, however slim, that she might hold her own against the giant Horace.

The tight clothes revealed her muscular upper body and toned legs. She had the thighs of an equestrian and the narrow torso of a dancer. Her upper body was almost masculine in its muscular definition.

What Regina saw, however, was markedly different from those around her. They compared little Lucy to the monster on the other end of the field. Unlike the hammer-wielding Horace, Lucy carried no weapons.

"Why is she empty-handed?" Regina demanded. "Why didn't you give her anything to defend herself?"

Leo raised his hands in front of his chest. "Whoa. Blood pressure, Regina. Take it down a notch. We offered her any weapon she wanted. She declined."

"Declined?"

"She didn't want anything. Said she could handle it without any weapons."

"That's suicide," Rebecca said. "She's giving up without even trying."

Leo said something in response, but Regina couldn't hear him. The crowd grew too loud. They chanted Horace's name. It sounded like a Gregorian chant. Rhythmic. Haunting. Like something from an old horror movie intended to drive the narrative into a dark place.

They stood and blocked her view. Regina struggled to her feet and then managed to stand on her seat. She craned her neck and found an opening. Her heart raced as if she were in the fight. She bit the inside of her lip. Nausea swirled in her gut.

"C'mon, Lucy," she muttered. "C'mon, girl."

In that moment, Lucy was not an enemy. She was her friend. An ally. And Regina wanted her to live.

Before the fight had even begun, it was over. Regina and everyone else in the stands were stunned.

CHAPTER 4

The giant Horace did not wait. He rushed Lucy. The hammers swung, and his wide gait carried him to her at lightning speed. She stood still, her arms at her sides, facing him with her profile, her left foot in front of her right.

While the crowd seemed stunned by the instantaneous attack, almost caught off guard by Horace's impatience, Lucy was not. She bounced on her toes like a boxer. Instead of cowering or running away from Horace, she ran straight at the giant.

The distance between them evaporated in an instant as Horace twirled the hammers at his sides, lowered them, and then swung in an upward motion as he reached Lucy.

Instead of the hammers striking her, Lucy leaned back and dropped into a slide. Like a baseball player coming in to home plate, she dragged her left hand out to one side in the dirt. As she slid underneath the twin swings, her hand caught the giant's ankle.

Timed perfectly with his step, she used his momentum to lift his foot higher than he intended. The move tipped Horace off balance, and he tumbled forward. Taking elongated strides to steady himself, he instead dove into the dirt chest first. He lay there motionless, clouds of dirt obscuring the view. When it cleared, the crowd gasped again.

Lucy had ridden her slide to perfection and was on her feet. She whirled to face her opponent, tense and ready for the next pass. As the dust settled, Lucy lowered her guard. Her shoulders relaxed, and she loped forward tentatively toward the felled giant.

Horace had fallen face-first onto one of the hammers. Its claw was buried deep into his head. His right leg twitched, an involuntary reaction to the shocking intrusion into his nervous system.

The man's eye, the one visible from the stands, was wide open. His mouth was too, as if the giant had something to say about the incredible end of the battle and his life.

Regina didn't know how to react. Disgust? Joy? Relief?

The emotions manifested themselves in laughter. An unstopping cackle, she herself found surprising, echoed in the stands.

Others turned. Their twisted expressions judged her with sneers and frowns. She ignored them and laughed even louder. Tears clouded her vision. Her stomach tightened from the relentless howl.

Lucy must have heard her. She took steps toward the stands and flexed her biceps. A show of strength. Then she roared like a lion before she too began laughing.

A smile flashed at the corners of Rebecca's mouth before she caught the infectious laughter. She giggled, then chuckled, before devolving into guffaws so intense she doubled over and had trouble catching her breath.

Others in the crowd began to laugh. Unsure of how to react, it must have seemed the most comfortable response. It was in that moment, when those cheering for Lucy's death now joined her in laughter, that Regina understood how easily

Leo had put them under his spell.

In the absence of leadership, people sought a strong voice. No matter to whom that voice belonged, people would listen. They would obey. They were lemmings. Lambs to the slaughter. Any number of metaphors danced through Regina's head as she took deep breaths to recover from her laughing fit.

Only Leo was stone-faced. He dropped to his seat and stewed, his mind working behind his scheming eyes. Regina considered a taunt but thought better of it. The man still had her in chains. She was on his turf. These were his rules.

Lucy stalked back and forth on the field. She pumped her fists. Tears streamed down her cheeks. Each passing moment seemed to breathe more strength into her, more confidence. It didn't appear to matter that Horace's death was as much a function of luck as it was her deft skill.

She was alive. That was all that mattered. It shone on her face and in the way she moved. The crowd's laughter devolved into applause, and Lucy bathed in the adulation. She encouraged it, urging the crowd to stand. She applauded them in return with sweeping, exaggerated claps over her head.

Perhaps sensing the turning tide, Leo shook himself from his stupor and stood. He pushed his way through the crowds in front of him and descended the bleachers to the railing that separated the stands from the field. He climbed between the painted bars and hopped onto the field.

Like a wave, the applause slowed as people in the audience realized Leo was in front of them. He approached Horace and crouched beside his body. The crowd silenced. Only whispers wound their way through the stands as Leo put his hand on the dead man's back. He muttered something to the corpse and plucked a claw hammer from the ground beside it.

Leo motioned to a pair of armed guards standing watch at

the edge of the stands, and they approached Lucy, their twin Sig Sauer NGSW rifles leveled at her chest. He waited for them to have her in their sights before he sauntered toward her.

He twirled the hammer in one hand and shot a glance at the crowd before returning his focus to Lucy. His walk was confident and deliberate. It was the gait of a man in charge, who knew how the game was played because he set the rules. He could also change them as he saw fit.

The crowd sat, almost on cue, as he drew close to Lucy. However, Regina stood. Despite the protests of those behind her, she would not take her seat. Rebecca joined her, and they stood shoulder to shoulder. Regina's heart raced. A sense of dread swelled in her chest as Leo took short, deft practice swipes at the air.

Lucy tensed at his approach. She pulled back her shoulders and lifted her chin in silent defiance. Her arms hung at her sides, her hands balled into tight fists. Her knuckles blanched white, and her jaw was clenched.

"It is better to be lucky than good," Leo said. His voice echoed in the stillness of the humid air and reverberated off the large structure of the grandstand. "Am I right?"

Lucy shook her head. "It's better to be lucky *and* good."

Snickers filtered amongst those in the crowd. No outright laughter. But Leo appeared to hear it. He lifted his free hand and put a finger to his lips. The noise quieted on cue.

Regina could barely control her breathing. Her pulse thumped in her neck and at her temples. Beads of perspiration bloomed above her lip and on the back of her neck. She felt it roll down her back and dampen her armpits.

Leo twirled the hammer. He admired it as it sliced through the air. "This is a powerful weapon with a rich history. Do you know it?"

Lucy eyed the armed guards as if contemplating her options, but remained silent and unmoved.

"It first appeared three million years ago. Hammer stones. That's what they were then. Smooth stones used as blunt striking instruments."

He took another swing at the space in front of him, ran his finger along the long, curved claw that ran from its head and tapered into a sharp fork.

"It was only a little more than thirty-two thousand years ago that something more sophisticated found its way into the skilled hands of men in the Upper Paleolithic era. Then the Bronze Age made the next leap in hammer technology."

He swiped across his body. He grimaced as if he'd struck an imaginary foe. This movement was close enough to Lucy that she flinched. Leo smiled, and the crowd collectively held its breath.

It took all of Regina's restraint to keep from calling out. Rebecca must have sensed her anxiety. She reached out with her bound hands, took Regina's, and squeezed them. The two exchanged a worried glance.

"It was the 1500s when the hammer really became a thing of beauty. So many refinements of iron. Hammers took on a host of varietals as workers employed them in countless professions. Yet they remained a valuable weapon. At its heart, the hammer is as much a weapon as it is a tool, am I right?"

Leo motioned to another pair of guards. These did not carry weapons, but they advanced with purpose and took Lucy by her arms. They held her in place, restraining her with some difficulty while she struggled against them. They forced her to her knees. She could not fend them off.

Regina's stomach turned, and she felt light-headed. Her vision darkened at the edges. No matter what differences she'd had with Lucy, they were compatriots. She didn't want to see her hurt, let alone killed.

Leo stepped close to Lucy. He was within a foot when he raised the hammer and swung down with incredible force.

Regina closed her eyes. She couldn't watch. Rebecca gasped and squeezed her hand so tight it hurt. She expected the sound of cracking bone or the wild cry of someone hit with so much power.

There was nothing. No sound. Except for laughter. Regina opened her eyes.

Leo stood above Lucy. He leaned back with a hand on his belly as he laughed. It was a cackle, something inhuman that echoed alone.

The hammer was in his other hand. It hung at his side. His swing had missed Lucy intentionally. It was a move intended to frighten, to belittle, to torture.

When he stopped laughing, he wagged a finger at Lucy and then at the crowd in the stands. His eyes found Regina and focused on her.

"Now *that* is funny," he said. "That is worth a good belly laugh, am I right?"

Regina exhaled, only realizing in that moment she had held her breath for so long she was almost faint. She wobbled, but Rebecca kept her upright.

"You thought I would kill our champion?" Leo asked. "You thought after her skillful victory in the arena, I would end her life out of spite?"

The questions were rhetorical, though Leo answered them himself. Of course he did. He was in his element. A captive audience and a stage.

"Of course not. What kind of person would I be?"

He laughed again. That drew some chuckles from the gathered minions in the stands. Regina's breath caught in her chest as he stared her down.

"No," he said. "I'm not going to kill her. You are."

He raised the hammer, extended his arm, and pointed the weapon at Regina. The crowd followed his aim, and all eyes fell on her. Heat flushed her cheeks.

"Or she'll kill you," Leo said. "Either way, it will be epic."

Regina's mind swam with possibilities, but she couldn't wrap her mind around what he meant. Why would she kill Lucy? Why would Lucy kill her? Then, in the split second before Leo spoke the words, she understood.

"You are next in the arena, my pretty," he said to Regina. "You will fight my new champion. To the death. One way or another."

CHAPTER 5

D-DAY + 4 YEARS, 6 MONTHS, 20 DAYS
LOUISVILLE, KENTUCKY

"A storm is coming."

Beck shouldered the pack and adjusted the chest strap. He stood at the edge of the track inside the historic venue. He could almost taste the mint juleps and see the broad derby hats atop the heads of aging debutantes. It seemed a tradition from a different era, as far removed from him as the Roman Colosseum or medieval tournaments. So removed from his reality was that vision that Beck questioned whether it was ever real. Had three-year-old thoroughbreds really raced here on the first Saturday in May on their quest for the legendary Triple Crown?

This oval lacked grandeur. It was anything but welcoming. Beck licked his lips. He was thirsty. Always thirsty. That mint julep would hit the spot.

The dirt was dry and veined with evidence of drought. The bourbon and mint. He blinked and repeated himself.

"No doubt. Storm is on its way. Within a few hours, we'll be in it."

Millie was bent on one knee, double knotting the laces on her boots. She looked up at him and squinted against the sun that shone bright on her face. It gave her an angelic quality and reminded Beck how much of her young life he had missed for one reason or another.

"How do you know?" she asked.

"I feel it in my joints. My knees especially. Whenever the pressure drops, they ache."

"I thought that was an old wives' tale," she said. "Didn't think it was true."

"Do I look like a wife?"

Millie smirked. She finished the knots and got to her feet. Hands planted on hips, she scanned the horizon and faced Beck. "You look old."

He laughed. "You're funny."

"So I've been told."

"Where is everybody?"

Millie's brow furrowed as if she didn't understand the question. "What do you mean?"

"You told me you'd have a big team ready to go," Beck said. "I don't see a team."

Millie narrowed her eyes at him. She looked just like her mom. It made his heart melt. It frightened him, too.

"I also told you I was going without you," she said. "I said you're in no condition to be traveling."

"I don't understand," said Beck. "What does one have to do with the other?"

"We're not taking a big team. It's you and me and two of my closest friends."

"What? That's suicide. Leo has an army. He might call it a militia, but it's an army."

"Exactly."

Beck took a step closer to his daughter. She lifted her chin and adjusted her hat. Held her ground.

"Exactly what?" he asked.

"I know you're John Beck, legendary giant killer, but

taking an army to face an army starts a war. I don't want a war, Dad. I want to get in and get out. Stealthy. You know? Like I said, we have a long-term plan for the militia, and I cannot afford to screw it up with an all-out war. Light and fast. That's what this needs."

Beck started to argue, but he held his tongue. He nodded. "How many on this light and fast team. Just four?"

"Just four."

"Where are they?"

"They're coming."

Beck twisted toward the sun. "It's getting late. We really should go."

"It's still early, Dad. We have plenty of time. Tons of daylight. Remember, this is my mission. I'm in charge. You're going to have to get used to that."

Again with the tone. Beck's gut told him his daughter was keeping something from him. Now was probably not the best time to address it. She narrowed her eyes at him, studying his concerned expression but mistaking the reason for it.

"We have time, Dad. I know what I'm doing, okay?"

Beck let it go. "Okay. I'm just saying there's a storm coming. That's all."

Millie picked up the pack at her feet and slid her arms through the straps. She adjusted them and snapped the chest strap. She whistled as she readied herself for the trek.

"I don't remember you being a whistler," Beck said.

She shrugged. "I guess I wasn't. Something I picked up along the way. When there's no streaming music everywhere you go and you can't charge your earbuds, you've gotta improvise."

"I guess you do."

Beck studied her as she loaded her rifle. He wasn't sure of the brand, but it held a long magazine underneath the vented barrel. It was a mean-looking weapon.

From behind her, at the opposite end of the track, four people emerged. They walked side by side, each of them rolling bicycles.

Beck jutted his chin toward the foursome. "What's that?"

"That's the team. Well, half of them. The other two are being nice enough to bring us our transportation."

"Bicycles?"

"Mountain bikes. Very nice mountain bikes."

"You've got to be kidding me. We're riding bikes?"

"What's wrong with bikes?"

Beck frowned. "What's *not* wrong with bikes?"

A smirk edged at the corner of Millie's mouth. "You don't know how to ride a bike, do you?"

"Yes, I do. I taught you, remember?"

"Mom taught me. You were…away."

"I could have sworn I—"

She raised her hand to stop him. "It's no big deal. Don't worry about it. Point is, bikes are awesome. They're faster than walking and don't need food or water like a horse. It's unreal to me the numbers of people who totally forgot about bikes when the power went out. Everybody is all about horses or the train."

"Stay off the train," Beck warned. "It's better to walk on hands and knees than ride a train."

The four bike men of the apocalypse drew closer. They steered the bicycles carefully as if they were constructed of gold foil.

"I've ridden the train, Dad. It's not so bad if you keep your head down. I like bikes better, though. Great cardio."

Beck laughed at that, and it drew a smile from Millie. She gestured toward the bikes and the men escorting them.

"The two on the left are for us. The one on the end is the

largest of the four. It should be the most comfortable for you."

"It's pink."

Millie's smile broadened into a grin. "It matches your cheeks."

Beck self-consciously touched his face. The heavy week-old scruff, close to a beard, was rough on his fingertips. He hadn't realized he was blushing.

The young man wheeling the pink bike rolled it close to Beck. He held it out, an offering, by leaning it toward Beck, who took the handlebar and seat into his hands.

The other bikes, all black, were smaller. Millie was right. This pink one likely was the best fit.

Millie swung a leg over the seat of her bike. She straddled it like a pro and rubbed her palms on the rubber handlebar grips. "Thanks, Keith. Justin. Appreciate it."

The two men who'd handed over the bikes nodded. The one called Keith put a hand on her shoulder. It was a familiar gesture. Too familiar. Beck clenched his jaw and resisted the urge to clock the guy in the center of his baby face.

"You sure you don't want us going, Sheriff? Justin and I are happy to help. You're riding pretty light."

Keith gestured to the other two bikers. Millie lifted an arm and put a hand on Keith's. Beck's stomach tightened. His blood boiled.

"We'll be fine, Keith," she said. "We've done more with less. Plus, I've got my dad. He's a legend. Unkillable."

Keith ran his thumb across Millie's hand. It was made all the more affectionate by Millie's apparent comfort with it. She didn't even react. Beck bit the inside of his cheek in an effort to stave off an explosion of protective anger.

His daughter was an adult now. She'd survived the wilderness post-D-Day for more than four years without his help. It was unfair to expect her innocence to remain intact. Not in this world. At least Keith was a good-looking kid. And the look in his eyes, the profound expression of concern that creased his squared features, betrayed his true feelings for Millie.

Millie must have sensed her father's stare. She squeezed Keith's hand and removed it from her shoulder. Keith blushed and looked down at his boots.

"It's not your dad I'm worried about," he said. "I wish you'd let me go with you. I can help you make sure this trip doesn't interfere with the long-term plan. With the—"

Millie shook her head. "Not gonna happen. I need you here. You have to lead the migration. Okay? Everybody knows you're in charge."

"But we've spent so much time and—"

"I've got this," Millie said. "This won't interfere with the plan."

Keith nodded. He forced a smile that disappeared when he caught Beck's glare. The kid backed away two steps from Millie.

"Dad," she said, "this is Keith."

The kid extended his hand. Beck looked at it and begrudgingly shook it.

"It's an honor," Keith said. "Mil—the Sheriff told me a lot about you. I've also read the stories. You're a genuine living legend."

Beck met Keith's stare. The kid seemed more sincere than sycophant.

"She's told me absolutely nothing about you," Beck said. He paused and watched the wind leave the kid's sails before he said, "But if she trusts you, I trust you. What's this plan you two are talking about? She won't tell me."

Keith smiled. "Sorry, Mr. Beck. Can't help you. If she

won't tell you, it's best if I don't either. I'll just say that—"

"Keith," Millie said, "that's enough. I'll tell my dad when the time is right. Now's not the right time."

He let go of Beck's grip and stuffed his hands into his pockets in an aw-shucks sort of way that threatened to produce an uppercut to the gut. Beck balled his own hands into fists before he flexed them to work out the arthritic stiffness in his knuckles.

Millie cut the tension with another introduction. "This is Justin. He's one of the guys who helped you when you first got here. He carried you to the infield."

This time Beck extended his hand first. "And he put a hood over my head?"

Justin was broad shouldered. Strong. "Yes, sir," he said. "That was me. You were in bad shape. I'm glad to see you doing so well."

They shook. Beck thanked him.

"Justin is staying with Keith to keep an eye on things," Millie said. "We move around among our various strongholds. It's seasonal. We're getting ready to migrate east. When we're finished doing what we have to do, we'll catch up with the rest of everybody on the way."

Beck nodded. "I have questions about that too. This mysterious militia plan is one thing. The migration is another. You've got a lot of balls in there. I'd like to understand more about—"

"You will when the time comes," Millie cut in. "There is plenty of time to unpack everything. Like you said, *Dad*, we need to hit the road."

Beck did not like the way she called him *Dad*. The tone told him he was annoying her. That much hadn't changed in the years since he had last seen her.

"I'm Chris," said one of the two men straddling bikes.

"I'm going with you to get back your friends."

Chris saluted with a flick of his wrist but didn't offer his hand. The other biker, a compact but muscular man named Tony, also introduced himself without a handshake. Both men carried identical packs on their backs. The packs had scabbards sewn onto their exterior to accommodate rifles. Their burdens appeared heavy, but neither Chris nor Tony seemed weighed down or off-kilter. They looked ready to ride.

"Let's do this," Millie said. "The faster we get there, the faster we get home."

"I don't like this," Keith said. "I wish you'd let me go."

Millie put a foot on a pedal and pushed off the ground with the other. She circled around Keith, gaining her balance and speed aboard the bike.

"We all have a role to play," she said as she passed him. "You have yours, and I have mine. See you on the migration, Keith."

Beck copied his daughter's kick start and pushed down on a pedal as he accelerated forward. It had been years since he'd ridden a bike. Longer than the amount of time between horse rides. He wobbled but steadied himself and followed his daughter. Chris and Tony flanked him on either side. As they rode from the infield toward the exit, Keith called out. His voice echoed, and his words repeated themselves. Each repetition was like a knife in Beck's back.

"I love you, Sheriff Millie Beck! Come back to me in one piece."

As much as that hurt, it was his daughter's response that twisted the blade and threatened to knock him from his seat.

"I love you too, Keith Appleton," she said. "I love you too."

CHAPTER 6

D-DAY + 4 YEARS, 6 MONTHS, 20 DAYS
LOUISVILLE, KENTUCKY

Beck's lower back ached with each revolution of the bike's pedals. He relished the glides downhill and cursed the ascension up the slightest inclines. The bike, while his size, was still small. It was designed for off-road maneuvers with its thick treaded tires. Performance was the first and last attribute. Comfort was not an aesthetic the engineer took into account.

Four hours into the ride, Millie slowed and coasted beside him. She seemed barely out of breath and guided the bike as if it were a part of her.

"You okay?" she asked. "We can stop."

Beck shook his head. He took a hand from the grip and wiped sweat from his face with the back of his sleeve. "I'm good, just out of practice and out of shape. I mean, not out of shape, but out of shape for this."

She wove the wheel back and forth to keep even with him as he plowed forward. Her touch was light on the handlebars. "I get it. It takes a little bit to get used to using the muscles you need for a bike. I guess I should've taken that into consideration. But I still think this is better than horses."

"I'm not so sure," Beck said. "Visibility isn't as good. We

could get ambushed more easily on these bikes."

She wrinkled her nose and surveyed both sides of the road. Chris and Tony were twenty yards ahead of them. Both appeared as unfazed by the cycling effort as his daughter.

"You think?" she asked. "I don't know about that. Sure, we give up some height, but we're faster zero to sixty on these bikes than we would be on horses. Plus we're so much quieter on wheels than hooves.

"Zero to sixty?"

"I know we can't go sixty miles per hour. I'm saying it's easier to go fast in a hurry on these bikes."

"Maybe."

"Definitely. We really got lucky with them. Couldn't believe it when we came across them."

The sun was high in the blue sky. No sign of rain. Beck wondered if his aches were a function of age and injury rather than meteorology. A quartet of blackbirds swooped low ahead of them and then climbed into the sky before they disappeared behind the tall pines lining the road on both sides. His daughter kept talking as he surveilled their surroundings. The talk of an ambush had him on edge. He took mental note of his pistol on his hip. It was fully loaded.

Millie's face lit up as she began the story. It brought back memories of her nonstop talking in the car on their road trips between Mobile and Tuscaloosa. He could listen to her for hours, which he frequently did back then. Before everything went to hell.

His mind shifted from surveillance to Millie. Part of him couldn't believe he had found her. Even though he'd always believed in his gut he would reunite with her, some small part of him harbored doubt. Those were the demons. The internal naysayers he somehow had managed to keep at bay since arriving in Louisville under less-than-ideal circumstances.

"We came across the bike shop when we were looking for tools," Millie said. "It was in a strip center next to a Home Depot. The Home Depot was looted. Plus, there were some rough people hanging out there, so we sorta staged at the strip center to figure out our next move."

"When was this?" Beck asked.

"Before my second trip back home," she said. "We were already beginning to form a little family and—"

Millie stopped mid-sentence and almost lost her balance on the bike. She bit her lower lip and rubbed her thumb across the brim of her hat. "I'm sorry, Dad. I didn't mean that the way it sounded. I just—"

"It's fine," Beck said. "I wasn't around. You had to do what you had to do. I'm proud of you. You figured out a way to survive. Thrive even."

She smiled and looked at him with the sort of admiration a child has for a parent for only a brief time. Beck felt electricity spark through his body. It was a quiet expression of love he was sure he'd never see again. Millie was a grown woman now, and he'd long fallen from the pedestal upon which a daughter puts her father. Beck caught himself smiling back at her.

"Thanks," she said. "Anyhow, we were waiting there by the bike shop. There were about fifteen of us by that point. Maybe twenty. Then Keith says, 'Hey, look at all the bikes.'"

"It was Keith, huh?"

Millie smirked. "You'd really like him, Dad. He's a good guy. Somehow he stayed good amidst all of this."

"When did you meet him? How?"

"He joined our group. He was alone. We found him on the trail and—"

"When was this?"

She shrugged. "Why does that matter?"

"Because I'm asking."

"Six months? Something like that. Hard to keep track of exact days and weeks. But about six months. It feels that long."

"And you trust this guy you just happened to come across on the trail?" Beck made finger quotes when he said "on the trail."

Millie rolled her eyes. At first, he thought it was playful. Her tone suggested otherwise. "I'm old enough to make my own decisions, Dad. I've been pretty good at it."

She let go of the handlebars and gestured to their surroundings as she kept pedaling. The bike stayed on course until she retook the grips.

"I'm sure," Beck said. "Sorry for the judgment. Just being protective. Tell me more about Super Keith and his brilliance."

Millie sighed. "Anyhow, Keith saw the bikes, and we were all like, seriously? How could there be all these bikes so long after the power went out? Nobody bothered to take them. It's like everybody forgot about bikes. So we broke into the place and took as many as we could. Then we loaded repair kits and extra tubes, tires, pumps into packs and took off. We made two more trips back to the shop until we cleaned it out. Crazy, right? All that time and nobody looted the bike shop? Bizarre."

Beck parroted her. "Bizarre."

"We still ride horses. We even have a truck that runs on solar panels. One of the girls—you'll meet her when we get back—she's super smart. She was an engineering major in college before…what do you call it, D-Day?"

"D-Day."

"She's super smart, and she figured out how to put these solar panels on a small truck. We only use it during the migration when we've got full support. It's not smart to take it on outings like this."

"Why not?"

"Too big a target."

Beck maneuvered the bike to maintain its course and pedaled harder. His thighs screamed from exhaustion, but he hid the discomfort. "I don't get it," he said. "If you're making an argument for bicycles running fast and silent as a deterrent to would-be attackers, why doesn't the solar truck trump it?"

"Trumpet?"

"No. Trump. It. Beat it. Best it. Why isn't it the better option?"

"It's just not. Like I told you back at Churchill Downs, we've had other rescue missions, Dad. This isn't the first. In our experience, we've found the bikes are the best option. Not infallible, just the best."

Infallible. That was a big word for a high school dropout. Did she have a dictionary, too? The mix of surprise and intrigue on his face must have been obvious. She smirked at him again as if reading his mind.

Beck noticed she held a knife in one hand. She had it pressed between her palm and the handlebar. The case was dingy, gray and brown, but there were hints of pink underneath the grime. It was the Buck knife he had given her all those years ago. The knife she'd used to cut off the ear of the man who'd kidnapped her and killed her mother.

Beck considered saying something about the knife, about its significance. It was a connection the two of them shared, a bond that transcended time and distance. Instead, he watched her dig the grime from under her nails and flick it to the ground.

"I learned the word from one of those books about you," Millie said. "One of them said your plans of attack were infallible. Nobody could beat you. I didn't know what the word meant, but the engineer, the one I told you adapted the solar truck, told me."

"Those books were full of it," Beck said. "They got most of it wrong, from what I've heard."

"Maybe," she said, "but if it weren't for the books, I might not have kept up hope you were alive."

The blue sky darkened ahead and to their left. Shelves of steel gray clouds rolled atop one another as they crowded against a building weather front. The storm was coming after all.

Tall evergreens that crowded the road's shoulders swayed or shimmied in a cool breeze. The scent of ozone portended the rain they would soon encounter. Wind gusts pushed against his efforts. Chris and Tony hunched over their handlebars and huffed up an incline.

Beck twisted his palms against his handlebars and braced himself for the exhausting trip still ahead. He lamented his conversation with Millie was over. It was nice talking with her, even about nothing. Hearing her voice, watching the expressions shift on her delicate but somehow hardened features gave him some sort of comfort he couldn't rationalize.

No matter the circumstance, he was with his daughter. He'd climb a thousand rises on a dirt bike in the rain and wind to be with her. Come to think of it, the things he'd done to find her were far greater obstacles than this. He hoped these new challenges brought him back together with the other women in his life. He felt responsible for all of them in some odd way.

Rebecca was his charge. He had led her from her home and the only people she truly knew. She'd lost the love of her life on the way. He was responsible.

Lucy was a frenemy. He'd chosen to bring her from her haunt in the southern woods as a way to keep his enemy close. She'd proved to be a worthy companion with a lot of fight and gumption. He was responsible for her well-being until he could find some suitable settlement. Even if she didn't feel the same way, he did. And while he couldn't implicitly trust her, something told him she would have his back when push came to shove. It would. She would.

Then there was Regina. Beck was unsure about her. Not her proven loyalty or willingness to put her life on the line for his cause, but rather how he felt about her in his heart.

Beck hadn't been with a woman since Millie's mother, let alone harbor romantic feelings. Not that he failed to have opportunities. But when Debbie had left him, he'd understood any physical transgression would put a swift end to the small chance he had of a reconciliation. He didn't change his course when the courts finalized the divorce or when she repeatedly told him they would never be a couple again.

Then she'd died in his arms, and he'd vowed to himself he would avenge her. He would find their daughter and keep her safe. Those parallel goals eclipsed any spark that might have existed between him and any other woman.

Regina was different, though. His attraction to her was something beyond a physical attraction. In fact, he hadn't found her physically attractive when he'd first found her armed and aiming a weapon at him. She was a big woman. Tall. Strong. Commanding even. Regina wasn't the petite flower to whom he had previously gravitated, yet he was drawn to her, and he was almost certain she to him. Something genuine and real seemed to connect them.

Debbie's death was avenged. Millie was beside him again. There was nothing to stop him from pursuing a future with

Regina other than their current distance. She was in enemy territory. While he was sure she could take care of herself, he wanted to rescue her. He wanted to prove himself worthy of her. She had, after all, survived in the post D-Day wilderness alone for years. In his mind, she was the legend deserving of a comic book. So was his daughter, the commander of an enclave of survivors. He was just a man with a grudge and a gun. Was he worthy of her? Did she even need or want him? Was he taking this foolish risk, putting his newly found daughter's safety at risk, for a second fool's errand?

The demons nattered away until the first raindrop shook him from his reverie. It was cold and hit him squarely on the nose.

Millie held out her hand. "Is that rain?"

"I think so," Beck said.

In the distance, the columns of clouds appeared like a steel gray curtain. They merged into a dark monolith that dumped sheets of rain south of their current position. No thunder, no lightning. Beck sensed the electricity in the air, however. The storm was coming.

"I wish we were in the truck," Beck said. "Would keep us dry."

Millie squinted up at the sky. She blinked against a spatter of raindrops but didn't acknowledge Beck's assessment. "It's not bad yet. A few drops here and there."

"This is just the start of it," Beck said. "We're about to get hammered."

Ahead of them, Tony circled back and rode toward them, retracing his path. Chris was behind him. Both appeared wary, their expressions drawn tight with concern.

When they reached Millie and Beck, they didn't stop. Instead, they looped again and rode alongside them.

Chris motioned toward the sky ahead of them and its

thickening opacity. "I don't like this, Sheriff. Roads will get slick. Our visibility is already diminished. If we come across any threats, it could be tough."

"We're not around the others," said Millie. "You can call me by my name."

Chris glanced at Beck before he nodded at Millie. "Yes, ma'am. That doesn't change my recommendation, though."

"What's the recommendation?" she asked. "I heard only a sitrep."

Sitrep?

Beck blinked. When did his little girl start talking like a soldier?

"Fair enough," Chris said. "I say we duck into these trees on the shoulder. Make camp and wait for the storm to blow through."

Millie appeared to consider as the foursome kept rolling toward the storm. The raindrops thickened in size and came in bursts now. The breeze was more of a wind. The air was colder.

"We have no way of knowing how long the storm will last," Millie said. "It could be five minutes; it could be five days. Last I checked, we don't have the luxury of waiting. There are people waiting on us. They have limited time."

The rain was steady. The shower's volume threatened to drown out the discussion.

"They'll run out of time if we push our luck," Tony said above the din. "Better we're later than we plan than not make it at all. These roads are going to get slick. And like Chris said, the visibility is really—"

Tony's eyes widened. His chin quivered before his expression softened, and he lurched forward on the bike. He fell forward over the handlebars and collapsed. His forward momentum drove him into Millie and knocked her from her bike. She tumbled onto the asphalt and grunted.

Beck saw the arrow buried in Tony's back. He drew his sidearm as he dropped his feet to the asphalt and skidded into a swerve to avoid Millie.

Chris was already off his bike, on a knee, his rifle pulled tight to his shoulder. "Sniper," he hissed. "In the trees."

Beck tossed his bike and raced the short distance to Millie. She was on her side. Blood trickled from a gash at her hairline. It mixed with the steady rain hitting her face. Her eyes were open, but she was dazed.

He crouched next to her and scanned their surroundings. Another arrow zipped past him. It bounced off the road and clattered against Millie's bike.

Chris returned fire. His rifle cracked with a pair of shots into the trees. They were wild shots. Guesses.

Another pair of arrows whooshed past them. The displaced air brushed Beck's face. He set his sidearm onto the road and pulled Millie's rifle from the scabbard on her pack.

She mumbled something unintelligible. Beck put a hand on her shoulder. "Stay down."

He pivoted to Chris as another pair of arrows sliced the space between them. One drilled into Tony's corpse.

"Chris," he said, "get over here and protect Millie. I'm going in."

"Going in?"

Beck snapped, "Just do it."

Chris crab-walked to Millie and put his body between her and the dense clusters of trees that hugged the east side of the road. He locked eyes with Beck and nodded. Beck returned the acknowledgment and made his way to the shoulder.

He stayed low and carried the rifle in one hand. Eyes up, he wove back and forth toward the cover of the trees and a drainage gully that separated the woods from the asphalt.

Twice, arrows bounced off the road behind him, just missing him. Chris provided cover fire with a trio of rifle shots that echoed in the cool, wet air.

Beck dove into the gulley and splashed into a thin layer of mud. The taste of it coated his lips, and he wiped it from his mouth with the back of one hand. He lay there for an instant and checked the rifle. Unfamiliar with the weapon, he found the safety and the fire select lever. He chose single shot over fully automatic to save ammo. He removed the magazine. It was full. Beck shoved it back into place. He chose single shot over fully automatic on the fire selector lever. Ammo was at a premium.

In amazed him the numbers of intact bullets that remained so long after D-Day. He remembered the days when the Second Amendment was a hot topic and every type of ammo available was suddenly unavailable. Or if a store or range managed to carry what he needed, they imposed limits on the purchase. No more than two boxes of this or a single box of that.

Ammo was one of the many things that surprised him about the post-apocalypse. People's willingness to engage in violence was another. Why wouldn't people conserve their ammo? Why wouldn't they do everything possible to live in peace? To make a virtually unbearable existence at least tenable?

These thoughts zipped through his head as another arrow sliced through the air close to him. It stabbed into the soft ground a foot from him. He was thankful they were not among those violent types who also had ammunition reserves. There was that, at least.

His heart raced, and he felt it in his chest and neck. It thumped at the rhythm of the heavy rain. Beck spat water from his mouth and cleared it from his nostrils as he rolled onto his stomach and elbowed his way through the thickening mud at the bottom of the roadside ditch.

Another arrow skidded along the edge of the ditch and rolled into the gulley next to Beck. The arrow's shaft was wood, its fletching feathered. He couldn't make out the tip, but it was obvious the projectile was handmade and not some relic of pre-D-Day purchased or looted from a sporting goods store.

Two more rifle shots snapped from Chris's weapon as Beck crawled from the gulley and into the woods. He got up from his knees and stood with his back against a thick oak trunk. The scent of pine mixed with the rot of moldy detritus beneath his boots.

His mind raced, and he worked to focus it. He couldn't worry about the severity of Millie's wound. She would be okay. Beck believed that. He had to believe it. They could not come this far for her to die at the hands of a post-apocalyptic archer. That was too absurd to be real.

Beck listened, trying to use sound as a way to place the snipers. Though the rainfall wasn't as loud under the canopy, it was enough that it masked any ambient noise. He cursed under his breath and dropped to one knee, readied the rifle, and spun. His body pressed against the side of the trunk, he tried to make his profile as small as possible.

The foliage was surprisingly dense. It was darker under the cover of trees. He scanned the clusters of trees with wider trunks close to the roadside. No movement. No return fire. So he advanced.

Beck stood and moved diagonally toward the next wide trunk. He dropped to one knee and leveled the rifle, then lifted it toward the top of the canopy. From beyond the woods, Chris's rifle cracked three more times.

It drew his attention to Millie. He lost focus for a split second. That was when the sniper, hidden amongst the trees, found his aim.

CHAPTER 7

D-DAY + 4 YEARS, 6 MONTHS, 20 DAYS
NEAR ELIZABETHTOWN, KENTUCKY

A lightning bolt of pain shot through Beck's left arm. He suppressed a cry and scrambled behind the tree as he dropped the rifle. He sank to the ground and reached for the arrow sticking out of his bicep, its shaft pinching the fabric of his shirt. Bright red blood leached across the sleeve, and Beck felt the warmth of it stream down his arm.

Sweat poured into his eyes and stung. It blurred his vision. He puffed his cheeks and worked to control his breathing. With his right hand he felt around the back of his arm, along his triceps. No exit wound. That was good. Maybe. Maybe not.

Beck studied the shaft for a moment to check the angle of entry. He noticed the nock, the part where the arrow's shaft rested on the bow's string, was hand cut. Striations in the carved wood lacked the smooth edges of something machine made.

He bit the inside of his cheek, braced himself, and took the arrow's shaft in his right hand. Not knowing the type of arrowhead, he risked doing a lot more damage to his arm if the head was broad. Broadheads were typically used for hunting. If these snipers were hunters, as they appeared to be,

57

this could be bad. Around him, mist fogged the air. The rain intensified, and more of it found its way through the canopy. In the distance thunder boomed. It rolled across the sky, unfurling until it drowned out the incessant rhythm of the rain.

Two deep breaths in and out through his nose, a count of three, and he pulled. The arrow slid right out. No broadhead. The bloodstained tip was whittled into a sharp point, like something a kid might carve with his first pocketknife.

Beck tossed the arrow to the ground and then stuck his finger into the hole in his shirtsleeve. He yanked down and tore the fabric until most of the sleeve separated from the rest of the shirt.

Awkwardly, he fashioned a rough tourniquet around his bicep above the wound and, using his teeth, tightened the strip into a knot. He flexed his left hand. Blood flow was restricted, but he was good for now. At least until he killed the snipers and got back to his daughter. Then he could fix the wound properly.

With renewed vigor, Beck gritted his teeth. He growled to himself and summoned the demons. Welcoming their derision and their vitriolic, self-loathing bile, he picked up the rifle and shouldered it.

He advanced quickly into the mist from one tree to another. Three times, arrows bounced off the trunks protecting him. Beck closed his eyes and listened to the rain. He focused on the moment, his finger on the trigger, the weight of the rifle's butt pressed tight against his shoulder. He let his anger course through his adrenaline-fueled muscles. He scanned his surroundings with purposeful sweeps of the rifle.

The first sniper was fifteen feet up. Beck spotted him. The sniper saw him, too. Before the archer could nock his next arrow, Beck applied pressure to the rifle's trigger.

The weapon kicked against him, but he kept his aim as he fired two more shots. One struck its target. The sniper dropped silently from the tree, bounced off a thick limb, and hit the ground with a sickening thud. If the bullets hadn't killed him, the ground did. His body lay twisted unnaturally on the detritus. Beck watched the mist curl around the corpse as if covering it from view, and refocused on the task ahead. At least one more sniper was sheltered in the trees. Perhaps more. He had work to do.

Beck advanced again. Two broad steps to the next tree. His heart raced, and the thick pounding in his wounded arm intensified. He clenched his jaw and tried to ignore the pain.

He was about to make another move when something caught his attention at the edge of his vision. He pivoted, protected himself as best he could, and redirected the rifle toward the movement.

His finger slid onto the trigger, and he tracked something coming toward him. It moved fast from tree to tree. In the fading light and the mist he couldn't get a bead on it. He waited. Watched. When the figure got close, he applied pressure.

The shot missed and drilled into a tree. Bark and shards of wood splintered into the mist. Then a voice called as Beck took aim again.

"Wait! Don't shoot. It's me, Beck. It's Chris."

Chris? What was he doing in the woods? Where was Millie? Had he left her alone to die? Was she dead?

Beck eased his finger from the trigger but reserved the right to put a slug in Chris if he didn't say the right things. Chris emerged through the mist, breathless. He had one hand on his rifle and the other above his head.

"What are you doing?" Beck spat through gritted teeth. "Where's my daughter?"

Chris eyed the bloody handmade tourniquet. "You're hurt. What happened?" Catching the expression on Beck's face, Chris took a step back. "It's okay. She's okay. She's okay."

"Where is she?"

"On the other side of the road," Chris said. "I got her off the road. She's got the bikes, and she's hiding. What happened to you?"

"By herself?"

Chris opened his mouth to answer but shook his head. "She's okay. You don't have to worry about her. The Sheriff, I mean Millie, is really tough and—"

"She's my daughter. I told you to keep an eye on her. You said you would. You left her. She's—"

Chris's expression darkened. "You left her, too."

Beck fought the urge to choke the kid. Or shoot him. Or shoot him and then choke him. He flexed his jaw and closed the space between them. He was much taller than Chris and looked down at the kid, trying to intimidate him. "What did you say?"

To his credit, Chris didn't flinch. His taut expression held. "I said you left her too."

"What happened in Alabama has nothing—"

Chris's expression twisted. "Alabama? I'm not talking about Alabama. I'm talking about right now. You left her in the street with a stranger. I'm a stranger to you. You don't know me. But you left her. You could've sent me to get the snipers, but you didn't. You went. You left her in the road."

Beck held Chris's righteous gaze but couldn't refute any of the kid's charges. He was absolutely right on all accounts.

Instead of admitting his guilt, Beck said, "We can talk about this later. Right now, we have a sniper or two to take out. Right?"

Chris nodded. "Right."

"Did you see anything on your way here?"

"No. Too foggy and the rain is too loud."

"You found me."

"Lucky, I guess."

Beck rolled his eyes. "Right. Luck. Lucky I didn't kill you when you flashed into my line of sight."

"You missed me," Chris said. "Was that luck?"

"I'm not doing this now," Beck said. "Focus on the job."

"How many you think there are?"

"I got one." Beck motioned with his head toward to his right. "He's twenty yards that way. I'm guessing the other one, assuming there's at least one more, has got to be in the same spot. Close by."

Chris's eyes widened. "You got one?"

"Yeah, though not before he got me, too."

"Your arm?"

"Yeah. He, or I guess it could have been another sniper, got me in the bicep. Hurt like a mother—"

"You pulled it out?"

"Yeah. No exit wound. Not too bad. Hurts, but I'll live."

Beck crouched. Chris did the same as Beck moved around the tree to point in the general direction of the sniper he'd killed.

"Over that way. He was three-quarters of the way up the tree. Spotted each other at the same time. I got the drop on him before he could fire off another arrow."

"Arrows. Crazy, right?" Chris said, all tension gone from his tone. "This is only the third time I've dealt with freaking arrows."

"Did you know about the threat here?"

"What do you mean?"

"Have you dealt with archers here, in this spot, before?"

"Not here exactly."

TOM ABRAHAMS

Beck furrowed his brow. "What does that mean? A little heads-up might've helped. Your buddy Tony might be alive. And I'd have a better handle on how to dispatch these f—"

"That's not fair. Tony's not my fault. Besides, I'd have thought that you, the great and powerful John Beck, would always be ready for an ambush. Then again, I did read about Oklahoma City. Colorado, too."

Rage simmered. Beck's face grew hot. He tightened his grip on the rifle.

"If you're gonna give it, old man, you'd best take it."

The demons won. Beck snapped the butt of the rifle into Chris's face. Cartilage or bone snapped, and the kid went down. He wailed through what was likely a broken nose.

Beck cursed at him. "Take *that*."

As soon as he said it, he regretted it. He'd broken someone else's nose to spite his own face. Chris was slumped over, whimpering. Blood leaked through his fingers as he cupped his hands over his face.

Beck considered an apology. Then didn't. He was mad at himself, but angrier at the kid for pushing him into an angry corner.

"Ever talk like that to me again and I'll aim lower. Got it? Now stay here while I fix this."

Without waiting for an answer or a rebuttal, Beck worked his way through the fog and rain toward the dead body. As best he could remember, he navigated in reverse the path he'd taken toward Chris. He was ten feet from the dead archer when he hit paydirt.

Another person hunched over the dead man. Their back turned toward Beck, they were oblivious to his approach. He slid his finger to the trigger and leveled the rifle. Then an odd voice cautioned him in his head.

"Why do you always shoot first?"

It was Lucas. The young kid he'd treated like a son who had died weeks earlier. Was it weeks? He had always asked so many questions. Too many questions. And he'd challenged Beck about his use of violence. Lucas was violent in his own right, but there was a morality to the kid's choices. A compass to which he stuck.

Instead of pulling the trigger, Beck checked his surroundings. The target, he or she, appeared to be unarmed. A bow lay on the ground next to an empty quiver.

Beck cleared his throat. The person jerked with surprise and whirled around to face him. The woman was middle aged, he guessed. Even in the haze, her swollen, red-rimmed eyes glowed with sadness.

Her gaze flitted to the rifle aimed at her chest, and she scooted back, falling over the body behind her. For a moment she scrambled like a beetle on its back, arms and legs flailing. Beck took two steps closer and eased his finger onto the trigger again as she rolled onto her knees and looked up at him, chin quivering. She lifted empty hands above her hunched shoulders. Her clothing, wet and stuck to her thin frame, was too large for her body. The sleeves drooped like extra skin from her upper arms, and her pants pooled around her squat legs.

"Are you alone?" he asked.

She nodded. Tears mixed with the rain that streamed down her sallow face. Her bony cheeks almost made her sad expression clown-like, a caricature of a griever. Her skin was paper-like and wrinkled in the places that betrayed age and experience. It also looked like a roadmap of loss and heartache. Wizened did not begin to describe it.

"Is there anyone else in the trees?"

The woman shook her head. Her hands wavered. They trembled.

Beck leaned his head toward the rifle's sights. He aimed the rifle at an angle that made it clear he was ready to fire. "Is there anyone else in the trees?"

She shook her head. "No," she said, her voice warbling. "I'm alone. It's just me. I swear."

Beck remained silent and held his position.

"I swear I'm alone. *Now* I'm alone. You killed my boy. I'm alone."

Beck held his aim. "Stand up and back away from the body."

She complied, though standing did not come easy. Her shoulders shuddered, and her knees appeared weak.

"Who are you?" he asked.

"Why does that matter?"

"Who. Are. You? You killed one of our people. Wounded me. Who are you?"

The woman lowered her hands. Her eyes widened, and she frowned. Genuine confusion clouded her features. "Why does it matter who I am? What does that matter at all?"

Beck was dumbfounded. She was right. Ultimately, it didn't matter who she was. He changed course. "What are you doing here?"

Again, the woman appeared confused. Her expression was that of someone who didn't understand a foreign language. "This is my home. These woods are where I live. I think the better question is, why are *you* here?"

Beck laughed. "I'm here because you shot my friend with an arrow. You killed him."

"You trespassed."

Beck smiled. The rain was colder now. A chill ran along his spine. "We were in the road. Not your woods."

"You trespassed. We were protecting ourselves."

"We would've kept going if you hadn't killed one of us."

"They all say that. All of them."

"All of whom?"

"The trespassers. They all say that. Everyone wants what we have. We have to protect what we have. My son and me."

Beck studied the woman's expression. She seemed to drift from the present and land somewhere far away. She was looking straight at Beck, but he was convinced she didn't see him.

"We have to protect what's ours. If we don't, others will take it. They'll take it all, and they'll leave us with nothing. That's what trespassers do. They come uninvited, and they take. They take and they take."

The woman sneered. Her face wrinkled into a snarl. She spat as she spoke, and drool rolled onto her chin. "That's all they do," she hissed. "They say they're just passing through. But they never do. They stop. They stay. They take. They leave us with nothing."

Beck saw her hands curl into claws. The woman's face was red. She was no longer trembling, and the quaver in her voice was gone. She pulled her shoulders back and lifted her chin. Eyes closed, she let the rain fall onto her face. She stretched out her arms, welcoming the storm, and she cackled. Loud. Shrill. Unnerving.

This time, the chill that ran along Beck's spine was not from the cold rain. He was unsure how to handle this. He'd heard of people losing their minds in the loneliness, isolation, and daily stress that befell countless D-Day survivors. Had it not been for his mission and Gabe Vazquez, Beck often wondered if he might've gone insane or died from a stroke or heart attack.

The longer he faced this woman, the clearer it became she wasn't all there. She blinked away the rain on her lashes, and her eyes darted around her. She studied Beck as if she had never seen him before that instant. Then, when her eyes fell to the body near her feet, she cupped her hands over her mouth and gasped.

"Oh, my darling," she said and hurried to the dead archer. She slid onto her knees and put her hands on the corpse. A cry that sounded like a balloon leaking air squealed from her tight lips, and she rocked back and forth. The woman shook her head and muttered, "No, no, no, no, no."

She grabbed the loose fabric and tugged it, shaking the body. Throwing back her head, she wailed. She sobbed. Her body shuddered.

Beck watched. He kept the gun aimed squarely at her.

She didn't appear to notice him for several minutes, and Beck considered leaving her there to mourn. However, he had learned never to leave someone alive and alone. That pity could come back to haunt him.

When she calmed herself and focused on Beck, her expression tightened. She leaned forward, tugging fistfuls of the dead archer's shirt with her hands. "You did this. You killed my daughter. My little girl. You left me alone. All alone. You trespassers. You dirty trespassers."

Daughter?

Beck glanced at the body on the ground. With the head turned away from him and the loose clothing draped over the corpse, he couldn't tell if the archer was a man or a woman.

The woman let go of the fabric and labored to her feet. She wobbled before gaining her balance. "All we wanted was some peace. To live our lives without harassment from trespassers like you."

She extended a long finger and shook it. Tears rolled down her face. Snot bubbled from her nostrils. Then her expression softened, and her eyes grew distant again.

Beck glanced over his shoulder. No sign of Chris. No

evidence of any other attackers.

"Why did you attack us?" Beck asked. He assumed that all memory of their previous exchange had evaporated like the mist that carried on the air between them.

She blinked. "Attack you? Who are you? Why are you here? What did you—"

The woman looked down at the body and back at Beck. Her features condensed with newly found anguish. "What did you do?" she asked. "Did you do this? Did you kill my husband? Why would you do this?"

Recognition clarified on her face. She nodded. The anger returned.

"You," she said. "You're a trespasser. You came here to take from us. I won't have it."

Beck expected the woman, suffering from dementia at the very least, would drop to her knees again. She would wail and bemoan the loss of a loved one. That wasn't what happened.

The woman lunged at Beck with a feral scream. She was remarkably fast. So fast, Beck didn't have time to reset his aim and fire. Her act, whether real or not, had dulled his reflexes and put him on his heels.

She was in the air, her clawlike fingers extended toward his throat, when the percussion of a rifle shot cracked through the rhythmic beating of the rain, cut through her scream, and the woman dropped to the ground, falling into Beck's legs. She was dead.

Chapter 8

Beck stumbled but maintained his footing. Refocused, he turned around to find Chris. The kid's rifle cracked again as he put the finishing round into the crazed woman. His eyes were swollen, his nose a purple and blood-red mess. But his aim was true.

The woman moaned at Beck's feet before her last breath rattled from her lungs. She exhaled, twitched, and lay still. Her body was on its side in a quasi-fetal position.

"You're welcome," Chris said.

His voice was thick and nasal-intoned. He stared at Beck for an instant, studied the two bodies on the ground, then spun around and marched away.

Beck's heart pounded. His hands trembled. The aftereffect of a near-miss adrenaline surge. He checked both bodies, then followed Chris and called after him.

"Hey. Hold up."

Chris ignored him. The kid pushed his way through the brush and among the trees until he emerged at the edge of the roadside ditch.

"Chris," Beck said, "wait up."

Chris didn't look back or stop. He went out into the pouring rain and trudged through the water-filled ditch. On the other side, he marched across the road toward where Beck presumed Millie was waiting.

"Damn it, Chris," Beck said. "Listen to me."

At the shoulder on the far side of the road, Chris stopped. He held his rifle at his side. The rain pelted him, but he stood still. Waiting.

Beck hurried through the gully, climbed up onto the road, and met Chris on the opposite side. He was winded. Post-traumatic exhaustion.

"Chris, first, let me say thank you."

Beck was to the left of Chris, even with him on the shoulder. The rain sounded like a torrent, a rushing river ready to spill its banks.

The kid held his ground but twisted to face Beck. "Then say it."

"Thanks for being there. I didn't expect her to move like that."

"Obviously."

"You saved me. I appreciate it."

A long pause filled the space between them. Chris lifted an eyebrow and winced. "Anything else?"

Beck sucked in a damp breath. He hated this part.

Chris shook his head. "Yeah, I didn't think you were man enough to apol—"

"I'm sorry," Beck said. "I shouldn't have clocked you like that. I mean, you probably had it coming, but I should've let it go."

"That's your apology?"

Beck didn't like this kid. It wouldn't matter how many times Chris saved his life or stopped a crazed wood gnome from attacking him, Beck would never like him.

He nodded. "That's my apology."

"If you include a 'but' in an apology, it doesn't count. That's what my mom told me."

"First," said Beck, "your mom sounds like a smart woman."

"She was. She died two weeks after the power went out."

"Sorry about that. I'm sure that was hard."

Chris shrugged. Rain bounced off his shoulders. Drops rolled down his face.

"*But* when I said 'but' just now, it was to explain I should've let your insolence go."

"Insolence?"

"It means disrespect. I read it in a book."

"Whatever. Your apology was qualified. It wasn't sincere. Millie said you have a hard time apologizing."

Beck was impatient with Chris's insistence on needling him, on finding the thing that would most make him angry. He considered another whack to the nose, but he let it slide.

A broad humorless grin stretched across his face. "You're right, Chris. It was qualified. It's hard to apologize to a punk like you. *But*...I am sorry. Let's move past it. Say I owe you one for stopping the woman in the woods. Okay?"

Chris stood motionless at first. Then he nodded. "Okay."

Beck was about to end the conversation when Millie interrupted. She stood in front of them at the edge of the woods. She held two bikes, one on either side of her thin frame.

Disgust painted her face. "What the hell is going on? And what happened to your face, Chris?"

Millie stared at Chris for a moment. When he didn't respond, she glared at Beck. "Dad, did you do that? Did you punch Chris in the face and break his nose?"

"How's your head?" Beck asked. "Are you okay?"

70

"I'm fine. Just got dinged. What did you do to Chris?"

"I didn't punch him, but I did break his nose. I think it's broken. It looks broken."

Millie rolled her eyes. "Chris, are you okay?"

"My vision's a little blurry, and I'm breathing through my mouth, but I'm fine. I'll be fine. Your dad apologized. Sort of. That was more surprising than the butt of his rifle against my nose."

Millie's eyes widened with horror before they narrowed with rage. "Moron."

"What?" Beck asked.

"Dad, I love you. I am beyond happy that you found me. I'm honored to help you rescue your friends. But *you* are a moron. Chris is here to help you. You thank him by doing *that?*"

Millie gestured to Chris's face. She shrugged as if to reiterate her disbelief.

"I said I was sorry."

Tears welled in her eyes. Or perhaps it was rain. Beck couldn't tell. But her anger shifted to melancholy in a split second. It was emotional whiplash.

"Oh," Millie said, "well then. It's all good. Tony's dead, Chris has a broken nose, but you said you were sorry."

Beck pivoted to look back at the road. Tony's body was gone.

"Where is he?" Beck asked.

"After Chris went to get you, I went and got Tony. I dragged him into the woods. He's back there with the two other bikes. We need to bury him. I can't do it alone."

"I told you to stay in the woods," Chris said. "I—"

Millie bristled. "Since when do you tell me to do anything?"

Beck was sure now the water in his daughter's eyes was

71

rain. She was stone cold. A leader. He saw it in her posture, heard it in the commanding, almost condescending tone of her voice, and he witnessed Chris's deference. In a way, the kid hadn't given him his due, but he certainly did his daughter.

"You're right, Sheriff," Chris said. "I only meant to suggest it was safer for you. That's all."

She rolled the bikes forward. "Take them. You can bring them back into the woods since you're here."

Without waiting for them, she let go of the bikes and marched back into the woods. Beck and Chris exchanged glances. Two boys scolded.

They followed her into the thicket and along a narrow, winding path that cut amongst the hardwoods. On this side of the road, the growth was denser. The rain had a harder time finding its way from the clouds to the ground.

Tony's body was propped against the wide trunk of a black oak. Beck didn't know much, if anything, about plants, but it surprised him the oak, with its broad reach, could survive in the cramped conditions of the roadside forest. He looked skyward into its canopy and blinked against the rain. The branches were thin, and its foliage, what there was of it, was brown. The tree was either dead or a zombie, a tree that appeared dead but still had some life in it.

Bugs paraded up and down its trunk, feasting on the oak's weakness and fragility. The closer he got, the more he noticed a lot of the trees in this section of the woods were in bad shape. The detritus was thicker underfoot, and the air smelled less like rain and more like moldy earth.

Millie shrugged off her pack and slung it to the ground. She crouched and pulled from it a collapsible shovel. She extended the telescoping handle and tossed it to Beck. He caught it with one hand.

Surprised at his own reflexes, he chuckled. "Where'd you get this?"

Millie put a hand on her hip. "I'm resourceful, Dad. Remember, I may be your daughter, but I'm not your little girl anymore."

The words stung. More than he imagined they would. Then again, Beck never imagined she would say them. The idea she was grown and no longer a child festered for a long time. When he saw her at Churchill Downs, it had manifested into reality, but it was unspoken and therefore not quite real. Now it was, and she hadn't even tried to be gentle about it.

It got worse.

She motioned to Tony's body. His eyes were open, his jaw slack. The poor man's tongue lolled.

"You did this. You bury him."

Beck couldn't think of anything valuable to say. What was the point? She was right.

He sucked in a breath and drove the spade into the soft earth. Leaves and dried needles crunched as he shoveled. Beck quickly got into a rhythm and tried to think of anything but the moment at hand.

Millie pointed at Beck. "You can help him, Chris. It'll go faster that way."

Chris found his own shovel and joined the effort. He stood several feet from Beck and started digging the other end of the grave.

His daughter was angry at him, furious really. Or was it worse? Was Millie disappointed? Had he failed to be the man she'd hoped would find her?

They had the frame of the hole dug when she spoke again.

She took a swig of water from a bottle and wiped her chin dry with the back of her hand. "Who did this?"

Beck looked at Chris. When the kid didn't respond, Beck stopped shoveling.

"A couple of loons. Loners. The woman was crazy. I don't know who the other person was. A family member or something. They're both dead."

"You killed them, too?"

Beck lifted the spade and drove into the dirt.

"What are they, Dad? What's the number up to now? Either directly or indirectly? How many dead people are you responsible for?"

Every word was like a dagger in his heart. His chest tightened, but he kept shoveling. Sweat clouded his vision, and he used his shoulders to wipe it away.

Why was Millie determined to hurt him? She'd chosen to come on this mission to help him. That was her choice. It was also her decision to bring a small group instead of an army. Wasn't Tony's death as much her fault as it was his? Or shouldn't the blame squarely fall on the archer who drove an arrow into Tony's back?

Millie pressed. "How many, Dad? One hundred? Five? A thousand?"

Chris stood ankle deep in his side of the hole. He leaned on the shovel but did not dig. His flat expression gave Beck the distinct impression the kid was both uncomfortable but enjoying the conflict.

Beck had enough. He slammed the shovel hard. The move buried half the blade into the ground, and the tool stood upright on its own. He walked away from the grave and closer to his daughter. He could only take so much.

"You want me to include your mom?" he growled.

Millie's eyes widened, and she frowned. Then she cried. She removed the hat from her head, and silent tears mixed with the rain on her cheeks. "You didn't kill Mom. What are you saying?"

"You said directly or indirectly. I'm asking, do you want me to include your mother? Because I can. I see her face along with everyone else whose life I took. I see them at night when I can't sleep. I hear them whisper my name. I feel their presence in the dark. Every single minute of every day and night. So, again, Millie, do I include her or not?"

Millie's expression softened, as if she now realized the depth of the wound she had probed. Before she answered, Beck offered her an out.

"Or would you rather tell me why you're so angry at me right now? That might be more constructive than counting off the notches on my belt."

She glanced at his belt. She tucked her lips between her teeth and glanced at Chris before eyeing Beck. "I'm angry because you came back."

Those six words almost knocked him over into the grave. Then she clarified.

"I mean, I'm not mad that you found me. I wanted you to find me. I wanted to find you. It's not that."

Beck edged toward his daughter and extended a hand toward her shoulder. She flinched at the gesture and backed away.

"I don't need your comfort. Not now. Not after all this time."

Beck dropped his arm and balled his hands into tight fists. A knot swelled in his throat. It ached as he swallowed past it.

"We shouldn't do this now, Dad. We need to bury Tony and get to your friends. They're what's important, right?"

And there it was. *His friends.*

"So that's what this is about," he said. "You're upset at me because you and I just reconnected, and the first thing I want to do is leave to go find three people you've never met."

"Three women I've never met."

"Why does that matter?"

She laughed. Chris laughed. Beck did not.

"Really?" Millie said, the incredulity as sharp as the point of her collapsible shovel. "You have to ask that question?"

Beck was never good with women. He failed to understand the intricacies of their needs and wants. Try as he might, he was ignorant. The kind of husband who bought a blender as a Christmas gift or a vacuum for a birthday. The kind of husband who went to a bar to meet another woman.

Millie brought her hand to her chest. "I shouldn't be mad at you, but I can't help it. We finally find each other after more than four years, you're clinging to life, and the first thing you ask about is your friends. Three women who must mean a whole hell of a lot to you, because you'd drag me into a dangerous mission to find them and free them."

"I didn't drag you into—"

Millie held up a hand to stop him. "You sure did. Maybe you didn't grab me by the wrist and pull me kicking and screaming, no. But my father asks for my help. What choice did I have?"

Although Beck was unsure if the questions were rhetorical, this time he kept his mouth shut. He looked down at his boots, at the splotches of water staining the leather.

"I'm a leader, Dad. It's what you made me. Or it's what I had to become. I don't know which. But I'm not a little girl. I've had to do tough things, endure tough things."

He narrowed his focus. "What tough things?"

She waved him off. "It doesn't matter. I shouldn't have put it that way. My point is, I made the decision to find these women with you. That's on me. But you asked, and the look in your eyes when you realized they weren't with you…"

"What?"

"More than asking me how I survived, how I became the leader I am, how I escaped from the lunatic who killed my mother, how I did a million other things, you asked about finding these *other* women. That was your priority."

He reached out again. This time, she didn't pull away, and he drew her close to him.

"That's not true," he said. "You're my priority, Millie. You've always been my priority."

Beck regretted the last sentence as soon as he whispered it into her ear. It wasn't true. His daughter hadn't always been his priority. Had she been, he never would have screwed up his marriage and ruined his family. Debbie would still be alive. Or she wouldn't have died alone in a house she'd rented to get away from Beck.

He half expected his daughter to pull away. Instead, she wrapped her arms around his back and buried her face into his chest. Her body shuddered as she sobbed.

Beck tightened his hold on her. "Shhh," he said. "It's okay. It's okay."

It was as good and as bad as he'd felt in a long time. His daughter hurt. He was the cause but enjoyed the opportunity to be the salve too.

Chris dug deeper into the earth and pretended to ignore them. He was bad at it.

The rain pattered on the canopy above. A stiff breeze rustled the dying foliage, and a shower of leaves and needles mixed with the rain.

Beck pressed his face against the top of Millie's head. He smelled the oils of her hair and the sweat on her skin. It was a combination of scents he had forgotten until that moment. It brought with it a cascade of memories. He closed his eyes and drifted into them. They reminded him of Christmas mornings and bedtime stories, playdates on the ballfield and lazy afternoons on the couch, streaming cartoons.

He gently kissed her head and moved his hands to her shoulders. "It's okay, Millie. It's okay."

What else was there to say? The words escaped him. As long as he had been a father, it wasn't like riding a bike. Neither was easy, but the bikes didn't grow up and become adults.

Her sobs diminished to whimpers, and she drew back from him, offering a weak smile. "Thanks, Dad."

"Thanks for what?"

"Letting me vent. I'll get over it. We'll find your friends. There's plenty of time to talk about us."

If nothing else, his daughter had mastered the art of emotional whiplash. Beck studied her and nodded.

"Let's finish," she said. "The rain's getting worse."

Beck rubbed his daughter's arms and went back to the grave. Chris looked away from him and redoubled his own efforts to finish the dig.

A half hour later, the grave was finished, and Tony's stiffening body was at the bottom of it. Beck climbed from the hole and then offered Chris a hand. The kid glanced at Beck warily but took the offer. Together, they filled the grave. All three of them took turns spilling over the dirt onto Tony. When they'd filled the grave, Beck leaned on his shovel and took a long swig of water from his bottle. Exhaustion pulled at his muscles.

He glanced over at his daughter. "So what's the plan?"

Millie stood at the head of the grave, opposite the oak. "I should say something, right? It should be me?"

"That's not what I meant," Beck said. "I meant what's this big secret plan you have to get rid of the militia? I've been thinking about it. Unless you've got hundreds of people I don't know about, you're not going to take them down. They're well trained, for the most part, and they're—"

"Dad," she said, "now is not the time."

"When is the time?"

"When I say so. Okay? When I say so."

Beck bit the inside of his cheek. "Fine."

She rolled her eyes. "Are either of you going to answer my original question? Shouldn't we say a prayer?"

Her eyes searched both men. It was obvious she wanted either of them to take the responsibility from her. Neither did.

"It shouldn't be me," Beck said. "I'm not in charge."

It was a childish thing to say. He couldn't help himself.

Chris shrugged. "You're the Sheriff, Millie. You should do it."

The rain was getting through to the forest floor. The wind whipped around them. The intermittent thunder from hours earlier was more frequent. Flashes of lightning strobed through the canopy. The temperature was easily ten degrees cooler than when they had dipped into the woods to bury Tony. Beck let go of the shovel, ran his filthy hands through his wet hair, and tucked his hands under his armpits. A shiver ran through his body.

Millie nodded. "Okay. I'll do it."

She closed her eyes and muttered to herself before speaking aloud. "Dear Lord, please admit our brother and friend Tony into your kingdom. He was a good, faithful servant who always gave his best. He was fair and kind and a valuable part of our family. If anyone deserves a spot in heaven, it would be Tony. He did not deserve to die the way he did. Nobody does, but especially not him. And even though he killed others, he did it out of necessity. He was trying to survive in a world where everything is hard and nobody respects anybody else. Please forgive him those things. A great gift would be his eternal salvation. We pray for this, Lord. Amen."

Two things struck Beck about the prayer. The first was that his daughter likely didn't know Tony's last name or if Tony was short for something else. Anthony? Antonio?

The second was the way she spoke about salvation. About forgiveness. About survival. Were those things all possible? Could one do the violent things needed to survive, seek forgiveness, and gain salvation?

Beck had never considered it before. He considered himself damned and beyond redemption. That did not preclude him from trying, as he had every time he put his own life on the line to help other less-violently-skilled people during his quest to find Millie. But he never believed he could achieve it.

Did Millie know something he didn't? Was her faith greater than his?

She opened her eyes and looked at him. Her expression sought approval. He recognized it.

"Good job," Beck said. "Very sweet. Tony would've appreciated it."

"Me too," Chris said. "You did a good job. You're better with words."

Millie flashed a sad smile at Chris. Lightning flashed, and thunder boomed overhead. It startled all of them, and Beck's heart pounded against his chest. Then he clapped his hands together, taking charge. He pointed at Millie, spoke to her with the kind of direction a father gives a child.

"We've got to find somewhere to hide," Beck said. "Somewhere to get out of the storm."

Millie stiffened. Her features hardened. She snapped her fingers at Beck. "I need my rifle. Could you put it back where you found it?"

Beck started to argue but thought better of it. He did as the Sheriff instructed. Chris slid his rifle in the scabbard and shouldered his pack.

"Mount up," Millie said and offered Beck the rifle in her hand. "Take this. It was Tony's. He probably wouldn't want you to have it, but we don't have a choice right now, do we?"

Beck took the weapon without saying anything. His warm conversations with his daughter just an hour earlier seemed like something relegated to the distant past. Or even like he had dreamt them and they'd never happened at all. The frost that had begun to thaw had reemerged. Whiplash again. It was his fault for pushing for answers about this secret plan she refused to divulge to him. Why wouldn't she tell him? What was the harm?

Whatever the issue, it was hers. He would have to allow her that. Other things were more important than secrets.

His own pack had a scabbard, and he affixed the rifle to the pack. It was awkward and made the bike all the more uncomfortable, but Beck didn't complain.

This was his mission. At the other end of it were his compatriots. But as they rolled away from the woods in which they had trespassed, Beck felt like the interloper the crazy woman in the woods had accused him of being.

Was she a witch? Did she know things about him she shouldn't? Could she commune with his demons?

They rode south without his daughter asking a single question about the archers in the woods. She led them in a straight line. Beck was in the back, and they weren't waiting for him, not even in the rain. Thunder boomed in the skies ahead of them. They were heading into the heart of the storm. Beck said nothing about the choice to keep moving. He had clearly said and done enough.

The sadness and guilt that welled in his core as they rode was too familiar. It was something he hadn't felt in a long time. Before D-Day. Before his wife had said they had no chance at a future. Before his daughter had first looked at him with disappointment instead of awe. Beck wondered if this mission was worth what he might lose and what, in that moment, he believed he had already lost.

CHAPTER 9

D-DAY + 4 YEARS, 6 MONTHS, 20 DAYS
HOPKINSVILLE, KENTUCKY

Leo sat in the empty stands. His arena was a mud pit. The pounding rain had worsened the field's already poor conditions. The wind shifted directions and blew spray into his face. The mist and the stiff breeze were cold. Surprisingly cold. He folded his arms across his chest and tried to insulate himself from the chill.

He surveyed his surroundings and tried to look at the bright side. He was alone. By himself. No sycophants or underlings or obsequious, sycophantic underlings stood ready to jump or dive or run at his command.

They were good for tasks but not for company. Not for friendship. Leo had no friends. That was the burden of leadership. People everywhere and not a one of them a trustworthy confidant.

Truth was, he had always been alone. Almost always. His wife, Gretchen, had left him for another man two years before D-Day. That man, she told him, was a real man. He worked with his hands, was a survivalist.

"You're a teacher," she said. "A teacher who makes less than a fast-food chicken manager. You will never be able to retire. I will never have the life I deserve."

A former soldier, his name was Darren. What kind of a man's name was Darren? It didn't sound like a name. Not like Leonardo. *That* was a name.

But Darren had invented some portable device that filtered water or a knife that also started fires or some crap like that. He was wealthy. Two Teslas and a house on the lake wealthy. Travel to Europe for the weekend wealthy. So Gretchen left him.

Those Teslas were useless now. So was money. What failed to evaporate when the banks' digital systems collapsed under the weight of powerlessness had little value in a new economy that favored brutal strength over negotiated prices or supply and demand. There was little supply, and everyone left demanded everything they could find.

Leo scratched the stubble on his chin and considered whether Gretchen ultimately got the life she deserved. If she had, she was suffering somewhere. Or she was slowly devoured by the nomadic cannibal tribes that roamed Kentucky, Tennessee, and West Virginia.

For a long time he imagined her watching them eat her a bite at a time while keeping her alive long enough to comprehend the horror of it. It used to make him smile. Not anymore. He was as dispassionate about it as he was a healthy dump.

Leo no longer hated Gretchen, although he had for a long time. Love blooms into hate when it's shorn at the roots. But had it not been for her infidelity and emasculation, he never would have pushed himself to become more than he was. He wouldn't have seized on the opportunity to fill the power vacuum and take charge. Anger was a powerful motivator.

He leaned back against the bleacher bench above him and rested his elbows on the cool aluminum. On the opposite side of the stadium and beyond the fence, a cluster of tall but spindly pine trees swayed as if dancing in unison.

Leo reminded himself of the weak man he had been. He had let Gretchen walk all over him. While he thought he did it because he loved her, it was something else. It was, he later determined after a lot of Southern Comfort and a lot of soul searching, that he allowed her to dominate him because he was afraid.

He was afraid she would yell at him. He was afraid she might stop loving him. He was afraid she would leave him for another man.

In the end, it was a self-fulfilling prophecy. She left him anyhow. She stopped loving him, assuming she ever did, and she yelled at him relentlessly.

Every time he considered being soft on his militia, each instance in which he pondered mercy as a viable solution, he forced an image of Gretchen into his mind. It was not to gin up anger. It was to remind himself of what he had once been. Leo never wanted to be that man again.

He'd transformed himself into the ruler of this hamlet. Governing a wide swath of land and commanding an army was no easy task. It required discipline, ruthless disregard for humanity, and the ability to see threats five steps ahead. He was a man who disdained surprises.

He wanted to know his opponent's moves before *they* knew them. It was critical to sustained power.

Outwit. Outsmart. Survive.

Leo repeated that mantra to himself on a daily basis. If he could have those three words emblazoned on a coat of arms, he would do it. He hadn't conceived of them. Had he? Had they been the slogan of a television program? Or something close to it? It didn't matter. Television no longer existed. But he was here. The turn of phrase was his now.

He had repeated those words—outwit, outsmart, survive—countless times since the Chinese, or whoever it was, snapped off the power and demolished one of the greatest civilizations in the history of the modern world.

Leo closed his eyes and listened to the rain. The wind whistled and whooshed around him. His mind drifted, thinking of nothing for several moments, as he cleared his thoughts and meditated. He considered the newly acquired intelligence that changed everything. Had he been a fool?

Leo had played the long game. His rise to power was calculated, and so was his hold on it. His strengths were his patience and his ability to see what others might do before they themselves settled on a plan. He prided himself in having an almost intuitive hold on future events. Always ahead of the curve, he was unbeatable.

He'd known John Beck would come to Hopkinsville. It was only a matter of time. Everyone in this part of the world knew about the bounty the Sheriff had put on Beck's head. If even a small part of Beck's legend was true, Leo imagined Beck was not the kind of man to let a bounty stand. Killer and vigilante that he was, Beck would seek out the Sheriff himself. He would run into the fire and not away from it.

So when Beck arrived in Hopkinsville with his harem and half a stable of horses, Leo was ready. The fight was short. He'd lost a few men. And he'd bagged Beck.

Beck was his entrée to a tête-à-tête with the Sheriff. Leo assumed that with Beck in his possession, the Sheriff would grant him an audience, and he could either broker an agreement or start a war. One or the other.

But the Sheriff hadn't seen him. The Sheriff had, in fact, used force to push him away. It had surprised him at the time. Angered him.

Now, with what he had learned, it all made sense. And it

made him want war. Damn the peace. Leo hadn't seen the Sheriff's actions coming, and that bothered him. It nagged at him. It gnawed at his calm.

He would take the offensive. Truth was, he already had. Things were in motion. The Sheriff would never see it coming.

This brought a smile to his face. He felt it edge at his lips and stretch his cheeks.

It was good to have this time alone. To recharge. He tensed and relaxed his muscles, sensing the strain as he worked to ease the stress from his body. He inhaled slowly through his nostrils and filled his lungs, exhaling through his parted lips.

He was seated in the optimal position, but this was good. The solitude was the most important part.

"Sir."

Leo didn't want to open his eyes. He hoped that if he kept them closed long enough, the intruder would go away. It didn't work.

"Sir, I'm sorry to bother you, but—"

Leo sighed and opened his eyes. "Then why are you?"

The man, whom he recognized as more of a go-fer than a soldier, stood at attention at the bottom of the bleachers. His face twitched with confusion.

"Why am I...what...sir?"

"Why are you bothering me? Can't you see I'm meditating? I didn't come out here to socialize."

"I'm sorry, sir. I didn't mean to interrupt. But I thought you would want to know."

"Know what?"

The go-fer's shoulders slumped forward. It was apparent he was rethinking his decision to bother the boss. "It's just that—"

"Spit it out."

"Your lunch is ready."

Leo considered ending the go-fer's life right then and there. No warning. Shot to the head. Before he put his hand on his holster, he remembered the instructions he had given the late predecessor to this now-trembling sack in front of him. He had warned that if he had to eat a cold meal again, he would do unspeakable things to everyone involved in the preparation and delivery of the food, and their loved ones if they had any. From that day forward, his food was always hot.

Leo wondered if he waited much longer to reply to the go-fer whether he might wet himself. Feeling relatively mellow in the immediate wake of his meditation, he let the go-fer off the hook.

He smiled broadly and revealed his sparkling teeth. "Well, then, why didn't you say so? I'll be along shortly."

The tension released, and a nervous smile flickered at the edges of the go-fer's mouth. "Yes, sir. Thank you, sir."

The go-fer turned and marched through the rain at a quick pace. Halfway to the fieldhouse, where lunch was served, he slipped and lost his balance. He loped forward with his arms flailing until he landed face-first in the mud and slid several feet along the sloppy field.

Leo chuckled. Then laughed. "Wonderful," he said aloud.

The go-fer pushed himself to a knee and stood, only to lose his footing and fall again. Now Leo was fully entertained. He stood and applauded, cupped his hands around his mouth and hooted. "Well done!" he shouted. "Well done, young man."

The hapless go-fer sat up in the mud. He was drenched and covered in slop. In that moment, Leo liked the guy.

He stepped over the bench in front of him and descended

to the railing that separated the stands from the track around the field. He pulled a hooded jacket from the railing, shook the rain from it, and slid into it. There was a hole in one elbow, but the hood was in good shape and cinched tight.

Leo climbed over the railing and hopped onto the track. The go-fer was on his feet, appraising his filth, when Leo waved to him and caught his attention.

"Stay there," he called. "Hold on a minute."

The go-fer looked over one shoulder and then the other, unsure Leo was speaking with him.

Leo pointed directly at him. "Stay there! Don't leave!" he shouted above a gust of wind that blew rain across his face and into his eyes.

The go-fer swiped at the layer of mud on his shirt. It did no good. He tugged on the sleeves and then shook his arms like a dog might try to dry itself. It was comical.

Leo smiled as he approached. "Hey, what's your name?"

The go-fer's wary eyes widened. He pointed his thumb at his chest. "My name, sir?"

"You're the only one here."

"Casca."

"Casca? What kind of name is that?"

Casca squinted in the rain. He blinked away droplets from his lashes. "It was my father's name. A family name."

"What's your last name?"

"You want my last name, too?"

"You ask a lot of stupid questions, don't you?"

Casca demurred. He looked down at his muddy boots. Rain streamed from his drenched hair, which hung over his eyes.

"What's your last name? You're not in trouble."

Casca looked up. "Long."

"Casca Long. I like it. Has a certain nobility to it. Prince

Casca Long. Senator Casca Long."

Casca shrugged. "I never thought about it."

Leo wagged his finger. "Wait a minute. I know you. From the cell. You gave me a rag to wipe the blood from my face."

"Yes, sir."

Leo threw his arm over the go-fer's shoulder. Casca flinched. He walked with Leo as the ruler started to move toward the fieldhouse.

"You never gave any thought to your name?" Leo asked. "What type of person doesn't consider their name? How it would sound with a title?"

"Not me, sir."

"Of course you didn't," Leo said. "You seem too focused on the task at hand, at being a good public servant. I like that about you, Casca, and I especially like that you make me laugh."

Casca smiled and glanced over at Leo as a son might a father after unexpected praise.

"I've been looking for someone to work by my side," Leo went on. "Someone who can do the things I ask, deliver a rag before I ask for one, and who makes me laugh."

"I just try to anticipate—"

"Anticipation is the key," Leo said. "That is the key to everything. Knowing what is next before anyone else sees it. Forward-looking. Always having your mind's eye on a swivel. You were with me at Churchill Downs?"

"Yes."

"What was your job there?"

"Same as it's been. Grunt. Doing what needs to be done. I helped with the cart."

"I think I remember you. Maybe. Who knows? To be honest, you all blend together. Unless you make me laugh. And you make me laugh, *Casca*."

Concern pinched Casca's brow. "Make you laugh? I'm not funny. Nobody ever tells me I'm funny."

"Oh, you're funny," said Leo. "In more ways than you recognize. C'mon, let's get something to eat."

Leo pushed open the door to the fieldhouse and gestured for Casca to go first. The go-fer hesitated, as if the invitation were a trap.

"Go ahead," Leo said reassuringly. "I insist."

The two marched the long, dark hallway to an open dining area with large windows. This space was a late addition to the complex, meant for team meals before or after games. It was arranged like a school cafeteria with a serving line and rectangular tables set in rows across the room.

They used large propane tanks to fuel the gas burners in the kitchen. The collection of tanks had been a magnificent find three years earlier during a reconnaissance mission south of Hopkinsville. All it took was some ingenuity and a few bullets to relieve the owner of the stockpile.

Moving them to the fieldhouse was another matter altogether. However, they managed over the course of weeks, and since then, one meal a day was served hot. The hot food was a morale boost for his troops, who worked hard in exchange for the shelter and supplies Leo afforded them.

Leo nodded at some of these men as he strode past their tables with his hand on Casca's shoulder. He sensed their confusion, perhaps even their envy. Leo rarely offered any sort of affection toward his militia.

"You go first," Leo said when they reached the serving line. "Take two helpings if you want."

Casca shook his head. "No, thank you, sir. You should go first. I don't need the two helpings. Maybe someone else could use it?"

This surprised Leo. Most would have jumped on the

opportunity for double rations. That was an almost unheard-of treat, reserved for leaders who won skirmishes or brought home bountiful spoils.

"No, you go first. I insist. I order it. But if you don't want the extra food, that's fine. I would never force a man to take what he didn't want."

They both knew this was a lie. Leo had a way of enticing people to do what they might not otherwise choose.

"Okay. Thank you, sir," said Casca.

Curiosity glinted in Casca's eyes as he slid ahead of Leo in line. It told Leo the kid was unsure of what Leo's intentions were. Casca interrupted his meditation and now the ruthless leader, who relished death matches among his prisoners, was as gracious as a longtime friend.

Leo questioned his own intentions. He had yet to sort out what drew him to Casca beyond the humor. Yet there was something there. Leo sensed an importance about the kid, and he was rarely, if ever, wrong about people. His own wife notwithstanding.

Whatever it was, he wanted to explore it. Or exploit it. Besides, he needed someone he could trust. There was nobody. Perhaps this Casca Long could be that person.

"Go ahead and find a seat when you've got your food," Leo said. "Wherever you want to sit. If it's somewhere that's already occupied, sit there anyway. Tell them I said it was okay."

Casca nodded. When he had his food, he moved from the line toward the tables. Leo faced the room and watched him. This was the test.

The kid studied the rows of tables and moved toward an empty one in the back of the room. Then he stopped, pivoted, and went straight to the table at the center. It was full. Eight of the militia's bigger, more experienced soldiers

ONE IN THE HAND

sat shoulder to shoulder. They ignored Casca as he approached.

The kid cleared his throat. "Excuse me," he said.

When the men didn't give him their attention, he repeated himself. Louder. Almost a shout.

The room fell silent. The men faced the skinny, muddy Casca. Annoyance twisted their expressions like they'd practiced it together.

"We're eating," said one of them. "What do you want?"

"I'm sitting here," Casca said. His Adam's apple bobbed in his throat. "You're in my seat."

The men scowled, then laughed. They ignored him and went back to their food and conversation.

Leo smiled. He folded his arms across his chest. This was the moment. How would his man respond? Had Leo been right about what he saw in Casca's face, the determination?

Casca held the steaming plate of food. "I told you, I'm sitting here."

The big man closest to him shifted his weight and pivoted to face Casca. Before he could open his mouth to respond, Casca took his plate of food and smashed it into the man's face. The cheap ceramic plate shattered, and the man howled as the hot food burned the side of his face.

The next closest soldier stood up to retaliate, but Casca drove his elbow into the man's jaw before he could stand. He fell back into his chair, which toppled over.

As the burned man whimpered and clawed the hot leftovers from his face, Casca pulled his chair out from under him. The wounded man fell back and curled into the fetal position. Casca took his seat and scooted himself closer to the table.

The resulting silence was almost deafening. The remaining men at the table raised their hands in deference to Casca and got up from their seats. They took their plates and moved to the empty tables at the back of the room.

None of them helped the two wounded soldiers, who both rolled on the floor in pain. Casca took the full plate from the man whose face he's smashed with his elbow and slid it over in front of himself. Then he took a fork from the burned man's empty plate and stabbed the fork into the food. He had a mouthful when Leo crossed the room, stepped over the burned man, and took a seat next to him.

"Where did that come from?" Leo asked. "I had high hopes for you back there in the arena. But I have to admit, I did not expect that."

Casca swallowed his food. "I don't like bullies."

Leo nodded. He put his hands on the table in front of him on either side of his plate, palms down. "I'm a bully."

Casca jabbed his fork into the meat on his plate and then squirreled it into his cheek. He shook his head as he chewed. "You're the boss. There's a difference."

"Is that so? Educate me."

"Bullies have no power, so they engage in oppressive, abusive behavior. They're compensating for their own shortcomings, their own insecurities."

Leo drummed his fingers on the table. He smiled and leaned back. Casca was a revelation. "Bosses can be oppressive or abusive. I can be both of those things just like these saps you've laid out on the floor."

The one with the food on his face had crawled away from the table and was staggering from the room. The other was still on the floor. Blood pooled around his head and drained through the cupped hands that covered his nose and mouth.

"I'm sure you could be or have been," Casca said. "But not to me. As long as I've been here, you've issued reasonable orders. I've followed them either directly from you or through your subordinates and my superiors."

Leo referenced the table. "Were any of the men here your superior?"

Casca slid the side of his fork along his plate to scoop up the last of the meat. He shook his head. "I don't know who they are."

"How long have you been with us, Casca Long?"

"Since March. I think it was March 15 or thereabouts."

Leo leaned forward on his elbows. Was he staring at a unicorn? "How would you know that?"

Casca squeezed his eyebrows together, wrinkling his forehead. "What do you mean?"

"The date. How would you know the date?"

"I keep a pocket calendar with me. It's from before the power went out. That year, you know? On the back of it, it has the next five years in very tiny print, but I can read it, so I cross them off and keep track of the date. After next year it gets a little tougher."

"Why haven't I seen you before today?"

"You have, sir," Casca said. "Several times. But yesterday was the first time I've spoken to you. I keep my mouth shut and do my job."

"Interesting."

"Which makes me wonder why you're talking to me now. What did I do that gave you confidence in me? I just interrupted your meditation and then fell in the mud."

Leo pushed his plate toward the middle of the table. Intrigue displaced hunger. "That was all it took, Casca. You interrupted my meditation. You had the guts to talk to me at a time when nobody else would do it. Then you made me laugh. Nobody makes me laugh. Not from my gut."

"Your gut, huh?"

"Yes, my gut. My gut tells me there's much more to you,

young Casca Long, than meets the eye. I like that. You and I are going to be spending a lot of time with one another."

Casca studied Leo for a long moment. Then he put his fork onto his plate. He ran his tongue along his teeth and smacked his lips. "Is that a good thing?"

Leo laughed again. "Is that a good thing? I love it. Good question."

"What's the answer?"

There was a tiny hint of insolence in Casca's voice, as if he went up to the edge of disrespect but took a step back before leaping.

"Yes," Leo said. "It's a good thing. Very good. I need someone I can trust. Someone who will tell me the truth and won't candy coat, but is also someone in whom I can confide. Could you be that person?"

Wariness sparked in Casca's expression. He tilted his head to one side. "I'm not sure," he said. "I mean, it's weird to me that someone like you wouldn't already have a confidant. You have plenty of generals or whatever. Leaders in the militia. Aren't they trustworthy? You just met me, sir."

"I don't trust any of them farther than I can throw them. I keep everyone at arm's length. That's how a ruler has to operate. It's the safest way to run a kingdom."

"Kingdom, huh? Interesting."

"Why is that interesting?"

"I always thought the rule was to keep friends close and enemies closer. That's what I've heard. Especially if you see yourself as a king. From what I remember of history, kings were always getting offed, right? A lot of times by their own family."

"True," Leo said. "That's very true. However, I don't subscribe to that philosophy in the literal sense. And I never said I trust you now. I said I *want* to trust you. I need

96

someone to trust. There are days when I feel my grip slipping. It would be nice to have someone holding onto my wrist from above."

Casca nodded. He sighed again.

A worry niggled at the back of Leo's brain as he studied Casca studying him. There was something about this newcomer that felt familiar. Was it his face? His demeanor? The way he questioned the obvious? Or was it something else altogether? He would think on it later. Right now his task was to secure Casca's loyalty.

He slapped his hands together. "Come with me," he said. "Let's go."

Casca eyed Leo's plate. "You didn't eat, sir."

"I'm not hungry. Not now anyway."

The two stood, and Casca stepped over the bleeding man in front of him. He ignored the man's plea for help, as did Leo. They left him there on the floor and went back out into the rain.

"Where are we going?" Casca asked.

"The dungeon," Leo replied.

"Why?"

"I want to play a game."

"What sort of game? I don't understand."

"You will when we get there, Casca. Just be quiet. Listen. Watch. Learn."

CHAPTER 10

D-DAY + 4 YEARS, 6 MONTHS, 20 DAYS
HOPKINSVILLE, KENTUCKY

Regina hated isolation. That was where they had put her after
the arena, after Leo had made it clear she would fight Lucy to
the death.

The room was small, dark, and without any circulating air.
For endless hours, she couldn't count how many, she sat on
the floor, trying to ease the pain in her lower back.

She didn't know where they had put Lucy or Rebecca. It
made sense they were together. No reason to separate them
as they had her.

"We can't have you conspiring with your opponent," Leo
had said when he'd shoved her in the back and closed the
door behind her.

Lucy and Rebecca were not opponents. Not yet. It
apparently didn't matter how much conspiring they did.

The one consolation was the rain drumming on the ceiling
of her prison. It was nonstop. At times, it was so loud she
had trouble hearing her own thoughts. Maybe that was a
good thing. Regina's thoughts tended toward the nihilistic.

How could she have survived so much to end up here,
facing a death match with a compadre? Was there a cosmic

force up there bent on making her existence pointless?

It seemed so. The isolation only served to cement her opinion that everything was meaningless. This was as low as she had felt since the attack that killed the power and changed her world. Beck called it D-Day.

Beck.

She missed him. This surprised her, and it didn't. It was surprising because she had only known him a short time. Not surprising because they'd shared an instant connection. From the moment he and Lucas had stumbled into her encampment, there'd been a connection.

She hated that characterization. *Connection.* It reminded her of a reality-television dating show pre-D-Day. It sounded cliché. Yet it was difficult to come up with any other word.

It wasn't love. It couldn't be that. Could it?

There was mutual admiration. She'd felt it. Physical attraction? Definitely on her part, and she'd sensed it when his eyes lingered on her curves. Regina had curves. Always had. They were too much for her liking, but no matter how much weight she lost after D-Day, and she'd lost a lot, the curves remained.

She remembered a country song that elevated curvy women. "Body Like a Back Road"? Was that it? Although Regina remembered few songs, that was one of them.

The tune hummed in her head as she sat in the dark. Thinking about Beck was perhaps the only thing that kept her from giving up. He would come for her, wouldn't he?

She chose to believe he was alive, somewhere, and he would find her. He would rescue her. The thought made her pulse accelerate. Then she remembered the severity of his illness, how sick he'd looked when Leo's men hauled him away.

John Beck was unkillable. Right? He was a survivor. Right?

Regina clung to this notion in the dark as her thoughts swirled in a confusing, almost delirious mélange of past, present, and future. Exhaustion crawled through her body, and she lay on her side, trying to coax sleep and ease the pain in her lower back.

It might have been a minute or an hour, she couldn't tell, when the door creaked open, footsteps echoed against the concrete floor, and a boot toe jabbed her hip.

"Wake up."

She opened her eyes but saw nothing. Another jab.

"Get up, princess. It's time."

Time for what? The death match? That couldn't be. It was still raining outside. The roof told her that. Leo had promised her they wouldn't fight in the rain, in the mud. That would be degrading, he'd said with a sinister laugh. He couldn't have women mud wrestling. That, he'd said, was undignified.

The third jab with the boot was more of a kick. It hurt.

"Stop it!" she cried out.

"So she *is* awake," said Leo. "Good. Let's get moving. We have things to do."

Regina used her elbow to lean up. A sharp pain shot like a lightning bolt from her lower back to the back of her right knee. She winced but managed to sit up straight.

Her eyes adjusted to the surroundings. Leo stood in front of her with another man at his side. The other man offered a hand.

She declined. "I'm fine. I can stand on my own."

Leo nudged the other man. "See? I told you she was self-reliant. Impressive."

Regina stood and shook off the head rush that threatened her balance. She tugged on her shirt and pulled up her pants.

"This is Casca Long," Leo said. "He's my new...consigliere."

"So you're a crime boss now?" Regina asked. "A regular Mafioso?"

"That's a pejorative term," Leo said. "I like kingpin."

"What do you and your consigliere want with me? I thought we weren't fighting in the rain."

Leo chuckled. "Oh, you're not fighting. Not yet. I figured I might give you an opportunity to avoid the arena."

"Avoid it, how?"

Leo motioned to Casca. "Help her along." Then he eyed Regina. "You'll find out soon enough."

The sidekick, Casca, took her bicep in his strong grip and led her from the room and into a dimly lit hallway. Only the gray light from the outside provided any illumination. Regina's legs were weak; her mouth was dry. She was certain dehydration had taken hold.

That was one of the deadliest things post D-Day. Dehydration. Countless people died from lack of water. Dehydration really was the scourge of the modern society. The first thumps of a headache knocked at her temples. She needed something to drink.

"I need water," she said as they trudged from one corridor to another. "Otherwise, I'll be useless. Whatever you have planned, I need something to drink."

Leo kept walking. "Of course. We're not barbarians. I'll make sure you have plenty to drink when we get to our destination. I might even have some old aspirin if you'd like it. It's not as potent as it used to be, might only serve as a placebo, but you never know. Truth is, I need you at your sharpest."

Regina imagined that whatever this sadistic piece of trash had in mind was worse than the isolation. It struck her that living through an apocalypse was like descending through the levels of Hell. At each stop, she pined for the awful conditions of her previous circumstance.

Leo rambled something falsely philosophical, and Regina ignored it. His diatribe was a warbling hum in the back of her mind. She focused on the man who held her arm and guided her along the maze of passages toward their unknown destination.

Casca Long. That name was familiar. Where had she heard it? Clearly, this man was no legendary figure. He was a young, strong henchman for a would-be kingpin.

Why was he an advisor to Leo? Since when? She hadn't seen him before. Not in all of her previous interactions with Leo.

"Where did you come from?" she asked.

Casca glanced at her but said nothing. He tightened his grip.

"I was talking to you, consigliere," she said as they turned another corner. This place was endless.

Leo answered for him. "He came from Tennessee, I believe. Is that right, Casca?"

"Yes."

"He has an important future in this kingdom," said Leo. "He has nerve, gumption, and he makes me laugh."

Casca's cheeks blushed at this. Regina was unsure why. The joke was lost on her.

"You have a sense of humor?"

Leo stopped at a door. He pulled out a set of keys and unlocked the deadbolt. After he shouldered the door open, he held it for Casca and Regina. They passed him onto a landing that led to a flight of stairs, which dipped below grade. When they went in, it felt like they were descending into a black hole.

"I have candles down there," Leo said. "Just watch your step on the way down. And yes, I have a sense of humor. It's particular, but it's refined."

"Of course it is," Regina said.

She took small steps, sliding her feet along the stairs. Casca guided her. Another level deeper into Hell.

"I thought you had generators?" she asked.

Leo was behind them, his boot steps clunky on the steps. "Of course we do, but I don't see a need to waste valuable resources down here. Your eyes will adjust. You'll be fine."

They reached the bottom step, and Casca stopped.

Leo took the lead again. "It's not long now. Less than a mile."

Regina was incredulous. "A mile? In this dark? I'd rather fight to the death."

"It's less than a mile. If you drag one hand along the wall, you'll have no problem navigating the tunnel."

They walked in quiet for several minutes. Only the echo of their footsteps in the tunnel provided any noise. That, and the occasional whistle from Leo.

"These are old tunnels," he said, breaking the welcome relative silence. "I don't know exactly how old. Maybe Cold War, perhaps before that. But they're wonderful. I can navigate much of the town without having to expose myself to the elements or the threat of an enemy."

"You have a lot of those, do you?" Regina asked.

Leo didn't hesitate. "Of course. What leader doesn't? I was just telling our good friend Casca that people are always sniping at a king. They want what he has. They scheme and plot and do everything they can to take what is rightfully his. I don't trust anyone. The more precautions I can take, the better."

"You trust nobody?" Regina asked.

"No."

"Not even our good friend Casca?"

"Not yet. As I told you, he's from Tennessee. He's new to the game. I like his guile, but I can't trust him yet."

"An advisor is no good without trust."

Leo laughed. "I beg to differ."

"Do beg."

He laughed again. "You're funny. That's twice today somebody has made me laugh. Genuinely laugh. Such a rarity. Perhaps I should rely on you as my consigliere?"

"Sure," Regina said. "I'll give you great advice."

Another chuckle. "I'm sure you would. Now watch your step here. We're nearing the end of the tunnel. We'll come up on the other side. It's twenty-nine steps to the surface. I'll go first and unlock the door."

Regina counted. It was twenty-nine steps. The light hit her eyes and blinded her until she could adjust. When she did and saw the room before her, she was taken aback. They stood in a large space that resembled a library or a study. Stained wood was the dominant feature, and tall windows stretched from the floor to a very high ceiling. Was it twenty feet tall?

Condensation fogged the rain-dappled windows, but enough daylight shone into the room to make it plainly visible. Leo turned around to face her and spread his arms wide.

"I love this place. A relic of a bygone era. A peaceful enclave for the high-minded."

Casca let go of Regina's arm, and she shook herself free. The room was incredible. Like something out of a movie. A set designer's rendition of the perfect home library.

Shelves lined the walls with endless volumes in leather binding. A tall ladder on wheels connected to the shelves via rail. A large crystal chandelier hung from the ceiling as its grounding centerpiece. Though the chandelier was not lit, the filtered sunlight through the opaque glass still managed to make the individual crystals sparkle.

Overstuffed chairs, leather and chenille, dotted the space. They sat on intricately designed parquet floors.

Although a fine layer of dust dampened the glamour, it was not enough to ruin the aesthetic.

"Where are we?" Regina asked, the wonder evident in her voice.

She almost forgot she was a prisoner. The wonder of it transported her to another time and place. She walked over to the largest of the bookshelves and trailed her fingers along the spines. She left clean paths the width of her fingertips in her wake. The books were a remarkable collection of works. She recognized almost all of them, even the ones she'd never read. More than anything, in that moment, she wanted to plop into one of the overstuffed chairs, curl her legs, tuck her feet behind her, and crack open a book. Any of them.

One of the many things lost in the aftermath of the EMP attack was idle time. It was gone. Snuffed out with the power grid. She could count on her dust-coated fingers the number of times she'd had time to chill, to escape the horrible and challenging reality of her circumstance.

She often chuckled to herself at the thought of all the things she'd taken for granted before the end of the world as she knew it. The list grew every time she considered what she, and almost everybody else in the former United States, had lost.

A good book was the beginning. It was the most crucial to Regina. She often wished she had somehow found refuge in a library, set up a fortress around it, and survived in a cocoon of fiction. How incredible that would be.

Books were not the only joy absent. Long, hot baths were gone, too. Short, hot baths. Hot baths. Baths at all. Unless one considered bathing in a river or a stream a bath. Regina did not. That was swimming, not bathing.

Grocery stores with fresh produce and cold milk. Regina was one of those shoppers who worked the exterior of the store. She stayed away from the aisles in the middle, with the boxed and canned foods. By sticking to the perimeter when she shopped, only fresh goods went into her basket. That, and an occasional chocolate bar at the checkout line. She missed cheese, too. Sharp cheddar. Good lord, she missed cheese.

The internet. That was a love-hate relationship. But in the wake of the attack, she hated how much she had loved the internet. The useless clickbait links on which she'd wasted mindless hours while scrolling through her Facebook, Instagram, or Twitter feeds.

Regina never posted much, and she was definitely not the selfie type. But she was a voyeur of sorts and enjoyed the time suck through other people's manufactured public lives. That was gone, too.

And it was weird, because during the pandemic in 2020, when she'd quarantined with most of the world, that digital connection had remained. She was alone without ever really being alone. That was an emotional luxury that had died on D-Day.

Music, too. And music she didn't have memorized. All she had to do was ask Alexa or Siri or Google to play a song for her, and there it was. She could listen to it over and over or skip to the next song. Music was omnipresent before D-Day. Now it too had vanished. Once, she found an old record player with an internal speaker in an abandoned apartment outside Austin. Next to the turntable was a modest collection of vinyl. She'd plucked Guns N' Roses' *Appetite for Destruction* from the stack and slid the disc from its protective sleeve.

She'd placed the disc on the player, lowered the needle,

and manually spun the record with her index finger. The speaker didn't work, so the exercise was pointless. She sang the chorus to "Paradise City" to herself and cried. It was another realization of the life she no longer lived.

Now in this library, she wondered if hope existed after all. Perhaps, at some point, she could settle down and read. She could stop wandering. Stop worrying. Stop killing.

Leo broke her reverie. "This is impressive, isn't it?"

"What is it? Where are we?"

"Does it matter?"

Regina shrugged. It didn't.

Leo motioned to a game table by the window. Two high-backed chairs faced each other on opposite sides. Now she knew what this was about.

"Come sit," he said. "I'd like to play a game."

She hesitated and stood her ground. "You want to play chess?"

On the table was an ornate chess set. The pieces appeared carved from marble. They were beautiful. The knights were tall, thin horses, the rooks stout battlements. Bishops held their hands in prayer at their chests, and regal likenesses were carved into the faces of the queen and king.

The board was cherry and pine, or something close to it. Walnut? She wasn't good with refined and stained woods. Get her in the forest and she could name them. Cut them down and repurpose them, and not so much.

Leo took his seat. Casca stood behind him, playing well the part of a consigliere. "Please," Leo said. "It's not as though you have a choice. This is your opportunity to avoid the arena."

Regina folded her arms across her chest. "What about Lucy?"

Leo shrugged. He folded one leg across the other. "What about her?"

"Can she avoid the arena?"

He picked imaginary lint from his pant leg. "Doubtful."

"I'm not playing."

He tilted his head. "I think you are."

"Why?"

"Why not?"

"I don't understand. What's your angle?"

Leo sighed. "No angle. I like chess. You said out there at the arena you knew the rules of the game and could play. I want to play. That's it, nothing more. My enticement is that if you beat me, you avoid the arena."

"What if I lose?"

Leo smiled. He stared into her eyes. "Haven't you already?"

Regina scanned the room. Suddenly, its dusty luster was gone. She could no longer see the rows and rows of beautiful books. Everything dissolved into a haze other than the chessboard and the man demanding she play.

"I'm not very good," she told him.

This was desperate, and she knew it as soon as the words slipped from her mouth. There was no choice here. Leo wanted her to play. He was her captor and she his prisoner. She would do what he demanded.

"I'll be the judge of that." Leo motioned to the empty chair across from him.

She relented and crossed the room to the chair. When Casca moved to help her, she waved him off. He stayed at his position behind his boss. She sank into the chair and pulled herself forward to sit up on its edge.

Leo was close enough to her that she smelled his dampness. It was something akin to mildew but somehow riper. It took everything in her not to curl her lip in disgust and cover her nose with the back of her hand. When they'd traveled the tunnel, she'd recognized the moldy odor but thought it was their surroundings. Now it was clear to her the dank scent was her opponent.

"I've taken the liberty of picking white for you," Leo said. "That means you go first."

Regina studied the pieces and reminded herself of their moves. This was more complicated than checkers, a game she enjoyed more than chess. Yet as she surveyed the board, she was confident she remembered how to play.

She put her hands in her lap and laced her fingers together. She inhaled slowly and tried to think of the best opening move. A pawn? A knight? Definitely a pawn.

Leo referenced the board. "Go ahead. Make your move."

Regina glanced up at him but kept her chin down. She lifted an eyebrow. "Are we on a clock?"

This drew a smile. "No. We are not. But I'm an impatient man. I only have so much time for fun and games."

"Then we should have played blackjack. It would have gone much faster."

He wagged a finger at her. "See? I told you that you were funny. There you go again with a sharp quip."

Regina worked through moves in her mind, trying to refresh her elementary knowledge of the game of kings. Then something clicked. She suppressed a wry smile and put her hands on either edge of the board. Without looking at her opponent, she spun the board one hundred eighty degrees.

"You go first," she said. "Just take it easy on me. Start with the pawns, please."

She looked up to find Leo studying her. He leaned back in his chair and rubbed his chin. Did he see what she was thinking? He nodded. Apparently not.

"Fair enough," he said. "I'm nothing if not a generous host. If my guest wants me to take the lead, I'm obliged to comply."

He leaned forward and moved his king's bishop's pawn one space forward. He let his fingers linger on the piece, as if there was more to consider, then let go and gestured to Regina.

"Your move, sweet."

Regina puffed her cheeks and held her breath. After she made a quick survey of the board, she moved her finger to several pieces before moving her king's pawn two spaces forward. She exhaled and sat back in her chair.

Without hesitating, Leo moved his hand to his king's knight pawn and slid it forward two spaces. He stayed on the edge of his seat, made a steeple with his fingers, and rested his chin on them, his eyes focused on Regina.

Regina suppressed another smile. Cognizant of Leo's intense gaze, she wiggled her fingers and let her hand hover over one piece, then another. She shifted in her seat. Then swiftly, she plucked her queen from its home space and moved it diagonally four spaces to the edge of the board.

Regina sat back and folded her hands in her lap. "Checkmate."

She looked up at a wide-eyed Leo. His eyes danced across the board. He opened his mouth to speak but said nothing. He tried again. Words apparently failed him.

"You can't move your king," Regina said. "You cannot defend it. Checkma—"

"I am aware," Leo hissed.

His face reddened, and he sucked in audible breaths through flared nostrils. Again, he scanned the board. When he accepted the inevitability of it, he tipped his king onto its side and offered his hand.

Regina hesitated. He gestured with his hand again. She took it, and he gripped it. Then he put his other hand atop both.

"Fool's Mate," he said. "I've never seen anyone do that in person, and I certainly didn't expect it from you. Caught me totally off guard. That's one game for you."

She tried to pull away, but he held on, and she couldn't. Regina shook her head. "I won. That's it."

"Best two of three."

"That's not what we agreed," Regina said. "You said I beat you and I don't have to face Lucy in the arena."

"We technically didn't agree to anything," Leo said. "I made a proposal, and I don't recall an agreement. I certainly never said it would be a single game."

Regina yanked away her hand, and he let go, though he held his hands in place, hovering above the board for several seconds before he raised them, palms out.

"It's fine," he said. "You can go back to your room."

He looked out the window. The rain beat against the fogged panes. The blurred images of green pines swayed in the yard outside.

"You can wait until this rain clears," he said. "Once it does, whenever that is, we'll wait for the arena to dry out a bit. In this heat, it won't take long. Water evaporates like that." Leo snapped his fingers. The volume of it startled her. "It won't be long, and I'll have you out on that field, facing off with Lucy. What weapon do you think you'd like? Anything but a gun."

Regina eyed the board, looked at his toppled king. She understood she had no choice. It was either play by his rules or not play at all. "Fine," she said. "I'm white this time."

A broad grin stretched across his face. His white teeth almost glowed in the dim light. He snapped his fingers again, this time at Casca. "Would you get us a drink? There is a bar cart on the far side of the room."

Casca stood even with his boss and searched the opposite end of the library. He pointed to a dark corner.

"Yes," Leo said. "Over there. We like to save it for special occasions. This is one, yes?"

Regina shook her head. "I don't drink."

Leo chuckled. "You'd refuse some of Kentucky's finest?"

She eyed the board, running through various permutations of the next game. She had an opening in mind, but she couldn't see more than two moves ahead. Regina was no expert or skilled player, not by a long shot. That she had remembered the Fool's Mate from her childhood was a miracle. That Leo hadn't seen it coming, had fallen into her trap, was even more miraculous. One in a million. She wouldn't be so lucky in game two. Regina sat forward and put her elbows on her knees.

Leo spoke to her, or spoke to hear himself talk, but she didn't listen. She had too much at stake and needed to focus.

While it was true that she was a bigger fan of checkers and that chess was not her game, in elementary school she had taken part in an after-school chess program. Mr. Steven Lawrence was her teacher. Patient and kind, his love for the game was infectious. Regina was not even close to the best student in his program, but she tried hard, and with a steel trap for a memory, she could win matches against other children her age. As long as they didn't know what they were doing, she was golden. When she faced classmates who actually had a penchant for chess, they would rub the floor with her.

All these years later, as she stared down at the board and tried to concoct some semblance of a strategy, some of those basic openings came back to her. She strained the memories tucked back into the farthest corners of her mind, urging them forward as if her life depended on them.

Because it did.

Casca returned with two half-empty leaded glasses. A brown liquid sloshed around in both. He handed one to his boss.

"I didn't want one," Regina said.

Casca flashed a smile and winked. "It's not for you."

He toasted her and tossed back the glass, downing the drink in a single, skilled swig.

Leo swirled his glass and eyed the contents. He chuckled. "Funny," he said. "I didn't say you could have some."

"That's true, sir," said Casca. "You also didn't tell me I couldn't have any."

Leo laughed. He raised his glass and gestured at the consigliere. "You do make me laugh. This is why I like you, Casca Long."

Regina heard the aide's name again, and now she laughed. Her focus on the game was lost for an instant as she placed where she had heard the name before, or a close facsimile.

Leo took a sip of his drink. He closed his eyes and appeared to relish it for a moment. Then he asked, "Why are you laughing?"

Regina pointed to herself. "Me?"

"Yes, you."

She glanced over at Casca. "Is that really your name?"

The consigliere stiffened. Fear flashed in his eyes, the kind of look one sibling gives another when hiding a secret from a parent. It was just a fleeting instant, and then it disappeared. His jaw set, and he pulled back his shoulders. "It is. It was my father's name, and his father's before that."

Leo rubbed his thumb along the edge of the glass. He studied both of them and took another long, slow sip. "There is nothing like Kentucky Bourbon," he said. "Nothing in the world. It was a treasure before the Chinese attacked us. Even more so now."

"Was it the Chinese?" Regina asked, trying to change to subject.

She decided to play this other game, too. Casca's charade. She was positive that was not his name, and she wondered if its significance might factor into something bigger. She had nothing to lose by helping Casca keep his true identity hidden for now. And perhaps, down the road, she could have something to gain.

Leo followed her lead after another, longer pull. "Of course it was the Chinese. It was their jets that dropped the electromagnetic pulse weapons all over the place. Everybody knows that."

"Everybody *thinks* they know that," Regina said. "I'll go along with the Chinese jets and all that, but nobody knows for sure who was behind the attacks. It could have been any of our enemies. It could even have been Americans. You know, flying Chinese jets to throw off the scent."

Leo laughed incredulously. "A false flag? To what end? No American political faction gained anything from the attacks. None."

"Who says it was a political faction? Maybe it was a collection of tech wizards. Or bankers."

"The financial elite? Also ridiculous. They had nothing to gain. If anything, those two sectors had the most to lose. No electricity, no internet, no computers, no online banking. Seriously, woman, I'm becoming more embarrassed by the second that I lost to you in a game of chess."

And distracted, she hoped. Between the alcohol and the fomented idea of an inside job, he might miss key moves. His ability to see five moves ahead might shrink to three or even two.

This was the chess equivalent of getting inside her opponent's head. Trash talk. Wasn't that what athletes used to call it when they played mind games?

Leo drained the glass and shook it at Casca. "A double for me. You may have whatever pleases you."

Casca took the glass, shot Regina a glance that seemed to convey appreciation, and walked toward the bar cart at the opposite end of the room. His boots left muddy prints on the floor as he marched away.

Leo referenced the board. "Reset the pieces. Let's go. I don't have eternity."

Regina reset the pieces and made her first move. She took her king's pawn and moved it forward two spaces. Leo quickly countered with an identical move.

Regina worked the moves in her head. Her basic understanding of the game only gave her an advantage in the opening. Once they moved to middle game, she was toast.

There were several possibilities, but she took her king's bishop and moved it even with her pawn. Leo hesitated and put a finger on another pawn, then changed his mind. He moved his queen's knight up two spaces and over one toward the center of the board.

Casca returned with two more bourbons, both doubles. Leo took his glass without looking at Casca or thanking him. His attention stayed on the board even as he took a long draw from the glass. He shifted in his chair and crossed his ankles.

Regina moved her queen diagonally four spaces to the edge of the board. This pinned a pawn in front of Leo's king.

He took another drink, his focus shifting from piece to piece. He touched a knight, then a pawn. He tried one and another. Finally, after several minutes, he moved his king's knight up two spaces and in one. This attacked Regina's queen.

He held his finger on the piece, looking at the board again, and let go. He sat back and drew the glass to his lips. Leo was self-satisfied, and Regina saw he had a plan now. It gestated and was about to birth itself onto the board. His win played across his face with twitches at the corners of a widening grin. How many moves into the future had he seen? Was she missing something?

Regina second-guessed her approach. She didn't expect the attack on her queen.

"Don't feel bad," Leo said. "We all outthink ourselves. Some of us imagine a false flag; others of us fall prey to a child's ridiculous opening salvo. It's not how we fail that matters, mind you, it's what we do after the failure. It's how we comport ourselves in the wake of momentary idiocy that matters."

"What's that supposed to mean?" Regina asked. She took her eyes from the board. Now he was playing the mind games, talking trash.

Leo leaned back and crossed one leg over another, no longer in a hurry to play the game. He relished this victory, having figured out her simple strategy. After another sip of the rare bourbon, he referenced her with the glass. "I doubt you'll learn from *your* stupidity. Conspiracy theorists like you always live in a world where things must be more complicated than they appear, that there is some grand cabal out to exact revenge on the little people. If you'll fall for conspiracies, you'll fall for anything."

"I don't track what you're saying. What does my suggestion about a false-flag attack have anything to do with chess? Anything to do with learning from my mistakes? Or you from yours?"

He feigned a pout. His tone carried a newfound condescension. "And here I thought you were smart. You're like a student I once had who came in on the first day of class all vim and vigor. Sits in the front row, asks questions, and engages. By week three, I've learned the student has no clue what's going on, can't pass a quiz let alone an exam, and is essentially all bluster, hoping that recognition and participation trumps actual knowledge."

Regina didn't follow his train of thought. If it was a train, it was off the rails. Clearly the liquor was not only dancing in his head, it had taken the lead.

"What are you talking about?"

"I'm saying you're not as smart as you think you are. I'm saying I thought you were smarter than you are. You talked a good game out in the arena when we watched the gladiators yesterday. But you lost me with the conspiracy stuff. You're unteachable, and that will be your undoing."

"So you're better than me?"

"I learn from my mistakes. I don't make the same error twice. I don't underestimate my opponents, those who would take what I have. That's why I'm sitting here and you're sitting there." He finished the double shot and motioned for her to get on with it. "Make your move. No sense in prolonging the inevitable. I can already see the checkmate."

Regina moved her queen diagonally forward and to the right two spaces. She took the king's bishop's pawn and removed it from the board. "I do, too. Checkmate."

She leaned back and watched Leo eye the board with an expression that conveyed confusion, horror, and anger. His face reddened, his grip tightening around his glass.

"What were you saying about learning from your mistakes?" Regina taunted, understanding full well she risked a violent wrath. "That was called the Scholar's Mate. It was the first opening I learned as a kid. You could've easily defended it with your pawn."

He sat stunned.

Regina touched the pawn in front of his king's knight. "This one. Move it forward a spot, and my opening is thwarted. You could've also used your queen. That would have been easy, too. But I suspect you were looking so far down the road, you couldn't see the forest for the trees, am I right?"

Leo hadn't used the rhetorical phrase in the last day. She threw it back at him, along with his pride.

Casca stood motionless beside the board. He had yet to drink from his double. His expression was taut and expectant. A volcano was on the verge of eruption.

Then it erupted. Leo threw the glass across the room, spraying bourbon onto the board and onto Regina's face. Then he stood and flipped the board over. The pieces flew into the air and tumbled. The board knocked against Regina's knees and dropped to the floor.

Leo arched his back and roared. The heavy wood and the volumes of books absorbed the echo of his rage, and he marched across the room. Fists clenched, he paced back and forth. Seething, he mumbled to himself through a flexing jaw.

Regina waited for him to stop pacing. Then she said, "Three out of five?"

Leo took two lunging steps forward and reared back. Regina froze from the shock of the quick, violent approach. His eyes bulged with anger, and she flinched, expecting blunt force. Before he reached her, however, Casca stepped between them and held out his glass.

"Sir," he said, "this is for you. I knew you'd want a third, and you seem to have spilled your second."

Leo huffed. His chest heaved, and his eyes darted between his consigliere and his adversary. He started to spit something but stopped himself. His nostrils flared and then constricted as he took rapid breaths in and out.

"Sir," Casca said, "take it easy. You'll get much less pleasure from hurting her here than you will from seeing her fail in the arena. Am I right?"

When he said the phrase, it came across as a reminder to his boss of who he was, of how many he commanded, and how high his station remained.

"Nobody knows what happened here. It was a friendly game of chess. You were distracted, and she blindsided you with tricks. None of that is worth the remorse you will feel after—"

Leo jabbed a finger into Casca's chest. "Don't tell me what I feel. Understood?"

Casca nodded and held out the drink. Leo took it and downed the entirety of it in a single long swig. He handed back the glass and adjusted his clothing. With both hands, he smoothed his hair and forced a smile.

"I'm fine, Casca. Step aside."

The consigliere did as instructed.

Regina wondered if her ploy was worth it. Now it seemed she might be worse off than if she had lost both games. Perhaps he was right in that she was too smart for her own good. Or not smart enough. She was unsure what his soliloquy truly meant.

"You won. Twice," Leo said to her, his tone softer. "Tricky as you were and untrue to the spirit of the king's game, you won. I am a man of my word. Not a barbarian, as so many would suggest. You have freed yourself of the obligation to compete as a gladiator. No arena for you."

A weight lifted from her shoulders. Relief swam through

her body, and she wanted to cry. Regina sat up straight and pretended his pronouncement meant nothing.

"What about Lucy?" she asked.

"What about her?"

"Is she also out?"

"Out of what?"

"The arena. Since I don't have to fight her, does she have to fight at all?"

Leo's brow relaxed, and the smile returned. It spread into that noxious grin, and he chuckled. "Of course she has to fight. She didn't best me in chess."

"Who is she fighting if not me?"

"Oh, that's easy, and it's so obvious," Leo said. "Apparently you can't see past the opening moves. Clearly if you could, you wouldn't have repeated your mistake."

Her mind raced. What did he mean? "What mistake?"

"Beating me twice. Now instead of you, your friend Lucy will fight to the death against that injured little one. The girl. Rebecca."

Regina shook her head. Her pulse quickened with panic. "No. You can't do that. That's not fair."

"Nobody ever said anything about fairness. And I can do whatever I want. In fact, I think after one of them kills the other, I'll kill the survivor. Right there in front of everyone. Including you. You get a seat front and center. What is it called? The duke's seat? It's yours. Keep it a secret, okay? I wouldn't want the surprise ending getting out too soon."

Regina choked back tears. She couldn't find the words. Her stomach churned.

Leo put a finger to his lips. "Shhhh."

CHAPTER 11

D-DAY + 4 YEARS, 6 MONTHS, 20 DAYS
NEAR ELIZABETHTOWN, KENTUCKY

Beck pedaled against the wind and into a driving rain. The movement was slow and painful. His clothes were drenched and threatened to rub him raw in all the wrong places. Each clap of thunder almost sent him tumbling over the front of the handlebars. After one that nearly deafened him, Millie stopped and waved at him. She straddled her bike, feet on the road. With one hand she pointed off toward the west. She said something he couldn't hear, the thunder ringing in his ears. So he pedaled closer to her, and she repeated herself.

"Over there," she said, her voice lifted above the pounding rain and howling wind.

Beck followed the aim of her outstretched arm. "What?" he shouted. "I don't see anything."

She pointed again as if to accentuate her words. "Over there. Smoke. See it? There's smoke."

Beck scanned the gray horizon through the curtain of rain. It took him close to a minute, but he found it. A thin finger of smoke lifting into the sky before it spread and disappeared into the low clouds. "That's a fire. Like from a fireplace or a camp."

"I know," Millie said. "I—"

The hairs on Beck's arm tingled, and lightning lit up the sky. In the millisecond before the crash of thunder knocked him from his bike to the ground, he caught the image of a farmhouse. It was less than a quarter mile from them. Probably closer. It couldn't be a quarter mile. Visibility was poor. Among the rain, the mist, the low clouds, and his exhaustion, he resolved there was no way it was more than one hundred yards.

Chris hopped from his bike and helped Beck to his feet. Beck thanked him and regretted his sucker punch to the kid's face. He steadied his bike and swung a leg over it as if mounting a horse. The three huddled close together.

"I saw a house," Beck said. "Close."

"I saw it, too," Millie said. "That's where the smoke's coming from. Someone's home. They could give us shelter."

Beck swiped the water from his eyes and, for the first time, was envious of his daughter's Stetson. He was never much of a hat guy. A full head of hair would do that. Besides, he never minded the beat of the sun on his face. The relentless rain was another thing. It annoyed him, distracted him from his focus.

He squinted at the house. It was closer than he thought. In a matter of seconds they were at the edge of a gravel drive, which sloped toward the house along a low rise before it looped back toward the road farther from them. They rode the bikes to the side of the house and left them there inside a thin waterfall of rain that fell from the farmhouse's gutterless roof.

The house itself was white. Or mostly white. The painted clapboard was missing paint. It looked as if some giant had come by with a sanding block and did a number on the place. Faded shutters framed the intact windows but hung askew. Some flapped in the straight-line winds and banged against the house with a precise rhythm, which complemented the regular intervals of thunder and constant patter of rain atop what Beck realized was actually a tin roof. The metallic ping of the rain should've made it obvious when they approached, but he was otherwise engaged in his surveillance of his surroundings. They walked along the side of the house, against one side of its wraparound porch, and Beck noticed virtually no dust on the covered front porch. The wide pine slats, though warped, cracked, and faded from heat and age, were spotless.

Beck also took stock of the property around the house. It was clear of debris. Even the wooden fence that lined the perimeter was in decent condition. New, fresh wood mingled with the weathered gray posts in spots where damage or age had necessitated replacement. The yard was absent the weeds that infiltrated every yard he had seen from Florida to New Mexico. The rain fell onto what passed for a manicured yard and into a neatly cultivated garden edged with rail timbers.

Whoever lived here took care of the place. That was obvious.

That was a good sign. Crazy people let the property go to hell. Caretakers typically took pride in their homes. Beck was sure he had read that somewhere once. Or Gabe had read it to him. Or maybe it was something the old friend had recited from a movie. Neither here nor there, it held true in Beck's experience. These observations gave him hope.

His boots sloshed in muddy puddles that pocked the rutted drive. He was thankful for the extra pairs of socks in his pack. Always carry extra socks. He had taught Millie that when she was young.

"Always have a flashlight, water to drink, and an extra pair of socks," he'd said more than once.

Debbie had challenged his logic. "What about underwear?

You can't wear that more than once. I'd pack extra drawers over socks."

She said drawers like a true country girl. *Drawwws*.

"Sure you can," Beck said. "Flip 'em around and that's two uses. Then turn them inside out. That's three. Then flip 'em again. Four uses. By then, you could probably go back to how you wore them the first day. Socks might get two uses. If you're lucky and they don't get wet."

Debbie had laughed and called him disgusting. She'd then accepted his socks over underwear ideology. So did Millie. All of these years later, the bag she'd packed him had extra socks.

He watched his daughter, the Stetson-wearing Sheriff, lead them to the front porch. She had her rifle leveled at the place and swept it from side to side as she approached with caution. Chris was equally defensive in his posture. He breathed through his nose, which sounded like a cat purring with a hairball in its throat. Beck wanted to apologize again. Instead, he took aim with his handgun and scanned the home's surroundings.

Like all houses post-D-Day, no electric lights lit the interior, but this one was absent the candlelight that warmed most homes with their orange-yellow flicker. From the front, the fire burning inside a hearth was not visible.

It almost gave Beck a *Texas Chainsaw Massacre* vibe. Not that he'd seen the film, but Gabe had told him enough about the plot to give him a good sense of the foreboding he now felt. He suppressed his apprehension and pressed forward.

"I'm going to knock," Millie said. "I'll lower my weapon. You two cover me."

"I can do it," Beck said. "You don't need to…"

He stopped himself. This was her mission and not his. She was in charge, not him.

"I got it, Dad. Women are less threatening. They're less

likely to open fire if I'm the one who knocks."

"Okay."

Their relationship, like any healthy one, was a give and take. For the moment, Beck was content to do the giving. He'd already done more than his fair share of taking. His daughter clearly wanted to prove something to him or to herself. Either that, or she was still hot and cold to her old man. It was another thing that reminded him of Debbie. Another thing he probably deserved.

Millie took two confident strides and lifted her hand to knock on the door with the heel of her fist. As she reared back, the door swung open. A woman straight from a Grant Wood painting stood at the threshold in a pink floral ankle-length frock and a powder blue apron. She had a long, almost equine face and stringy hair pulled tight into a bun at the back of her head. Round, frameless glasses perched on her button nose. She had one hand on the door and the other on her narrow hip.

She smiled, revealing poor dental hygiene. Actually, post D-Day, her lack of teeth was average dental hygiene. She didn't hold a chainsaw or any power equipment as far as Beck could tell.

"Well, hello there," she said like she was welcoming family to a holiday supper. "So nice to see you. What can I do to help you folks? Is it the rain? Do you want out of the rain?"

The woman shifted her weight. Her toes curled under her bare feet. She studied each of them with friendly but curious glances. When none of them spoke immediately, the woman took her hand from the doorknob and waved it in the air above her head. She laughed, and it only amplified her horse-girl energy.

"I do apologize," she said and pressed a hand to her chest, fingers spread. "Bless your hearts. I tossed out a feed bag full of questions, didn't I? Let me start over. What can I do to help?"

"We would like to come out of the rain, if you don't mind," Millie said. "We're on a long trek to find some friends, and the rain's getting the better of us. We won't be any trouble. Just a dry spot until the rain passes."

Millie had slipped into a different drawl, one that almost mimicked the woman at the door. It was impressive. Beck suppressed a smile. Like a chameleon, she adapted to her surroundings.

She extended her hand to the woman. "I'm Millie. This is my friend Chris, and that's my dad."

The woman's smile disappeared for an instant as she looked at the men. Her gaze lingered on Beck the way someone who recognizes a face but can't place a name. She took Millie's hand.

"I'm Dolly. Like Dolly Parton. She's an angel, isn't she? My daddy said when I came into this world, I was singing sweet like Dolly, so that's what they named me."

"Nice to meet you, Dolly," Millie said. "Again, we don't mean to impose."

Dolly waved her hand as if the idea were preposterous. "Of course not. We get travelers from time to time. It's tough out there. They come here seeking shelter or food. We're happy to oblige."

She leaned forward and put her hand next to her mouth as if sharing a secret. "Truth be told, it's nice to talk to someone other than Daddy."

Another voice bellowed from inside the house, "Who's at the door, Dolly?"

The young woman smiled and glanced over her shoulder. "It's visitors," she said. "Travelers looking for some shelter from the storm."

A large man appeared at the door. He stood beside Dolly and filled the empty space. The man stood at least six feet five and was almost as wide. He wore a long-sleeved T-shirt underneath ample blue denim overalls and a long calico beard. A swirl of gray hair atop his head almost resembled soft serve atop a waffle cone. The sides were shaved. His daughter had more teeth remaining than he. His smile appeared warm and inviting, which belied his imposing stature.

He appraised Beck and his companions. His gaze, like Dolly's, lingered on Beck a little longer than the others.

"I'm Dale. You already met my daughter, Dolly."

"Nice to meet you, Dale. I'm Millie, this is my dad, and that's Chris."

Dale looked at Beck but spoke to Millie. "Your dad got a name?"

"I'm John," Beck said, taking the onus from Millie. No need to give away his last name.

"Where are you three headed?" Dale asked. His tone reminded Beck of a state trooper at a traffic stop. Benign questions whose answers revealed more than was obvious.

"Hopkinsville," Millie said. "We have friends there."

Dale's expression tightened. "Your friends are with the militia?"

Millie shook her head. "No. The militia has our friends. We're going to get them."

Dale's features softened. He nodded as if he understood the predicament. Or was it something else? Did he know something about the militia he didn't divulge? He tilted his head to one side. "I don't envy you that," he said. "C'mon in and take a load off. You can get dry, rest up."

Dolly pressed her back against the door to make room and gestured them into the house.

Millie went first, Chris followed, and Beck was last.

"Thank you," he said to Dolly as he crossed the threshold. The wood planks creaked under the weight of his boots.

When he entered, Dale shifted his weight, almost blocking Beck. He extended a hand. Beck took it, and they shook. Dale studied him, his eyes dancing across Beck's face, looking for clues.

"You look familiar," he said. "We met somewhere before, John? Maybe before the power went out? You farm near here or work in town?"

Beck held Dale's gaze, resisting the urge to look away. "I don't think so, Dale. I get that a lot, though. Must be I have one of them faces."

He stepped in and tripped. There was a collection of boots, different sizes, by the front door. Dale tugged and tightened his grip, drawing Beck's attention from the boots and back to him.

"Must be that," he said. "Must be."

Dolly closed the door behind them. Then she locked it.

CHAPTER 12

Beck stared into the fire. He half-listened to the conversation as he focused on the flames and the radiant heat on his face.

He remembered how the ocean used to have this effect on him. He could stand on the deck of the *Charybdis*, the large deep-water drilling platform on which he worked before D-Day, and stare for hours at the Gulf waters. He studied the horizon and the distant ships passing along the line between air and sea, which stretched in all directions.

The vastness of the water, the sense of diminution he felt standing alone far from shore, was awesome. It gave him peace and helped him compartmentalize his worries. Everything, when compared to size of the ocean, was relatively small.

Fire now replaced the water. He could stare into the flames, the shifting licks and colors, and lose himself. The incredible power of the fire made him feel as weak as the ocean made him feel small. It also helped him understand how nature was in control. He could only do so much to change the course of things.

He studied the oranges and yellows, the hints of blue that wavered along the base of the flames where they emanated at the logs, and reminded himself of how blessed he was to have found his daughter. How the demons were wrong about him. How he was doing right by his friends to go find them. Perhaps, in all of this, he was salvageable, and his soul was not damned.

Or it could be his comfort with fire was a pretext for the conditions of his eternal home? Did he even believe in Hell? And if he did, was it fiery, or was it a place where he would have to relive all of his sins again and again?

Dolly put her hand on his knee, interrupting his internal dialogue. "Mr. John," she said, "would you like another drink? We have plenty."

Beck blinked from his daydream and looked at the cup he held in his hand. It was almost empty. He finished the dregs and handed her the cup. "Yes, please. That's very kind of you."

She smiled at him, the fire glinting on one of her teeth, and took the cup. She stood and crossed the room, disappearing into the kitchen.

Dale was midsentence. "...died, it was just me and her. Dolly took her mother's death pretty hard. I did everything I could to keep her alive, but I'm no doctor, and we didn't have the medicine she needed."

Dale sat in a large fabric recliner in the corner of the wood-paneled room. The house was neat but not clean, and it was evident they had never updated the property. It had a distinct 1970s vibe.

"It was pneumonia?" Chris asked.

Dale rubbed his hands on the worn fabric along the chair's arms. His drink was on a block wood table next to the chair, no coaster. "We think so. She had a bad cough. Couldn't breathe. Could have been the Covid too, you know? People still got it all those years later. Whatever it was, she couldn't lick it. Died in that chair right over there where Millie's sitting."

Millie's eyes widened. She lifted her hands from the arms of the formal wingback chair and studied herself as if she'd spilled milk all over her.

Dale laughed. He waved a hand at Millie. "I'm just kidding. She died in our bed upstairs. Couldn't move in the end. It was a sad sight to see, for sure."

Millie offered a sickly smile and eased back into the chair.

Dolly returned with Beck's drink. "Here you go, Mr. John."

"Thank you." Beck took the glass and a sip of the water. It tasted good. Despite having been soaked in the rain, he was thirsty, and water did the trick.

Dale gestured to the glass in Beck's hand. "We catch the rain. There's a nice five-hundred-gallon rain catchment system. Cost me a pretty penny back in the day, but it's worth it now. Bought it first for irrigation, help with the garden and such. It was overkill at the time. Not so much now. Holds the rain, filters it. I rigged it so we can still get water into the house for drinking and cooking. We have to pour water into the toilets to get them to flush, and I have to say, I can't imagine our septic tank's got too much room left. But it'll do for now. It is what it is, right?"

"How's it work?" Beck asked.

"The catchment?"

Beck nodded. He took another sip of the water.

Dale shot a quick glance over at Dolly and shrugged. "Simple physics. It catches the rain, runs it through the filter, cleans it out—"

"I mean how did you rig it?" Beck said. "Sorry, I should have been more specific."

Another glance between the father and daughter. Dale

took a drink from his own cup. "A couple of bypasses here and there. Simple plumbing. Took some patience. A little trial and error. But it worked."

Dolly added, "My daddy is so handy. It's a good thing, too. I don't know what we'd do if he weren't that way. I think about all the poor people out there in the world who don't know what they're doing."

Millie tugged on her socks, pulling them up her calves. They had all changed into dry clothes. Their wet clothing hung in a laundry room on a line that stretched from one side of the space to the other. The clothes dryer and washing machine were both stuffed with tools and spare parts. Neither worked without power. Beck wondered if their clothes would dry before they had to leave. If they did, they did. At least his feet were dry now.

"What do you mean?" asked Millie.

"I mean all of them city folk," Dolly said. "What skills did they have? They get people to cut their grass, clean their houses. They need milk, they go to the store. They have a problem with their car, they take it to the shop. How many skills did they have? Really, the farther away we get from the land, the farther away we get from being self-reliant. You know what I mean?"

The wood logs cracked and popped inside the fireplace. Above the stone hearth was a painted wood mantel. The chipped paint peeled like that on the house's exterior. Beck studied the items displayed on the plank. There was an old tea set complete with dainty cups and a pot embossed with a floral pattern. A pair of wrought-iron candlesticks held thick beeswax candles, which bent at odd angles from their melt. A fake floral bouquet was at the center. It was displayed as if spilling from a wicker cornucopia.

Beck scanned the room and noted similar tchotchkes

perched on tables or on the shelves of an open decorative cupboard. Something bothered him about the room, as it did about the house and their hosts. While he couldn't quite put his finger on it, his compass pointed to something being off. Something serious.

Dale leaned forward in his chair. He rested one hand on a knee and, with his other, wagged a finger. "Think about all the simple skills them city folks never learned. You think they could can food? Or tend a garden? Well, maybe some of them, but not a lot. They was far more concerned with eating at them fancy locally sourced organic bistros than they was with sourcing the food themselves. Were any of them prepared? I heard a lot of them big cities are nightmares now. New York, Miami, Houston, heck, most of California is like one big prison. People are at the mercy of whatever government exists or sprang up. I wouldn't trade my left nut for—"

Dolly frowned. Her cheeks blushed in the firelight. "Daddy, watch your mouth."

Dale raised both hands in apology. "Sorry to the mixed company. I mean, I would give my left…eyeball…to be where we are. Them city folks looked down on the country people, you know?"

Dale had a point. And while Beck was not city folk, he also was not as prepared as he could have been. He had no stash of food, couldn't grow his own vegetables, and had it not been for his single-minded quest driving his survival, he might've perished along with all of the other people who refused to prepare for an eventual and likely unavoidable apocalypse.

"Think about all them people who laughed before the pandemic. Then they rushed to buy toilet paper. Toilet paper! They didn't learn their lesson. Power goes out, and they're screwed like a pooch in heat."

Outside the house, lightning strobed. Thunder rumbled above them.

Dolly groaned. "Daddy…"

"Sorry," he said. "They're up the creek without a paddle. You know?"

"I get your point," Beck said. "You make sense. I've met a lot of people who were unprepared. What struck me most was how fast civilization devolved. Not overnight, but pretty close."

"What's that old saying?" Dale asked rhetorically. "We're only nine meals away from anarchy?"

"I hadn't heard that before," Beck said. "I guess it's probably true."

"Oh, it's true," Dale said. "Think about it. Within three days of the power not coming back on, you had riots in the cities. People looting just to stay alive. Killing for water and food and diapers. It was a mess."

Beck had heard rumors, although he hadn't seen any of that firsthand. His early days were surviving the *Charybdis*, getting to shore, and making his way from Mobile to Tuscaloosa. He had seen the desperation along the way, the wide-eyed panic in the young people on the streets of the college town when he'd arrived. He had even seen evidence of looting. However, Dale spoke of it as if he had experienced it all firsthand.

"Riots?" he asked.

"Oh, yeah," Dale said. "Mobs of people smashing windows and doors, taking whatever they could. I saw—"

"Daddy," Dolly interrupted, "would you like some more to drink? You're almost empty."

Dale's eyes narrowed for a moment. Then the tension eased with an expression of recognition, as if he'd forgotten something and just now remembered what it was. He held out his cup. "Sure. Thanks, sweetie. You always think of me."

Beck prompted, "You were saying you *saw*—"

"I heard about," Dale clarified. "I *heard* about the riots. From folks like you who stopped by here on their way someplace else. They tell it with such detail, I feel like I was there."

Beck considered challenging Dale, asking him who he really was and where he was from. He thought better of it. No need to poke a sleeping bear, especially when the bear was sharing his cave with him in the middle of a storm.

"How do you keep the yard so nice?" Millie asked. "Without a power mower and all?"

Was his daughter attuned to the same frequency, doubting the veracity of Dale's story? Beck tried meeting her eyes, but she was too focused on the man in the easy chair.

"Manual mower. Old four blade that I push and walk behind. It's good to keep the yard nice. Lets people know the place is occupied. Maybe keeps some less-desirables from thinking they can squat here."

"How long does it take?" Millie asked.

Dale puckered his lips and puffed his cheeks in thought. He whistled. "Oh, better part of a day. Lots of land here, you know."

"How many acres?"

Dale hesitated. He had to sense her misgivings, but he played along. "Ten acres."

Beck bit the inside of his cheek to keep himself from speaking. He might not be country folk, but he'd grown up in the Deep South. He could guess acreage, and this place was more than ten acres. Easily twenty. Anyone who owned the land would know that.

Beck caught Millie's eye and shook his head at her almost

imperceptibly. She caught his drift and backed off.

"That's a nice piece of land," she said. "You're really fortunate to have it, smart to keep it up, and generous to allow us to dry out here. We're eternally grateful."

Millie offered a generous, if not entirely genuine, smile. The tension building in the room eased. A little.

Beck looked past his host out the six-pane window behind him at the back of the house. Rain thrummed on the glass. It was dark outside, and the ambient glow from the fireplace reflected the interior of the house in the panes like mirrors. He was almost certain it was past sunset, though the rain and heavy, dark clouds made that nearly impossible to know at first glance.

Lightning flashed again. The crack of thunder was close again. Almost immediate.

As if reading his mind, Dolly said, "Y'all might as well spend the night. No sense in heading out in this mess."

Beck hated the idea. Every bone in his body told him they should go, damn the weather. But he had to leave the decision up to his daughter. It was her mission, after all.

Demons chirped at him for doubting himself, for being weak-minded. He ignored them. "What do you think?" he asked Millie.

Millie studied him for a long moment. "I think we'll be okay. We can make it in the rain. We appreciate—"

"Nonsense," Dale said. "I won't hear of it. It's too dangerous to be out there. Get some rest. Leave first thing in the morning. Even if it's still storming, you'll have the benefit of daylight to guide you."

"Absolutely," Dolly said. "We have plenty of room. Each of you can sleep in your own bed. How long has it been since you slept in a bed?"

Only a day, Beck thought. He was no longer a fan of beds.

They were too soft, made him stiff in the morning. Beck said nothing. He didn't want to upset his daughter.

Millie sighed. "Chris, what do you think?"

Chris sat up and lifted his eyebrows in surprise. He appeared as shocked as Beck by the question. By whose opinion she wanted. He shrugged. "I don't know. It is a mess out there, Dolly's right about that. I don't think we could see two feet in front of our own faces. On the bikes that would be even worse."

Dale laughed. "Bikes? Y'all are on bicycles?"

Millie nodded. "Mountain bikes."

Dale slapped his leg. "Well, I'll be. Of all the people I've seen, and it's been a few, ain't none of them been on bikes. On foot, on horses, sure. I even saw a solar-powered truck roll past here once, but never a bicycle."

Beck found it hard to believe Dale and Dolly hadn't seen them ride up on the bicycles when they'd arrived. That could've been his total mistrust of the father and daughter. Were they even related? Was all of this a sham? A trap? Or was he being paranoid?

"We'll spend the night," Millie said. "Thank you. But we'll plan to leave first thing in the morning."

Beck's chest tightened. He gritted his teeth. His daughter didn't trust his gut instincts, but he would go along to get along. It was just one night.

Dale clapped his hands together. It was too eager. "Excellent. We love having company. Not that I don't love spending time with Dolly, but you understand how dull it can get for both of us."

Beck smiled an acknowledgment. "Thanks again for the hospitality. Would you mind showing me to my room? I'm going to make it an early night."

"You don't want any dinner?" Dolly asked. "We have

some stew we could share. There's plenty to go around."

Beck shook his head. "I'm good, thanks. I'm more tired than hungry."

Turning down food generally was a bad idea. One never could be certain where they might find their next meal. But Beck would rather be paranoid, hungry, and alive than risk eating anything from someone he didn't trust.

He wanted to override his daughter and get them out of there, but his tenuous relationship with her might fray beyond repair if he challenged her in that moment. So he kept his mouth shut and resolved to keep his head on a swivel. Beck would neither eat nor sleep that night. Not that he ever really slept without the help of a near-deadly infection.

He stood up and brushed nonexistent wrinkles from his pants.

Millie stood as well. She twisted at the waist and stretched her back. "I think I'll go to bed, too. Tomorrow is probably a big day."

"Me too," Chris said. "It's smart to get a good night's sleep when we can. Are the rooms upstairs?"

Disappointment clouded Dale's features. His mouth curled into a resting frown and accentuated his beard-covered jowls. He lifted his chin and scratched his neck. "Okay then, if y'all insist. I'll have Dolly show you to your rooms."

He didn't get up to wish them a good night. Dale sank back into his chair, his gaze drifting beyond the walls of the farmhouse, and he absently stroked the scruff on his thick neck.

Dolly forced an uncomfortable smile. "Okay, then. Let me show y'all upstairs. Like I said, we have enough rooms for each of you to have your own."

She motioned to follow her, and they did. Millie went first, then Chris, and Beck took up the rear. Lightning flashed simultaneously with a pealing crack of thunder that shook the house. The windows rattled, and the old tea set on the fireplace mantel clinked as if it might shatter.

Dolly stopped at the base of the stairs, one hand on the finial at the bottom of the wooden baluster. She put her other hand to her chest and gasped. "Oh my! I thought that one might blow the house down."

A nervous giggle followed, but she didn't wait for anyone else's reaction as she started up the steps. Each one creaked under her weight as if complaining about the guests following her to the second floor.

"Don't mind these old floors," she said. "They're just cranky because of the weather."

When she reached the landing on the second floor, with her arms spread wide, she offered a near-toothless grin. "Home sweet home," she said. "All of the guest rooms are to my left. Right over there. Three bedrooms and a bath. You'll have to share the bath. If you do relieve yourself, mind you, please refill the tank with water. There's a bucket next to the commode."

Unlike the main floor, lit with the shadowy ambience from the large fire, the upstairs was dark. If not for the lightning that flickered outside, the layout would have been impossible to see.

It was a narrow hallway with a bathroom directly behind Dolly. To her right, their left, was a trio of doors. Beck assumed they were more bedrooms. Or maybe two bedrooms and another bath. The layout mirrored itself on the side of the house to which Dolly directed them.

Millie gestured into the black. "Any room?"

Dolly nodded. "Any of them is fine. All of them have beds. They have curtains too, so you could pull them closed over the windows if you like. Give you some privacy."

That struck Beck as odd. As far as he knew, nobody was within miles of the place. How much more privacy could they need?

"Give you some privacy" was a simple phrase. It probably meant nothing. Beck second-guessed his suspicions. It could be Dolly and her daddy, Dale, were just weird. Hospitable, but weird in a socially awkward way.

An image of the crazy woman in the woods flashed in his mind. If isolation had stolen her sanity, what had it done to this father and daughter? Before D-Day, they might have been perfectly regular folks. In its aftermath, what normalcy they'd carried probably drained over the years. Now they were weird. Not sinister, not untruthful or adversarial, just weird.

Beck was weird. He knew that about himself. He'd come to terms with it sometime over the last four years. Or it was earlier, when he'd sat in a jail cell, contemplating his misfortunes and misdeeds. It was okay to be weird. That was forgivable. Being judgmental was not. And if his daughter, who led an army of people and had survived on her own without his help, thought it was safe enough to spend the night, he should too.

Some of his misgivings sank to the back of his mind as he used the wall to guide him along the hallway toward the room at the end. Behind him, Millie stopped at the threshold of her room. Chris was in the room closer to Beck's.

"Thank you, Dolly," Millie said. "We're so grateful, and someday I hope we can repay your generosity."

"Yes," said Chris. "Thanks so much."

Beck stood with his hand on the brass doorknob, ready to shoulder his way into his room. He hesitated and peered through the dark toward the spot where he barely saw the vague shape of the woman at the top of the stairs.

"Thank you, Dolly. Thanks also to Dale. See you in the morning."

Dolly disappeared down the stairs, her footsteps creaking on the steps. When the creaks stopped, and it was evident she had reached the first floor, Beck moved away from his door.

"Sleep tight," he said, "and keep your gun close."

"Will do," Chris said. "You too."

"Goodnight, Dad," said Millie. "And thanks."

"For what?"

Beck closed his eyes and focused on her voice. He could not see her in the dark, so he hoped the nuance in her tone might tell him what she was saying that her words would not convey.

"For not disagreeing with me down there. For letting me take the lead."

He played dumb. "About what?"

She lowered her voice and whispered, "C'mon, Dad. You and I both know, heck, Chris could even sense it, you're not comfortable with staying here tonight. Something pinged your radar, and you're worried."

"What do you know about my radar?"

"I saw it in your eyes. You don't trust them."

Beck let her accurate assessment hang in the silent darkness among the three of them.

"I don't trust them either," she said, "but what choice do we have? We can't head out into the rain. If they sense we're onto them, whatever it is they might try to do, they'll just ambush us before we can leave anyhow. We lose nothing by trying to get some rest, making them think we're oblivious."

Beck smiled. He wished she could see it. He pulled back his shoulders with pride. Even if he hadn't had the chance to finish raising her, something he'd taught her had stuck.

"I don't trust them either," Chris whispered. "But bolting

out of here tonight would've set off their alarms. We stepped into the mess when we knocked on the door. We've gotta ride it out now."

"Okay," Beck said. "We're all on the same page. Just stay ready. Be alert, and don't be surprised if we have to get violent."

"Understood," Millie said.

"Hey" —Chris held up a finger— "shouldn't we all sleep in the same room?"

"Why?" asked Millie.

"Well, if they think we're in rooms by ourselves, then they think we're more vulnerable. Right?"

Beck sighed. "He has a point. Wish I'd thought of it."

Actually, he had thought of it, but decided against suggesting it. He wanted to remain deferential unless and until all hell broke loose. It was a good thing Chris had raised the possibility.

"Okay," Millie said. "Let's all sleep in Dad's room. It's at the end of the hall. Maybe the last place they look."

"Okay," he agreed. "Use the wall to guide yourself here. Make sure the doors to your rooms are closed."

Beck opened his door. Millie and Chris brushed past him and into the darkness beyond. He stepped inside behind them and closed the door.

This would've been a great time to use his crank flashlight if he still had it. He missed it. Maybe more than his shotgun. He faced the room as another long succession of lightning flashes lit up the space. Millie was on the edge of the bed, Chris on the floor next to it.

Thunder rumbled in the distance. Wind howled outside and pushed at the twin windows opposite the bed. The lone branch of a scrub oak scratched against the glass.

Outside, in that brief flash of light, Beck saw movement in

the expansive yard out front. He moved to the window and stood beside it, pulled the sheer drapes closed but peered through them through the glass. He waited and watched, trying to keep his focus on the spot where he thought he'd spotted something. Or someone.

"Tomorrow's going to be a long day," Millie repeated. "I'm going to try to get some shut-eye if that's okay."

"Me too," Chris echoed.

"That's fine," Beck said. "I don't sleep."

In the instant after he spoke, another long strobe illuminated the expanse between the road and the house. Standing in the rain, soaked and armed, were six figures. They were shoulder to shoulder, looking up at the house. None of them moved when the thunder boomed. Beck felt it in his chest and a chill along his spine.

"We have to get through the night first," Beck said. "Otherwise, we may not see tomorrow."

CHAPTER 13

Lightning flashed. Thunder cracked. The six figures stood their ground as if the wind and rain were imaginary.

Chris took his peek through the curtains. "Who are they? Where did they come from?"

He stood close enough to Beck that the concern creasing his brow was evident. The gears in his mind spun as he likely calculated the odds. It didn't take a mathematician to understand they were unfavorable. But Beck had faced worse.

He and Chris were on one side of the window, Millie on the other. She stole a glance outside, then asked Beck, "Did you notice there were no family photographs downstairs?"

"I did. Couldn't put my finger on it at the time. But yeah, this isn't Dale and Dolly's house."

Millie dropped to a knee and checked her rifle. "It is their house, Dad, but they took it from somebody. I bet those men outside are with them."

"You're right," Beck said. "When I tripped over the boots in the hallway, I should've put two and two together right then and there."

Millie shook her head. "It was too late by then. Chris was

right. The second we knocked, we were in too deep. This place is a trap. We walked right into it."

Beck cursed himself. He should've known better. Millie was a distraction. Not her so much as his concern for her, his deep desire to please her and rebuild their relationship. He had been a better soldier when his focus was on the idea of his daughter and not the physical manifestation of her. One gave him focus, and the other made him sloppy.

Survival was a straight line. Nothing complicated. No curves. Anything that forced a deviation from that line might as well come with an eraser because it meant the end.

He set his jaw and silenced the demons. His attention squared on Millie. "What's done is done. We cannot change it. It's what we do now that matters. It's all that matters."

Millie nodded. "So what's next?"

Beck flinched at the question. She was asking his opinion after telling him repeatedly she didn't want it. "What do you mean?"

"Dad, I want your help here. So I'm asking, what's next?"

Beck offered a smile, although he was unsure if she could see it. The answer was obvious. "Open fire," he said. "Right now. They're sitting ducks. They won't expect it."

"Kill them where they stand?" asked Chris. "But we don't know who they are. We don't know why they're here. We're making a lot of assumptions."

Beck closed the small distance between him and Chris. "I'd rather kill them and be wrong than die and be right."

"But that—"

"Put their souls on mine," Beck said. "This is my call. I commit the sin."

Beck moved past the window and took the rifle from his daughter's hand. She didn't resist. He went back to the glass, poked the barrel between the sheers, lifted the weapon to his shoulder, and eyed the scope. His finger eased to the trigger. Exhaled.

They were gone. The yard was empty.

Beck cursed again.

"What?" Millie asked.

"They're gone."

"Gone?"

"They're not there," Beck said. "Look."

Millie edged to the window again. She scanned the yard and cursed, too.

"What do we do now?" Chris asked.

"The plan hasn't changed," Beck said. "We still kill them before they kill us."

He moved away from the window, the rifle in his hand, and crossed the room to a closet door and pulled it open.

"What are you looking for?" Millie asked.

Beck used his free hand to rifle through the hanging clothes. "I'll know it when I find it."

His mind raced. They had made a huge tactical error by stepping foot inside this house. That error was compounded by insisting they go upstairs to bed. Now they were cornered.

He couldn't wrap his mind around a couple of oddities, though. Even though they had left their clothes and gear in the defunct laundry room, Dale and Dolly had let them keep their guns. Not that either would've been able to keep Beck from his, but it still seemed strange. Only for a moment had they been without their respective weapons, when they'd left them in the home's small entry. Dale and Dolly hadn't batted an eye when their three guests toted their weapons with them into the sitting room. Beck was certain both were armed. Concealed carry. Small of the back. Hip. Underneath a piece of furniture.

If Beck understood one thing in the post-D-Day world, it

was that good and bad survivors had weapons. Especially the good. Because if they were unarmed, they didn't survive very long. It was likely Dale and Dolly expected them to keep their weapons, and it was better not to make a deal of it. Asking them to stay in the house unarmed was more of a red flag, perhaps.

Maybe they did it to keep them off balance and unsuspecting of the onslaught to come. What did it matter if they had their weapons if it was eight people versus three and those eight had the element of surprise?

Then it hit Beck. He stopped checking the closet and faced his daughter. "Did you check the ammo?"

"Ammo in what?"

He held up the weapon and shook it. "Your rifle."

She glanced at the weapon, then back at Beck. "No. I checked the fire selector, but—"

He tossed the weapon at her. She caught it.

"Check it. Chris, check yours."

Beck pulled his sidearm from his waist. As soon as he held it in his hand, the weight felt off. He released the magazine. It was empty.

Beck gnashed his teeth and cursed again. "It's empty, isn't it? Your rifle."

Millie looked up; terror streaked her face. Chris nodded. His concern had shifted to fear.

"Our gear is in that laundry room. Along with the extra ammo. We've got to get into that room."

Millie's voice quavered. "How do we even know the ammo is still with our gear? They could've taken all of it by now."

"Maybe. But we can't leave here without any ammunition. Even if we jumped for it and made a break for the road, we're screwed. We can't infiltrate the militia empty-handed. We have to fight. Or I do."

Millie's body tensed. "What?"

Outside the room, a chorus of voices echoed from downstairs. It was loud enough the rain didn't mask it. Beck crossed the room to the door and pressed his ear to it. No more voices, but the stair steps creaked. Once, then twice. He holstered his nine-millimeter.

Beck backed away and crossed to Millie and Chris. "They're on their way up. They'll be here in a second. They'll probably hit the other rooms first. We've got a minute."

He marched back to the window, looked outside, and then threw back the curtains. His thumbs found the twin latches and unlocked the casement windows. With a heave, he opened the window. Wind blew rain into the room. A cold spray hit Beck's face as he braced himself and stuck his head through the opening. He surveyed the surroundings and dipped back inside.

He pulled Chris and Millie close and whispered, "There's a narrow overhang beneath the window. Lower yourself onto it and jump. Both of you."

"What are you doing?"

"I'm getting our ammo."

Millie grabbed a handful of the fabric on Beck's shirt. "You're not staying here, are you?"

Beck shook his head. "I'm coming with you. But I'm jumping last. Then I'm getting the ammo."

"Dad—"

"Just do what I say. Got it? When you get down there, don't turn around. Run for the bikes and start pedaling. Ride as hard as you can for ten minutes, then pull off the road. Hide in the woods off the shoulder and watch for me. I'll be right behind you."

"But—"

He narrowed his gaze, affecting his most paternal look, and lowered his tone. A father telling a daughter to listen and do as he says. "Millie."

Millie tightened her hold and nodded. Then her features hardened as if she readied herself for the struggle to come. "Okay."

Chris went first. He climbed into the window, slid out, and disappeared into the dark below. Millie was next.

"Be careful," Beck said. "It's slippery."

"I got it." She slowly released her grip on his arm. Then she mimicked Chris and dropped from sight.

Beck peeked his head back into the wind and rain. Heavy, whipped drops stung his face. He squinted and saw the faintest hint of his daughter as she got to her feet and ran around the side of the house where they had stashed the bikes. He smiled to himself. For once, she'd listened.

He backed into the room, considered closing the window, then thought better of it. He went back to the closet. There had to be something he could use.

Without the benefit of light, he relied on his touch. The closet was packed. He groped along the shelf that ran atop the hanging bar and felt something sharp. He grabbed it and pulled it from the closet.

It was a rectangular picture frame. Made from metal, one corner was damaged and razor sharp. Half of the corner was peeled away from the rest of the frame as if shorn.

This could work.

Beck pulled a shirt from the clothing rack and wrapped his hand with it as he worked loose the edge of the frame. The piece loosened, and he pried it back and forth until it snapped. Then he picked at the adjacent corner and pried that piece of metal loose. He tore the shirt in half and wrapped his other hand. This would protect his fingers and palms from injury. He hoped.

Before he replaced the remaining frame on the shelf, he glanced at the photograph inside the frame. Beck held it close so he could study it in the dark. His stomach tightened as the photograph held his gaze. Anger boiled in his gut.

The photograph featured the house in which he now readied himself to commit extreme violence and a family in its neatly manicured front yard. But it wasn't Dolly or Dale in the photograph. It was a young family. A father with close-cropped blond hair and a look-alike, scrawny preteen son. The wife was angelic. Her genuine smile was intoxicating. Their young daughter was a wonderful mix of her parents. The four of them held each other in a family embrace. Their dog sat obediently beside them, tongue wagging and mugging for the camera as if it knew the importance of the snapshot in time. Beck flipped over the photograph and read the date scribbled on the back. It was a date he knew well. The day before D-Day. Underneath the date was the calligraphic inscription, *Our family, our home. The Torgersons. Greta, Bob, Robby, and Camille.* This had been their home. Dale and Dolly and whoever else had stolen it from them.

Beck's imagination ran with the horrible visions of what had happened to this family. He had so many questions. He would get answers. He would avenge them.

This was a sensation he missed, the idea of helping those who couldn't help themselves. Although the Torgersons were long dead, or worse, he could make things right in the karmic sense. Adrenaline surged as he tucked the picture into his pocket, adjusted the cloth binds on his hands, and brandished the twin shards that would serve as instruments of retribution.

The aluminum, or whatever it was, was thin but strong

enough for Beck's purposes. It would do the trick.

He moved to the door and listened. Outside in the hallway, the bustle of boots on the floor told him they were close. Had they already tried the first room?

He heard one of them curse and whisper, "They're not in there. Nobody is in there."

Beck reminded himself of their names. *Greta. Bob. Robby. Camille. Greta. Bob. Robby. Camille.*

The sounds of the boots grew louder. A key slid into a lock, and a handle turned. They were at the second room.

Beck's heart pounded. His pulse thumped in his neck and at his temples. He tightened his grip on the shards and planned his attack. He would have to stun them into inaction. It was a gamble, but it was his best shot.

He turned back and studied the room. His eyes had adjusted enough he could make out the shapes of the furniture and the general layout. Where was the best place to hide until the moment was right?

In the hall, more cursing. They'd discovered another empty room. Beck tried to count voices or footsteps. It was impossible. He moved to the spot he thought best and waited. Any moment now, they would enter the room. Any moment now, he would have the upper hand, stealing from them the element of surprise. Now all they had was the numbers, and that wouldn't be enough for Beck's skill, his rage, and his comfort with extreme violence.

He closed his eyes and pictured Millie. For more than four years, she was his inspiration for all things. She was his…what did Gabe call it, a *raison d'etre*? Nothing changed. He imagined her on her bike, pedaling as fast as she could into the gloom, Chris on her heels or beside her. Millie would look over her shoulder for him and wonder where he'd gone. If she listened to him, she would keep going, keep pedaling. If she didn't, and he failed at his task inside the house, she might not survive. She might circle back and return to the house. In it, she would find him dead and risk her own end. He had to win this fight. For his sake, of course, for his friends in Hopkinsville, sure. For the Torgersons, too. They deserved their justice no matter where their souls were now. But most of all, he had to summon the most valuable and vile parts of himself for Millie. *For Millie most of all.*

A key slid into the bedroom door lock, and it clicked. The old mechanism was loud enough Beck heard it over the beating of the rain on the closed windows and the howl of the wind whooshing through the open casement.

Beck opened his mouth, stuck his tongue to the roof of his mouth, and breathed in and out. It was a way to keep his respiration silent and eliminate any chance of the intruders hearing him before he wanted them to know exactly where he was.

The knob turned against its dry mechanism, and the door swung open on creaking, unoiled hinges. Beck braced himself and waited. He balanced the shards in his hands and positioned himself on his toes. A tiger. Ready to pounce.

The first intruder crossed the threshold. Water sloshed in his boots. He moved into the room, and another man followed. Beck waited. Bounced on his toes. Gripped the blades.

A third person entered. Then a fourth. Beck held his ground. Breathed through his mouth. Waited for the right moment.

They spread out as a fourth person, likely also a man, crossed the room and stood at the window. None of the intruders saw Beck.

Every muscle tensed. He was a loaded spring. Flooded

with anger and adrenaline, it took everything in him not to attack. But he waited.

Two more entered the room. One of them was Dale. Beck recognized his gait and his voice when he spoke, though his Southern twang was gone.

"They leave through the damned window?" he asked.

The man closest to the window slapped the wall with one hand. "Haven't I told you to nail these shut? This is the second time it's happened."

"We caught the other one," Dale said. "We'll get them, too."

"This is not how to run the operation. Leo would cut your throat if he knew how sloppy you are, Dale. I'm the only thing standing between you and the arena."

"The militia owes us," said Dale. "And Leo doesn't need to know. Not unless you tell him. We've provided plenty of people for their games. Plenty of—"

The man at the window spoke with his back to the others. "Where's the girl?"

"In the kitchen where we left her. She's—"

Beck kicked closed the door that blocked him from view. Lightning flashed as he backhanded a shard across the neck of the man closest to him. The attack was so quick, so precise, the man made no sound as his body slumped.

Beck spun away from him and jabbed both shards into the next intruder. As that man fell into him, Beck dropped to the floor. In the dark, the others didn't see him as they opened fire. Chaos became Beck's third weapon.

On one knee, he dragged a shard across the Achilles of a third man. Then he punched it upward into a soft target that drew a wailing cry from a dying man.

Beck rolled onto his back and caught the fourth victim across the back of his ankle, into his knee, and then between his ribs as the wounded man twisted.

Four down within six seconds. Only Dale and the man at the window remained. They fired into the walls, into their dead comrades. But now Beck was armed. He was in a corner of the room, invisible to the men until the muzzle flash and crack of the rifle gave away his position. He fired two rounds into the man at the window. A pair of shots slugged Dale in the gut, and two more knocked the other through the open window to the ground below. His body made a sickening sound when it hit the muddy earth. Beck advanced on the empty-handed Dale. The host was on the floor, sitting cross-legged and holding in his guts.

Beck kicked clear a rifle not far from Dale's feet and dragged him by his collar into the hall. Then he pulled him down the stairs, tugging him against the wood planks and enjoying the thuds and grunts behind him.

When he reached the first floor, Dale was barely conscious. Beck pressed the rifle to one of the wounds, and Dale's eyes popped open wide. He groaned and cried out for help and mercy.

Beck kicked him in the side. "Don't die on me, old man. Not yet."

He scanned his surroundings but didn't see Dolly. She was the lone survivor. For now.

"Dolly," he called out, "where are you?"

No response. Beck eyed Dale and moved from the hallway into the living room. The fire crackled and popped. Its ambient heat hit Beck as he swept the rifle across the room. Beck backed toward the fire, making sure Dolly couldn't sneak up on him, and called out again.

"They're all dead, Dolly. I'd like to keep you alive. Give you a shot in the—what do they call it—the arena? Whatever that is, I'm sure it's—"

A deafening blast stopped him cold. It would have killed him, but Dolly's aim was awful. Beck dove for cover as she pumped the shotgun and fired again. From behind an easy chair, he found his aim and popped a round into Dolly's arm. She dropped the shotgun and cried out in pain. Beck raised himself to his feet and kept the rifle pointed at Dolly as he approached.

In the flickering light, the dancing shadows made it tough to see if she had another weapon. But she was so consumed by her injury, Beck was unconcerned about another threat.

He gestured to Dale's chair with the rifle. "Sit down."

"I can't," she said. "I'm hurt. You shot me."

Dolly unleashed a tirade of unladylike language and besmirched the memory of his long-dead mother. Beck was undeterred.

"Sit. Or I sit you down myself."

Whimpering, Dolly took a seat in the chair. The wound was a nick. Enough to make her bleed but not enough to incapacitate her. Infection would be the rub. If she lived long enough to risk dying from it.

She spat at his feet and snarled. A feral animal trapped and alone.

"Get it out of your system, Dolly. If that's even your name. Get it out now, because you're going to tell me what I want to know. Understand? If you don't, I'm going to make your daddy's final moments worse than they have to be."

She laughed. It was more of a cackle. "He's not my father. Are you thick in the head?"

All of the sweetness Dolly had shown Beck when they arrived hours earlier was sour. She sounded like a completely different person. Even the expression on her face made her nearly unrecognizable as the affable hostess who'd greeted them at the door and invited them out of the rain and wind.

Beck was thankful he'd refused an offer of her cooking. Who knew what she'd put in it?

"You can do to him whatever you want," she said. "Be my guest. I don't care."

Beck shot her in the leg.

The percussive crack startled her, and she jumped in the chair. Then the realization hit her, and she screamed in pain. "You shot me? You shot me! You—"

Another string of expletives mixed with wails and groans. She grabbed her shattered leg. The compound injury was gruesome. She had earned it.

Beck put a finger to his lips. "Shhhh. You'll wake the dead."

His sense of humor was lost on her. Oblivious to him, Dolly's sallow skin gave her a sickly glow. Sweat poured from her forehead and matted her bangs against her skin. She panted and moved aimlessly in the seat, her ruined limb dangling by exposed meat. Infection from the graze wound was an afterthought now. Dolly would die from this injury. Or if she somehow survived, she would never walk again. Not on two legs.

He waited for the cries to dampen before he spoke again. Beck didn't enjoy this. He was never one for picking on women. But he needed information she had, and she wouldn't give it to him without an incentive.

Beck sat on the table in front of her and pointed the rifle at the other leg. She calmed down and huffed labored breaths from puffed cheeks.

"I'll shoot the other one if you don't give me what I want."

Dolly shook her head. It was not a dismissal. If anything, Beck took it as acquiescence. He sensed he didn't have much time. The shock would set in, and she would pass out or be useless. Her mind would be so focused on the pain, Dolly would be unable to provide him any credible answers.

"Where's the ammo?" he asked.

Spit flew from her lips. Her teeth chattered. She shook her head. "In the kitchen."

"Kitchen? Where?"

"Cupboard."

"Our packs?"

"Laundry."

"You left them in the laundry room?"

She nodded. Streams of sweat rolled down her face and glistened in the firelight.

"Tell me about the arena."

Dolly groaned and threw back her head. Strings of saliva bridged her mouth, and she lay back in the chair. More groans, heavy breaths, grunts. He was losing her.

"Tell me about the arena, Dolly. I'll stop the pain if you do."

She was gone. Her skin was gray, her lips blue. Too much blood loss.

Beck cursed himself for his itchy trigger finger. He should have winged her again. That would have done the trick, and she'd be more coherent. But what was done was done. Before he lost her, he needed something else from her. He had another question. One more important to him in that moment than the arena or the militia.

"What happened to the Torgersons?"

She leaned forward. Her eyes fluttered. Confusion slid into the pained expression that painted her face. Dolly looked much older than she had minutes earlier, as if her life force were traveling up the chimney with the wood ash and fire smoke. "Who?"

"The Torgersons. The family who lived here. Greta, Bob,

Robby, and Camille. Beautiful young family. This was their house."

Recognition erased the confusion. Dolly chuckled, then coughed. She shook her head. This time, it was not acquiescence. "Those losers? They begged for their lives. It was pitiful."

She stuttered and slurred through an explanation of their arrival, their betrayal of their host family, and their demise. Most of it was incoherent babble, but Beck caught enough of it to understand the depravity of Dolly's and Dale's actions.

She was mid-sentence when Beck shot her in the other leg. He waited for the echo of her howl, counted slowly to ten, and put her out of her misery.

As he watched her take her last, struggling breath, he whispered, "They send their regards."

CHAPTER 14

D-DAY + 4 YEARS, 6 MONTHS, 20 DAYS
NEAR ELIZABETHTOWN, KENTUCKY

Dale was bleeding out, but he was alive. Beck had shot him clean through twice, so as long as he kept the holes plugged, Dale would keep his wits about him long enough to answer the questions Dolly had failed to satisfy.

He leaned against the front door. The thick lids hung over his eyes, and he snorted through an open mouth.

Beck had yet to ask him a question when Dale surprised him. The man wagged a weak finger at him. "I know you," he said. "I know you."

Beck lifted an eyebrow.

"The legend is true. You're unkillable."

Dale coughed. His eyes fluttered. Beck thumped him on the shoulder to refocus him.

"Not that we would've killed you," Dale said. "There's a bounty on your head, John Beck. We were going to take you in."

Beck suppressed a smile. He played dumb. "Take me in?"

"The Sheriff wants you. Put out a bounty on you. Worth more alive than dead."

"The Sheriff, huh?"

"Yeah, he runs parts north of here."

"What else do you know about him?"

Dale shrugged as best he could. "Has an army bigger than the militia. People say he controls West Virginia, or parts of it. Has friends from here to Canada. Runs a path back and forth."

"For what?"

"People. Modern-day underground railroad. Couple of times a year, he takes people to Canada. Supposedly has a utopia up there."

Beck studied the dying man's features. He couldn't get a good read on his pale, slimy complexion. Even his beard seemed to lose its color. Was this true?

"So how would you find the Sheriff? If you got me, turned me in, what would you do?"

Dale laughed, then winced and coughed again. Blood glistened at the corners of his droll mouth. He slowly lifted a hand and wiped the back of it across his face.

"What's so funny?"

"You really don't know anything, do you? The comics never said you were thick in the head, John Beck."

"Humor me."

"Churchill Downs. Everybody knows Churchill Downs is the place. The Sheriff controls it. It's like the gateway into his world, but he's very particular about who he lets in and who he helps."

Beck leaned in close enough to breathe in the odor of blood and sweat and urine. He glanced at the floor and noticed the firelight-reflecting puddle that spread out from underneath Dale's legs. The man had wet himself.

He fought the urge to gag and focused on his next question. "How do you know this?"

"I thought everybody knew it. It's—"

Dale coughed again. This time, a spray of blood spattered

Beck's face and chest. Beck blinked away the blood, smeared it across his cheek with his sleeve.

"It's what?" Beck asked.

"Common knowledge. The Sheriff helps people who can't help themselves. He also goes and takes care of anyone who gets in the way of his mission. He's like you…but better."

This brought about another coughing fit. Beck backed away to avoid the bloody sputum. When Dale stopped, his breathing was labored. He didn't have long now. Beck had seen this before, too many times to count.

"What about the arena?" he asked. "What's that about? You work for the militia?"

Dale shook his head. His chest heaved, but his breathing was shallow. His voice lost its tenor. "I work for whoever pays. The militia pays for people. Me and my posse, the ones you killed up there, we're good at finding people."

"Your posse."

"Well, really, it's Dolly's posse. We all worked for her. She was in charge. Smarter than the rest of us. Smarter than you, too."

The revelation didn't surprise him. He had come to understand the power of women in the apocalypse. Underestimate them at one's own peril.

They were smarter than men. More deliberate, less reactionary. Less prone to violence as a first resort, but perfectly fine with it as a persuasive or survival tool. He imagined his ex-wife Debbie would've been a force in this new world. Despite men's greater physical strength, they were no match for cunning, armed women. If those women led armies of men, they might as well be unstoppable.

Beck pressed Dale. Not much time left. Not for Dale, and Beck had to be on his way.

"You found people for the militia? What for?"

"They pay for them and make them fight. Like gladiators. Like that movie."

Beck had no idea what movie he meant. He did know what Roman gladiators were. "So you were going to sell us to the militia so we could fight to the death?"

Dale's expression compressed. Tears drained from the corners of his eyes. "You are stupid. Damn, it's something you're alive. Really something. I said we were taking you to the Sheriff."

"But the others…"

Dale nodded. "They'll get 'em anyhow. No way you survive your little trek. Whatever it is. I know you're John Beck, the legend, but the militia can't be beat."

"What if the Sheriff took on the militia?"

Dale laughed. It was weaker though and seemed to drain the last of his energy. "Well, that would be something. I'd pay to see that."

Beck had a lot of questions left but only one for the dying man in front of him. He stood up, and his figure cast a long shadow over Dale's body, as if the grim reaper were about to steal the man's soul and take it where it belonged.

"Why did you kill the Torgersons?"

Dale's brow furrowed. "Who?"

"The family who owned this house."

Dale looked away from him and dipped his chin to his chest. Was he losing consciousness, or was he gaining a conscience?

"That was Dolly's call. She found the house. We needed a place to stay, a good location to set up with plenty of room for all of us."

"So you killed a family. You killed children."

Dale lifted his head, and for the first time, Beck sensed anger in the man's face. "You're judging me? That's rich. I did what I had to do. Just like you, John Beck. I've read the books, and if half of what they write about you is true, you've got no room to talk."

Beck clenched his teeth.

"You're a disappointment, John Beck. Yeah, you're a killer, and you can't be killed. That's something. But you're as stupid as a rock and a hypocrite at that."

Somehow, the man managed one last volley of words. A final salvo that dripped venom. Then he closed his eyes, and his head drooped. When Beck didn't move or respond, Dale opened his eyes and sneered. The final missive from a dead man.

"Now let me die in peace and get out of my house."

The demons hissed in Beck's ears. They sounded like Dale as they whispered his words and uttered his accusations. They stung like shards of metal into his chest and the back of his head. Beck had for the most part kept them at bay and essentially silenced them for so long that the cacophony of their collective voices ignited a sensation in his gut he barely recognized.

Beck was simultaneously angry and sad, defiant and acquiescent, victorious and defeated. All of it dizzied him before he steadied himself. He turned to walk away, to give Dale his dying wish. Yet he couldn't do it. Not the killer that he was at his core. It was who this apocalypse had made him. The irony of it almost made him laugh as he adjusted the cloth wrapping his right hand and picked up the razor-sharp piece of the Torgersons' picture frame.

Before D-Day, he'd spent time in prison for a killing he didn't commit. That wrongful charge had broken apart his family and left him irreparably damaged. Now, in this apocalyptic world in which he thrived, he'd killed countless people without account. No repercussions, no fear of reprisal.

It felt good when he grabbed Dale by the sweat-mopped hair on his head, yanked back, and drew the shard across the man's neck.

"This was never your house, and it never will be," he said as he dropped the blade to the floor. The fire crackled behind him. Lightning flashed outside. No thunder this time.

The ammunition was in the kitchen where Dolly had said it would be. Their packs were still in the laundry room. Beck worked as fast as he could to consolidate their belongings into something he could carry on his back before he rode the bike toward his daughter and Chris.

He walked back through the sitting room one more time and stared into the fire. The flames danced in different shades of yellow, orange, and red. They were weaker than they'd been earlier in the evening. The logs that fueled them were little more than char now. Unstoked and unfed, the fire would die alongside the home's occupants. Beck lost himself in the fire for a long moment before he reminded himself how late he was. A small part of him wondered if Millie would be there when he reached her hiding place.

She will be there. Of course she'll be there.

He couldn't wait to reunite with her and tell her what he'd learned. Beck also had unanswered questions about who his daughter really was and what she had done during their time apart. *Was* she running an escape route to Canada? How could that be? She was only twenty. Was that how old she was? How old was she?

In that moment, as he blinked and looked away from the smoldering fire, he couldn't remember her birthday or her age. He had trouble with her middle name. What color were her eyes?

Beck sighed. He carried the consolidated packs on his shoulders, and he walked through the house one last time.

Someone would find this mess. Someone would clean it up. Or they wouldn't.

Beck had spent years now making messes other people had to clean up. He also cleaned up messes others left behind. His was a complicated life. Complicated and conflicted. He reached the front door, muscled through the narrow opening, and out into the night.

Sheets of rain descended from dark clouds above, but the wind was less than before. And it was cold again. Or maybe that was him and not the weather.

Beck paused on the porch for another moment, wishing he were less contemplative. It was easier when he didn't think about his actions. Then he stepped out into the rain and let it wash him clean.

CHAPTER 15

D-DAY + 4 YEARS, 6 MONTHS, 20 DAYS
HOPKINSVILLE, KENTUCKY

Casca Long stood in the rain. He had never read the Bible, but he knew the story of Noah, the flood, and the ark. Forty days and nights of relentless rain. Enough water from the heavens to flood the Earth and cleanse it. Noah, his loved ones, and animals two by two survived the relentless deluge aboard the ark, and when the skies cleared, God promised Noah he would not cover Earth in water again.

Casca wondered when he might see a dove, an olive branch, or a rainbow. Staring toward the milky gray horizon, where the storm met the undulating Kentucky landscape, he imagined he might never see any of them. They required peace and hope. In his young life, Casca Long had never really experienced either. His leader, however, the one for whom he fought, was an inspiration and did make him believe in the possibility of a life beyond subsistence.

Was that hope, or was it wishful thinking? Casca tended to think it was the latter. But to shift from realist to optimist, he took on this new role with as much enthusiasm as he could muster.

Sure, it came with risk. What didn't in these times? Everything was a risk. In a world where each breath might be his last, Casca chose to take his destiny into his own hands and dive headlong into the deep waters from which he hoped to emerge unscathed.

He raked his fingers through his hair and shook the water from them as he marched along the track that led from the arena to the building in which the gladiators lived. He checked over both shoulders, thankful for the absence of security cameras in this powerless world, and walked out of the rain and into the dank environs that served as stables for the unwitting, conscripted warriors.

He moved from room to room, unsure of his destination, through the dark hallways illuminated by candles set on the floors every twenty feet. They cast their light onto the walls and floors with a golden shimmer. Casca would know the room when he found it.

At the end of the hallway, he found the room. A guard sat on the floor next to the door, his legs stretched out in front of it, partially blocking the pathway. He snored softly, like an asthmatic cat purring. His head dipped against his chest at an odd angle.

Casca nudged him. "Open the door."

The guard snored awake. His eyes fluttered, and he cleared his throat, the grogginess and confusion apparent on his face as he tried to pull focus on the man standing over him. "What? Who are you?"

"I'm Leo's consigliere. Casca Long. I want to see the gladiator. Open the door."

"I don't have any order from—"

Casca placed his boot heel on the guard's ankle and applied pressure. He stared hard at the confused guard. The guard shifted his weight and tried to free his ankle. Casca pressed harder until the guard cried out in pain and reached for his foot.

"Open the door."

The guard cried out again but complied. He begged for Casca to move his foot. When Casca did relieve the pressure, the guard sighed and took heavy breaths as if to ease the lingering pain.

The guard struggled to his feet, fished the keys from his pocket, and opened the door. Casca stood at the threshold and moved close enough to the guard to feel his hot breath on his face.

"Lock us in the room. When you hear me call for you, unlock it, and let me out. Understood?"

The guard nodded.

Casca set his jaw and growled. "I need verbal confirmation. Do you understand me? I would hate to report you to Leo and find you on the other side of these cells."

The guard's eyes danced as they held Casca's sharp gaze. "I understand. I'll lock the door and let you out when you ask."

Casca turned away and stepped into the room. The sharp odors of mildew and excrement hit him before the door slammed shut behind him. He gagged and held the back of his hand over his nose, taking a moment to gather himself.

A small voice called from the dark. "Who's here?"

"It's me. Casca Long. How are you?"

"How do you think I am?"

He took another step deeper into the dark. He covered his nose as he spoke. "I asked because I don't know. I'm not one for pleasantries."

"What time is it?"

He chuckled. "Late."

"What's funny?"

"I haven't heard anyone ask what time it is in a long time," Casca said. "It's a pointless relic of the past, isn't it?"

"What do you want?"

Casca took another step. The odor was stronger. His eyes watered and failed to adjust to the abject blackness of the space. "I want what you want, Regina," he said. "You and I have similar goals."

Now it was Regina who laughed. "I doubt that."

Casca wanted to say more. He wanted to lay it out and tell her everything right then and there. But he was unsure if he could trust her. Not yet. He had to play the game, move the pieces, and try to predict how she would respond.

"Why?" he asked.

"Because I don't know who you are, but I know who you're not."

"Really? Who am I not?"

"You're not Casca Long," she said. "Casca Longus was the first to stab Julius Caesar. I doubt you're related."

A broad smile stretched Casca's face. It was involuntary and caught him by surprise. How long had it been since he smiled? Weeks? Months?

"What's your real name?" Regina asked. "And who are you planning on stabbing in the left shoulder above the collarbone?"

"You know your history," Casca said.

Regina was closer now, her voice louder. Footfalls echoed in the dark. "What's your real name?" she asked again.

"Carl."

"Carl? Really?"

He stiffened. "Why? What's wrong with Carl?"

"Nothing. I've never met anyone named Carl."

"I've never met anyone named Regina."

"How do you know my name? I never gave it to your boss."

"I overheard the others. Lucy and Rebecca. They

mentioned a Regina, and I put two and two together."

Regina was close enough now he smelled her scent. Sweaty but familiar. He'd caught it when they marched to the library where she had played chess.

"What do you want?"

"I want to help you escape."

"Why? What did your boss do? I thought you were his consigliere?"

"I am, but he's not my boss. My boss doesn't live here. My boss isn't in the militia."

"Who's your boss?"

He hesitated. This was the moment of truth. If he told her whom he worked for, she could use the information against him. Regina could barter the intelligence for her own freedom. Then again, he'd already given her enough to do that without revealing his true identity.

"Why don't we sit down," he said. "Take a few minutes to—"

The door clicked and creaked open a crack. A sliver of dim candlelight shone through the narrow opening.

"You okay in there?" It was the guard.

"I'm fine," Casca said. "I'll be out in a minute."

"I just—"

Casca raised his voice, his tone sharp. "I said I'll be out in a minute."

The door closed, and the lock clicked again.

"I don't want to sit," Regina said. "I've been sitting. Anything you have to say, I can take standing up."

He squinted and tried to find her in the dark. He couldn't. Not even a vague shape or shadow. This place was like a tomb.

"I'm sorry you're in here," he said.

"Why are you sorry? You didn't do it."

"No," he said, "but this is pretty awful."

"Cut the small talk, Carl. I've played games once today. That's enough. Say what you have to say, and then let me decide if I'm at all interested in whatever you propose."

Casca exhaled. "Fair enough. Have you heard of the Sheriff?"

Regina didn't respond. When the pause reach the uncomfortable, he repeated himself. "Have you heard of the Sheriff?"

"I've heard of him," Regina said. "He's got a bounty out on my friend."

Of all the things she might've said, this was by far the least expected. This was like a checkmate on the third move.

"A bounty?" he asked. "Who is your friend?"

Even before she gave him the answer, he knew it. The Sheriff, his boss, was Millie Beck. The only bounty she had offered in the years he had known her was for her father, John Beck. This was not something he was ready to divulge. Not yet.

"Have you heard of John Beck?" Regina asked.

He played it coy. "Everybody's heard of John Beck. He's the unkillable avenger in the comic books. You know him? He's your friend?"

"I know him. I knew him. I have no idea whether he's still alive. I'm told he's dead, that Leo killed him or the Sheriff killed him. I don't know what to believe, but I like to think he's alive."

"The Sheriff wouldn't kill him."

Hands gripped his shoulders, and the sudden contact startled him. He backed away, but Regina held onto him.

"Do you know where Beck is? Have you seen him? How is he? He's alive, right? I knew he was alive. Where is he?"

Casca shook his head. "I have no idea where he is. I've

never seen him. When I left the Sheriff, Beck was still out there somewhere. It was before Leo caught him at the hotel and took him north."

Her grip tightened on his biceps. "Then how could you know the Sheriff wouldn't kill him?"

"Because the Sheriff—"

Regina's fingers dug into his arms. "Wait, how do you know about the hotel?"

He hesitated. "I was there."

"You were there? Where? I don't remember seeing you. I—"

"I was there. On the ground outside the hotel. I was part of the team that dealt with Beck. He was pretty sick."

"I know he was sick. That's why I—"

Her voice cracked. Her grip on his arms loosened. She let go and turned away. Her figure disappeared back into the dark.

"I'm pretty sure he's alive," Casca said. "He was when I last saw him, when they left for Churchill Downs."

"Churchill Downs? The racetrack?"

"Yes."

She came close again. Her eyes searched his. Then her expression stretched with recognition. "That's right. I remember. That's where we were headed. The racetrack. I'd forgotten."

Regina brought her hands to the sides of her head, elbows out. She looked at him, but her vision was clearly elsewhere, outside this cell.

"My mind is a mess," she said. "I can't even tell you how long I've been here. How long it's been since that day at the hotel."

Casca checked over his shoulder. He didn't have long. If he spent much more time in the room, the guard's suspicions would grow. That would be bad. Very bad. "Look, I need to go. But I'll leave you with this…"

She lowered her hands. "You're leaving?"

"You'll see me again," he assured her, "but I need something from you."

"What?"

"I was planning on doing this alone, but since you're here, I could use your help."

Regina edged closer. A mask of intensity sharpened her features. He had her full attention.

This was a gamble, yet Casca believed he could trust her. She was a friend of John Beck. That should offer enough credibility. "When the time is right," he said, "I'm going to kill Leo."

"You can't do that alone. You're his consigliere now, right?"

"Yes," he said, "but then I'll die. I'll never escape. I was okay with that if it was the only option. But now I see another play, one that involves you and your friends."

"I don't understand."

He backed away from her. "You don't have to understand right now. Not yet. Soon enough."

"Soon enough might be too late," she called after him as he turned to leave.

He didn't reply, and banged on the door. "Guard, I'm ready."

"Did you hear me?" Regina asked.

He ignored her as the key slid into the lock and turned. The door slid open. Casca expected her to rush him, force him into unnecessary violence to quell suspicion. She stayed put, however, and the guard moved away from the opening.

Casca stepped into the hall and relished the fresher air, the dim light. He thanked the guard.

The sentry slid the door closed and locked it, then asked, "What was all that about?"

"The future of the militia," Casca said. "That prisoner has valuable information."

"Like what?"

Casca smiled. "Like none of your business. Go back to sleep."

The guard's shoulders drooped almost imperceptibly as if someone had leaked air from a balloon.

Casca marched along the hall toward the rain. When he went back into the night, he took in a deep breath and filled his lungs with cold, humid air that almost made him cough.

Things were starting to come together. Perhaps it was time to hope. And then it wasn't.

From the gloom stepped a familiar figure.

"What were you doing?" asked Leo.

The leader stood with his arms folded in front of him. His feet were shoulder-width apart. He had been standing there for some time. Casca couldn't tell for how long.

Shadows cut across Leo's face, hiding his expression, but Casca need not see it. His boss was serious. In that moment, he made the calculated decision to tell the truth. If Leo knew it already, he lost nothing. If he didn't know, Casca might better earn his trust with candor. Even the truth came in shades of gray.

"I was visiting the chess player," he said.

"Why?"

"I believe she has information that can help us."

"Us?"

"The militia, sir."

Leo shifted his weight from one foot to the other. He remained silent.

Casca took that as a hint to elaborate, which he did. "She's aware of a plot to assassinate you."

Leo lifted a hand and rubbed his chin. "Is she?"

"Yes, sir. She's willing to help in the plot."

"Whose plot is it?"

Casca didn't hesitate. "The Sheriff's."

"How did you know she was aware of the plot?"

Now Casca strayed from the truth. "There were rumors among the men, sir. Nothing concrete. But I heard it enough to take the smoke and fire approach."

"Smoke and fire?"

"Where there's smoke, there's fire."

Leo nodded. "Ahhh. Yes. Smoke and fire. Go on."

Casca shrugged. A gust of wind carried a spray of rain that washed across his face. He tasted it on his lips. "I didn't know specifics, only rumblings. Since the women you detained were looking for the Sheriff, I thought they might have information that could help us."

"That's industrious of you," Leo said. "The kind of initiative you showed when you interrupted my meditation."

"I'm trying to be helpful, sir. I want to be useful in as many ways as possible."

"Is that so?"

"Of course," Casca said. "I want to earn your trust."

"That makes sense. Though I do have a question for you."

"Yes, sir?"

"Does the Sheriff trust you?"

Casca's stomach lurched. "I'm sorry, what?"

"The Sheriff."

"I don't under—"

Leo closed the gap between them. He put a hand on Casca's shoulder and gripped it hard. His hardened expression was visible now. His mouth curled into a snarl. "Does the Sheriff trust you, *Carl?*"

CHAPTER 16

Rebecca was physically in her cell, but her mind was in New Mexico. She was home. Well, where home had been when her mother was alive. Before the marauders. Before John Beck.

In the dark of her cell, she didn't need to close her eyes to spark her imagination, but she did anyway. She focused on her breathing, on the slow, rhythmic beat of her heart as she drifted into a vision of what life had been.

It was far from perfect. Single mom. Quaker values. Rebecca never felt like a normal teenager, whatever normal was. But love surrounded her. It grounded her. It gave her the hope she could no longer muster. Not in this place. Not without the man who should have been the love of her life, Lucas. His death had hit her harder than she'd realized. It wasn't until she spent so much time in the dark, in the stink, and with her own thoughts that she understood the depth of his loss. It was so sudden. So violent. Like her mother's.

In her trance, the pain of her wounded ankle evaporated, the survivor's guilt that threatened to consume her waned, and she was again in the hot, dry environs of New Mexico.

She could almost feel the sun on her face as she escaped her cell.

The mountains to the west of their village rose in jagged peaks toward the sky, and she shielded her eyes from the fiery sunset. On the other side of those mountains was Albuquerque. Incredibly, she'd never gone there. She never saw the city or what was left of it. Her mother had kept her insulated in the village, making sure she had books to read and food to eat.

The Quakers were good people. They treated Rebecca and her mother with incredible kindness and never judged them. There was a reason they called each other Friend, and it was well-founded.

Rebecca focused on a particular memory. It was a highlight she played over and again in her mind when she felt lost or particularly hopeless. She'd hit replay a lot in recent days, but she never tired of it.

In the memory, she was with her mother in the small home they shared on the eastern edge of the village. It was an especially hot day. Cloudless, the air as still as dead mice. That was how her mom would put it. She liked odd colloquialisms.

"I've got something fun planned," her mother said. "Get dressed and meet me outside."

Rebecca hurried to her room, slipped off a long T-shirt she wore as a nightgown, and pulled on a pair of shorts and a tank top. The clothes were too big, but fit her well enough they didn't fall off. They just served to make her look even thinner than she was.

Her mother was already outside when Rebecca emerged barefoot from her room. She padded through the living room and bounded onto the narrow street that ran in front of their home.

"Have you ever played hopscotch?"

Rebecca shook her head. She eyed something in her mother's left hand.

"It's a game."

"What sort of game?"

"A fun game."

Rebecca giggled and motioned to her mother's left hand. "What's that?"

"Tree bark."

Without explanation, her mother crouched and used the bark to draw a square on the cracked pavement. Then she drew another and another. The bark grew smaller in her hand until it was a nub. Her mother produced another piece from her pocket and finished the drawing.

Rebecca stood next to her mother, hands on hips, staring at the squares. She studied the array. Her quizzical look must have drawn a chuckle from her mother because she laughed.

"I've never seen you so serious."

Rebecca looked up at her mom, squinting in the late day sun. She raised a hand to shield her eyes and shrugged. "I don't get it."

Inside the boxes, her mother drew numbers. The numerals ascended from the box closest to them to the one at the top of the drawing, one through five. Numbers three and four were next to each other, so the squares looked to Rebecca like a cross or a lowercase letter T.

"It's a game I used to play when I was a little girl. My friends and I would play for hours. We would play to ten, but I figure we'll start simple. I can add more boxes later if you want."

The image of her mother as a child, a girl playing with friends, was jarring. Rebecca never thought of her mother as anything other than...her mother. To think of a world beyond the one that devolved after the power went out only added to the surreality of it.

"How do you play?"

Her mother held up the bark. It was rounded on one end and looked like a brown rock. "You toss this onto the squares, then you hop on one foot in the single squares. When you reach the double box, use both feet. Skip the square where the bark lands, then go all the way up and all the way back if you can. When you pass the marker, the bark, pick it up while still staying on one foot."

"Where do I toss it? Does it matter which number?"

"Start with the first box. If you finish your turn without falling over, toss it to the second box. If you don't, you stay on one. First one to go all the way up to five and back down again wins."

The game was a little girl's game. Rebecca understood that. She was a teenager and on the verge of womanhood. That was what her mother kept telling her.

"You're on the verge of womanhood. Almost there. Childhood is almost over. Enjoy it while you can."

Her mother had said it with love. But Rebecca was convinced her childhood ended the day the power went out. Like a switch flipped, she went from kid to young adult in the split second it took for the EMP to kill electricity across most of the country.

True, she looked younger than her age. She could probably pass for a tween even now, if it weren't for the hard expression she almost always wore. It was a mask to ward off trouble as much as it was to hide the depths of her sadness. The apocalypse sucked.

Back then, in front of the modest, clean home she shared with her mother, she'd looked and felt especially young. Perhaps her mother understood the dichotomy of apocalyptic youth. Circumstances forced them into adult situations far earlier than they otherwise experienced. Yet their maturity, in so many ways, was stunted. Socialization, verbal and visual communication, the first butterflies of a romantic crush were lost on a generation of children devoid of classroom schooling, playgrounds, computers, and social media. As much as Rebecca's mother was convinced the latter plagued two generations of young people, its absence, she lamented, was worse.

So hopscotch it was.

"Go ahead and draw the squares to ten," Rebecca said. "Let's start there."

Her mother smiled. It was a genuine, warm smile that brightened her face as if lit from within. A glow that Rebecca rarely saw. She wondered to herself, as she relived the memory of that afternoon and evening too many times to count, if it was the game that gave her comfort or her mother's smile. Was it both?

Rebecca had won all five games they played. Her mother called her a natural.

"You've got the gift," she said. "Athletic, smart, and beautiful. You are blessed beyond measure."

In retrospect, Rebecca was convinced her mother let her win. No way could she beat her five times in a row without the fix being in. They'd stayed in the street until it was too dark to read the numbers or see the dim outlines of the boxes.

It rained that night. Rebecca remembered going outside after the clouds gave way to a hazy afternoon. The hopscotch blocks were gone. Vanished, as if they'd never been there at all.

They never played again. The marauders who raided their village from the mountains to the west were increasingly aggressive. The village elders warned of kidnappings and murders. Rebecca's mother kept them inside as much as possible.

Their world, as tiny as it had become, was even smaller. She watched time pass through the grimy windows, which gave the outside an opaque, otherworldly appearance. The day her mother died, the day she met John Beck, was the first she had been outdoors in…she couldn't remember how long.

The glorious memory was gone again, and the image materialized of her mother lying dead not far from where they'd played hopscotch. She felt the grip of the marauder's hand around her neck. The warmth of the sun on her face was gone. A chill ran along her spine as her reverie grew dark.

Rebecca was barefoot, and the woman marauder forced her down the concrete steps that led from the front door to their dirt yard. When she reached the bottom, the woman shoved her, and she fell into the dirt. Rocks cut her hands and scratched her face.

She remembered thinking she would die there. Her number was up. No counting to ten and hopping. Just lying there, bullet to the head. The woman surprised her with an order.

"Get up. I ain't got time for this."

Then she heard an unfamiliar man's voice. It carried weight. There was nothing friendly about it, and she was sure, even without seeing who belonged to the voice, the man was not a Quaker.

"Hey, you."

That was all he said. He pumped a shotgun and blew away the marauder without another word. The woman's face fixed with a strange mixture of horror and total surprise. She dropped the pistol and staggered. When she fell, the crack of her head against the side of the house startled Rebecca almost as much as the shotgun blast. Her body twitched. Then it stopped. Still as dead mice.

In that moment, all of the emotion flooded from her. She released it and cried in front of the stranger who'd saved her life. Although it embarrassed her, she couldn't help it. She tried to suppress her cries with repeated swallows against the knot in her throat.

The man checked over both shoulders and spun in a circle as he swept their surroundings. Apparently seeing no other immediate threats, he motioned her toward him. She was frozen in place. He came to her and crouched next to her. The sun blocked his features. He smelled of sweat and blood. His voice was softer than before.

"You're okay," he said. "I've got you now. Nobody's going to hurt you."

The man extended a hand to her, and she studied it before reaching out to take it. What did he want with her? Why had he saved her? Did it matter? She was alive. If he wanted to hurt her, he would've already done it. Wouldn't he? She pulled on his grip, and Beck stood as she did, helping her to her feet.

When he did, the sunlight hit his features, and she knew who he was. He was the man hired to save her village. He was legendary.

"What's your name?" he asked.

"Rebecca."

"Rebecca, I'm John Beck."

She knuckled snot from her nose. "I know."

"How old are you?"

She squinted. "How old are you?"

Beck ignored her question and motioned to the other houses on the street. "Is there anyone else here?"

She motioned to a neighboring street. "I think they're on Coaster."

"How many?"

Not really interested in talking because of the ache in her throat, Rebecca held up four fingers and a thumb. Then she glanced at the dead marauder at the steps of her home, lifted an eyebrow, and folded her thumb into her palm.

"Four more," Beck said. "No problem. You go back inside and—"

"I'm coming with you."

Beck studied the girl's fearful expression.

"Okay," he relented. "You come with me, but you do exactly as I tell you."

She nodded. "I agree to that, for now. We can reassess the arrangement later." They had never reassessed. She'd stayed with Beck as they traveled east to Alabama and then north to Kentucky. Not once had she regretted her decision to leave her village and follow the man who had saved her life. Even in those frightening moments when she fell from a bridge and thought she might die in the waters below, Rebecca was at peace with her choice. Until now.

She missed the high desert. The sunsets. The people. Despite the violence, they never lost hope. They held onto their faith. They looked forward. The more she thought about it, the more she wondered if it was the sunrise she loved more than the sunsets. Sunrise was a promise of the day to come. It was confirmation she had survived another night. Yes, it was the sunrises she missed.

"What are you thinking about?"

Lucy's voice startled her. She had been asleep and snoring softly a few feet away in the dark. Rebecca hadn't noticed her stir. She blinked herself into the present, and the images of home dissolved.

"I want to go back to New Mexico."

Lucy laughed. "New Mexico? You can't walk to the next

town, let alone half a continent away."

A vague outline of her cellmate shifted in the dark. Rebecca narrowed her gaze and tried to focus. "I need to get back there, Lucy. Some day. Not tomorrow, not next week. But that's where I need to go. It's my home."

"Okay," Lucy said. "But if you like it so much, why did you ever leave?"

Rebecca considered the question for a moment. She sniffed the dank air. She was accustomed to the worst of the odors, but faint whiffs of it still made her gag.

"Where are you from, Lucy?"

"Nowhere. Everywhere."

"What does that mean?"

"I don't really have a home. I've drifted for so long I—"

"Before D-Day. What about then?"

"All over. I don't think I remember where I was born. We never stayed in one place too long. Always one step ahead of the bill collector. I actually like the apocalypse better. No taxman, no bills to pay. If you can get past the whole 'I might die a violent death today' thing, this lifestyle is a lot less stressful."

She had a point. It was flawed, but she wasn't wrong.

Rebecca shifted her approach. "Okay, what was your favorite place? If you could pick one?"

"Before or after D-Day?"

"Either."

Lucy sighed. It was the type of exhale that gave the hint of a thoughtful answer to come.

"The Outer Banks," she replied.

"Where's that?"

"North Carolina."

"What's it like?"

Another sigh. This one carried the faintest hint of melancholy.

"It's beautiful," Lucy said. "They're barrier islands, and they feel like another world."

Rebecca tried to imagine the islands. She tried to think if she had ever seen an island in person before.

"They're so peaceful. There's a breeze. Everywhere you look, there's water, and the beach is still. It was untouched."

"Untouched?"

"That's not the right word," Lucy said. "I mean, it wasn't touristy, you know? It was mostly locals. It didn't feel like a theme park like some beaches, if that makes sense."

Rebecca thought about the places she had seen before and after D-Day. So much of her travels merged together. Endless walks on endless roads or trails, survival by the skin of her teeth. Rivers and lakes? Sure. Deserts and mountains? Of course. Oceans? Not once. Not even the Gulf of Mexico. The closest was maybe Lake Pontchartrain. She and her mother had crossed it twice on their way west. It was more than twenty-three miles long, took a full day to walk, and it felt every bit like they were in the middle of an ocean when they reached the middle.

"We should turn back," her mother had joked. "It's too far to the other side."

The humor had sailed over Rebecca's head. "Wouldn't it be the same distance?"

"Yes," her mother said. "I'm joking. Thought it might make you smile."

She had smiled, and laughed about it later. When a checkpoint on the northern shore prevented them from coming inland and soldiers, or militia, or whoever they were, turned them around and they had to walk twenty-three miles in the opposite direction, the joke was no longer a joke.

Rebecca tried a smile. "I'm sure it was beautiful," she said. "I've always thought beaches would be beautiful."

Not catching the nuance of Rebecca's admission, Lucy continued with her story. She edged closer and lowered her voice. "Did you know the Wright brothers first flew their plane in the Outer Banks?"

"Who?"

"The Wright brothers. They were brothers who built the first plane that actually flew."

"Oh," Rebecca said. "I've read about them. Kitty Hawk?"

"No," she said. "People think it was called Kitty Hawk, but the plane was called Flyer One. My mom took me to the exhibit they have set up in Kill Devil Hills. That's where they flew."

"Kill Devil Hills. Sounds like the perfect place to spend the apocalypse."

Lucy chuckled. "I'd like to go back someday."

Rebecca sniffed. Her eyes watered at the pungent odor of the space. She blinked away the tears. "Let's do it, then," she said.

"Do what?"

"Let's go to Kill Devil Hills. Then back to New Mexico."

"What? Together?"

"Why not? Let's plan on it."

"We're not in a position to go anywhere," Lucy said. "Look around, Rebecca."

There was nothing to see in the dark. Rebecca understood her point, though. They were captives and had no control of their destiny at the moment.

"When we get out of here," Rebecca said. "Once we are on the road and my ankle's better, we can do it. You and me."

"What about Regina?"

"She can come, too. But I'm pretty sure she has a thing for Beck, so she'll want to be wherever he is."

"He's probably dead."

Rebecca's throat tightened. She clenched her jaw and held the sudden rush of emotion at bay. Even if her gut told her Beck was dead, she couldn't bring herself to accept it. Hearing the words aloud made it too real.

"Either way," she said, "we should make a plan. East Coast first. Then out west."

Lucy reached out and put her hand on Rebecca's. She squeezed. Tears rolled down Rebecca's cheeks. "Okay," Lucy said. "It's you and me. You'll love the beach."

Rebecca nodded. "And you'll love the high desert. There's nothing like it."

As if on cue, the lock on their door clicked, and a figure trudged across the threshold and into the room. Dim light from the hallway drew an outline of the recognizable form. His voice confirmed it, but Rebecca already knew who it was.

"Ladies," said Leo, "it's time I update you on your circumstances."

Another figure handed him a candle, and Leo held the flame close to his face. His eyes glowing, he moved deeper into their cell. Leo appeared every bit the demon they knew him to be.

He stopped several feet from them, far enough away that a sudden move wouldn't catch him off guard. He checked over his shoulder and motioned for the person at the door to keep it open.

"This won't take long," he said. "But it's necessary to give you an update. It's what the newspeople in the previous world would have called breaking news."

His eyes widened at this revelation. His voice accented the drama of it.

"Your friend Regina has made an arrangement with me," he said. "And suffice it to say, it benefits her, at least in the short term. Actually, it benefits all of us. By all of us, I mean everyone here except for the two of you."

Rebecca's pulse accelerated. Her ankle throbbed from the increased flow of blood to all parts of her body. If she were at one hundred percent, she would've lunged at him like a cat and clawed out his eyes. With her injury, however, there was no way she could take him down let alone take him out.

"I'm here to tell you that once the rain clears and the arena dries out, you two will be our feature attraction. The main event, as it were. You two will fight."

"How is that news?" Lucy asked. "You're telling us what we already knew."

His smile broadened, and his teeth glistened. "Oh no, that's not true. You had no idea you'd be fighting one another."

Rebecca's heart nearly stopped. Her breath caught. "What do you mean 'one another'?"

Leo's brow wrinkled. "I mean each other. You two ladies will fight to the death. If you don't, I'll kill both of you. Shots to the head."

He lifted his free hand and pointed his finger as if making a pretend gun. He aimed it at Lucy and pulled the pretend hammer, then did the same at Rebecca.

"Then kill both of us," Lucy said. "We're not fighting."

Leo held his gaze on Lucy for a long moment and then shifted his attention to Rebecca. "Is that how you feel?" he asked. "You're letting her make up your mind for you?"

Rebecca played out the scenarios. Then she shook her head. "I don't believe you. Regina wouldn't sell us out. What have you done with her?"

"What do you mean? I haven't done anything with her.

She had a choice, and she chose to have the two of you fight to the death."

That made no sense. Regina wasn't the sort of person to do that. At least, Rebecca didn't think so. She would call his bluff.

"Then yes," Rebecca said. "Kill us both. I'm not fighting Lucy."

Leo sighed. He frowned in a way that feigned real disappointment. "Have it your way. Once the sun shines, we'll head out to the arena. I'll gather everyone to watch, and then I'll execute both of you."

He turned to leave and walked across the room. He blew out the candle and spun around to face them, his figure again in shadow at the doorway. "I'll kill Regina, too. Just for the fun of it."

Before either of them could react, Leo slammed the door shut, leaving them in the dark. Their dreams of the beach and the desert seemed as far as the moon.

CHAPTER 17

D-DAY + 4 YEARS, 6 MONTHS, 20 DAYS
HOPKINSVILLE, KENTUCKY

The sting of a slap across his face awoke the man formerly
known as Casca. His eyes opened, and Leo stared down at
him, hands on hips.

Candlelight flickered around them and cast a fiery,
flickering glow on the four walls of his cell.

Leo jutted his chin at his consigliere. "Carl, Carl, Carl. Is
that a family name, too? Something handed down for
generations?"

Despite his consciousness, Carl didn't have his wits about
him. Everything was blurry. A swollen bruise closed one of
his eyes, and his lips felt three times their size.

Leo slapped him again. "Look at me, Carl. When I speak
to you, you look me in the eyes. Understood?"

A string of bloody drool stretched from his lower lip as he
lifted his head. He squinted with his one good eye and tried
to focus on Leo.

"Your sheriff isn't the only one with spies," said Leo.
"He's a little late to the game, am I right? Well, I think I'm
right. Because my spy knew about you before you ever
showed up here."

Carl's mind swam with confusion. There was a spy within

Millie's team? A spy who knew about him, his fake identity, and the assassination plot? His heart raced. He struggled against the binds at his wrists and feet. It did no good.

"Did you really think I would fall for your ruse, Carl? I mean, first of all, the name? A little on the nose, isn't it? The first man to stab Caesar? Ridiculous, if you ask me. It speaks to the Sheriff's hubris. You know that word, hubris?"

Carl tried to lick his lips. It burned. His mouth was dry aside from the metallic taste of his own blood.

"I'm mixing Greek and Roman mythology here," Leo said, "but hubris means excessive pride. Its root, in Greek tragedy, has to do with a mortal's excessive pride related to the gods. And here, young Carl, I *am* a god. Your hubris is tragic."

Who was the mole? How had they infiltrated Millie's inner circle?

"I knew from the moment you brought me that rag in the cell next door that you were a problem child. Then you volunteered to deliver news to me while I was meditating. You've been here a short time, and all of a sudden you think you've laid low long enough that you can make an obvious play and nobody will notice?"

Carl's chin dipped against his chest. He closed his eyes. This was a nightmare. The worst of all possible outcomes.

"I'm so disappointed that the Sheriff wasn't smarter about this. The crazy thing about it is that you had your chance, Carl. You had your chance to knife me or shoot me or do whatever you wanted to do. You could have killed me."

Leo was right. There had been opportunities. However, Millie wanted something dramatic. She wanted Carl to find the right moment, with a lot of witnesses. He should've gone with his gut and done the job when he'd had the chance.

"But you thought I had no clue about who you were and why you were here. You underestimated me, Carl. That's your biggest mistake. The Sheriff's biggest mistake. He thinks he's smarter than me. But he isn't."

Carl looked up. His face hurt. His neck hurt. Speaking hurt. "Who is it?" he asked.

Leo grinned. Hands on his hips, he leaned over and turned an ear toward Carl. "What was that? I can't understand what you're saying. You've got something wrong with your lips."

Carl tried again. "Who is it?"

"Who's what?"

Leo stood up and put a hand to his chest. "Who is my spy? My mole? The one who was in place with the Sheriff before he ever sent you here?"

Carl nodded. His good eye blinked and watered. The image of Leo standing over him blurred. He did his best to keep his fading focus on his tormenter.

Leo, perhaps sensing a loss of consciousness, slapped him again across the face. The sting clarified his vision.

"Stay with me, Carl, because I want you to hear this. I want you to understand something. If I tell you who the spy is, it's because I've decided you're no longer useful to me. I don't think you want that to be the case."

Carl was sure of one thing. He would die here. Either in this chair or on the arena field, his life was over. He would never leave this place. He was resigned to that, had accepted it long ago when Millie first approached him with the plan. His mind drifted as he recalled the conversation.

"It's a suicide mission," she'd told him. "Chances are, you won't come back. You have to be okay with that. If you're not, I'll get someone else to go."

"No," he told her, "I owe you my life as it is. It's an honor you would choose me to do this. It's the least I can do to repay you for what you've given me. What you've given so many people."

Carl didn't regret his decision. He was still proud to be the one to carry out what could have been a game-changer. As much as he didn't like pain, and nobody of sound mind did, death didn't scare him. If anything, the prospect of dying meant a better eternity came faster than it otherwise would.

While he was not a proponent of murder, Carl believed that ridding the post-apocalyptic world of a horrible man like Leo would save thousands of people. His net gain would ensure him a bright future in the afterlife.

So he did his best to nod and looked Leo square in the eye. "Tell me. I'm okay to die. I'm fine with not having a use to you anymore."

A hint of surprise, or something close to it, twitched on Leo's face. His expression shifted from smug to intrigued. "First, tell me why you're here."

Carl shook his head. "You already know."

His words were rounded at the edges, and he hardly understood what he was saying. Leo seemed to deduce his meaning.

"I know you're here to kill me," Leo said. "But what else is there? If the sole mission was to kill me, you'd have done that. There's something more. Something you're not telling me."

Carl's throat hurt. He tried focusing on Leo but found his mind drifting again. Leo was right. There was something more. His intuition was impressive.

When Carl first saw Leo in the flesh, he'd wondered how this thin man, without any military or tactical skill, had managed to amass an army of violent soldiers. How had he essentially taken control of an entire region?

As he'd observed Leo work, he better understood the man's appeal. He was smart, engaging, and intuitive. He often seemed to know what his men and women were thinking before they did. He could talk his way into and out of everything.

Carl, as Casca, had seen it firsthand when they delivered Beck to the Sheriff's people at Churchill Downs. There was a cult of personality unrivaled among anyone else Carl had ever known. Even Millie, who was dynamic in her own right, lacked the magnetic tractor beam Leo possessed.

"Do you remember when I told you that you made me laugh?" Leo asked.

Carl's temples throbbed. The binds at his wrists bored into his flesh as he shifted his weight.

"I said then that you made me laugh because I already knew who you were. I knew when you got assigned to our trip to deliver John Beck. I wanted to see how you'd react at Churchill Downs. I watched you. You did nothing. You stayed back, avoided the fray."

Carl was shocked by the revelation. Everything he thought he had done was a ruse. Leo had made him from day one because of a traitor within Millie's ranks.

"There's another thing I know, Carl," Leo said. "And this will blow your mind."

Carl ignored the pain to focus solely on his captor.

Leo stepped closer and grinned. Self-satisfied. "Your Sheriff?"

Carl sat still. The dramatic pause lasted forever, though it was only seconds.

"Your beloved Sheriff isn't a he, it's a she. Millie Beck. John Beck's daughter. I let her have him."

"You knew?"

"Of course I knew. I let Millie have John for one reason."

Carl bit. "What?"

"So I could kill them both. That's the whole reason I kept your friend Regina here. It's the only reason she and those other girls are alive. It's a trap for Beck and his girl, Millie."

"A trap?"

"They're coming for them, Millie and Beck. I'll let them think they're going to do it. They're going to walk in here thinking they're going to win. But they won't. At the last second, right when they think they've done it…"

He snapped his fingers, and Carl jumped in his seat.

"I'll kill 'em all. The Sheriff, Beck, and his three girls. All of them in one fell swoop. Then *I'll* be the legend. I'll be the one they write books about, am I right?"

Carl's mind swam with confusion. How could this be? How could they have fallen into this trap? Maybe it *was* hubris. Or stupidity. Or both. For certain, none of them had seen the game as clearly as Leo. He was five moves ahead. Checkmate was only a matter of time.

Now, Carl did not want to die. He wanted to live. He wanted to warn the others and somehow redeem himself. If he did nothing, this part of the world would fall under evil rule. The migrations would end, and his friends would die horrible deaths or live horrible lives.

Leo leaned back and stretched his back. "So if you're ready to go, I can tell you the name of my beautiful spy. The one who made all of this possible."

Carl shook his head. "Give me a minute. I need to think."

"Of course you do. I'm in no hurry. Take all the time you need. I'll let you think about whatever it is you need to think about, and I'll be back. We can have another chat and go from there."

Leo started to leave. He turned and walked back to the door. Carl sucked in as deep a breath as he could muster.

"Leo," he called out, "you're not going to win. Beck and Millie will kill you. You will *lose*."

Leo paused with his hand on the door, tilted his head to

one side; then he marched back across the space and drove a knife into Carl's side. He leaned in close.

"*Et tu*, Carl? *Et tu?*"

CHAPTER 18

Beck hopped from his bike. Streaks of pain arced across his lower back towards his legs. He took labored breaths and stood astride the bike, packs hanging from his shoulders. Drenched in rain and sweat, he leaned on the bike for balance.

Every muscle in his body pulsed with the thickness of exhaustion. His clothes stuck to him as he weathered the battering rain. This was the third time he'd abandoned the bicycle's speed for the comfort of a slow walk. He had to be close though, assuming Millie had waited for him.

He licked his lips and tasted the diluted brine of his perspiration and trudged forward in his boots. He stayed in the middle of the road, avoiding the deepening puddles of water that edged from the shoulders.

In the dark, it was hard to know where exactly he was headed, and the driving rain made it worse. Even as he called out his daughter's name, he imagined she couldn't hear him.

"Millie? Millie, can you hear me? Chris?"

It was almost as though the percussion of the wind and rain swallowed his voice as soon as he spoke. Beck dipped his chin and slogged south, trying to keep the rain from driving

197

into his eyes and nose.

Another ten yards. "Millie? Chris?"

His throat was raw from the volume. Everything hurt.

He wobbled but kept his balance and pushed ahead. Lightning strobed in the sky. It was a prolonged flicker that gave him a moment to get a better sense of his bearings. The weight of his clothes threatened to sink him to the road, but he called out again.

"Mil—"

"Dad."

He looked up. Two figures stood in front of him. They were twenty yards south.

He shielded his eyes from the onslaught. "Millie? Chris?"

Another flash of lightning confirmed it. Millie stood next to her bike. Chris was behind her next to his. She wore her hat but held it atop her head with one hand since the wind threatened to tear it from her.

Beck approached and smiled. "Sorry I'm late."

He half expected a lecture. Or three. However, Millie chucked her bike to the side and ran to Beck. She threw her arms around him and embraced him.

Stunned, he didn't move for several seconds. Then he let go of his bike and returned the hug.

It was only when she looked up at him and lightning flashed that he noticed she was crying. Her eyes glistened in that flicker.

"I thought you were dead," she said. "I thought they got you and I'd never see you again. I thought—"

Her chin quivered. She closed her eyes and buried her face in his chest.

As horrible as he felt, Beck also hadn't felt this good in a long time. It was the most confusing combination of emotions that coursed through his body as he strengthened his hold on Millie. "I'm okay. We're both okay. Everything will be okay."

The world melted around him. Beck no longer felt the wind or rain, only his daughter's sobs into his chest and her hands gripping his back as if clinging to him for her life.

Beck thought about saying something, about another volley of assurances to assuage her emotion, her worry. But he stayed quiet and waited for her to calm on her own. When she did, she punched him squarely in the chest.

"Ow!" he said. "What was that for?"

"For scaring the living daylights out of me."

"Yeah, but—"

Millie punched him again. "And that's for lying to me. You said you were right behind me. You weren't. You stayed behind. Why did you stay behind?"

"I had to get our gear. Without our ammo, we're as good as dead anyhow."

She studied him. It dawned on her he wore two heavy packs that tugged at his shoulders.

"So you got it?"

"Yeah."

Chris joined them, holding both his and Millie's bikes. "Glad you're okay. We almost gave up on you."

"I'm glad you didn't," said Beck.

Millie spat rain from her mouth. "How'd you do it?"

"Can we get out of the rain? Talk about it later? There's a lot to talk about. I don't think we should do it here in the middle of the road."

Millie checked over her shoulder. She looked at one side of the road and then the other. A distant flicker of lightning and low rumble of thunder gave her a moment of pause. Then she shook her head. "I don't think we're getting out of the rain, but you're right, Dad. Not the best place to stand around and talk. Let's help you with that gear and get going. We can try to move slow, make some progress until the rain eases or stops. It can't keep up like this forever."

Beck shrugged off a pack and handed it to Chris. "Never thought I'd say this, but I miss the weatherman. That's something you never think you're gonna miss, but knowing the weather is huge."

Millie took some of the ammo out of Beck's pack. That lightened his load and armed him with a weapon that could do some damage.

"Weather*woman*," she said and patted his back.

"What?"

"You said weatherman," Millie said. "It's not always a man, you know."

Chris loaded his rifle and shrugged. "It's nobody now."

Millie rolled her eyes. "Okay, but you get my point. It wasn't always a weatherman. There were women, too. What did they call them? Their official title?"

"Meteorologists," said Beck. "And I stand corrected. You're right. There are—*were*—as many women on television telling me about the rain and sunshine as there were men. Especially in the morning. Lots of women in the morning."

They hopped aboard their bicycles almost in unison. Beck pushed down on the left pedal and propelled himself forward. His thigh muscles sang with pain, but he gained some momentum and slowly rode forward, keeping pace with Chris and Millie. He was sure they took it easy on him.

"Why was that?" Chris asked.

Beck glanced at him. "What?"

"Women in the morning? Why did they put the women meteorologists in the morning?"

"Good question," said Beck.

"I know," Millie said. "It's because women are cheerier."

"Cheerier? Is that a word?" Chris asked.

Millie pedaled effortlessly, even in the driving rain. "It's a word, and it's true. If you're waking up early to watch the news, who wants to see a grumpy man telling you about anything?"

"While that's a good theory," said Beck, "I would take even a grumpy meteorologist right now if he or *she* could tell us when the rain would stop."

"You're right though, Dad," Millie said. "It's gotta stop sometime."

An hour later, the rain stopped. A cold mist hung in the air as the clouds cleared and revealed a pale white moon, which was low on the horizon.

"Only a few hours until morning," Beck said. "Then we'll have some daylight to guide us."

It was the first time all night he'd been able to hear himself think. And while he was grateful for the lack of rain and wind, his clothes were beginning to give him a rash. The repetitive motion on the bike was rubbing his skin raw in all the wrong places.

All of them were exhausted. It was evident on their sallow features. Yet they kept moving. Beck was afraid if he stopped, his body would seize, and he might not be able to start again.

He opened up a conversation as a distraction from his ailments. "We have a lot to talk about. I learned some things before Dale and Dolly met their maker."

Millie steered her bike closer. All three of them pedaled at a slow pace. They avoided the standing water and further exhaustion.

"Oh really?" she asked. "Like what?"

Beck detailed what the pair had told him about the arena and how the militia's reach stretched well beyond the confines of Hopkinsville. He explained how Dale and Dolly's plan was to take him to the Sheriff. They had recognized him shortly after his arrival. They would take him to Churchill Downs.

Millie laughed at that. "If they only knew."

"Yeah," Beck said, "but they think the militia is cooking something. Dale didn't come out and say it, but I got the sense that Leo and his army aren't content with the territory they have. They want more. They want to heat things up, stir the pot."

"What's with the food metaphors?" Millie asked.

"I guess I'm hungry," Beck said. "I didn't even realize I was doing that."

Chris shifted the conversation back to its focus. "If they were going to take you to the Sheriff, what were they going to do with us?"

"Put you in the arena," Beck said, "which I think is an old football stadium or something. It's like Leo is the emperor and he lords over gladiators."

Beck didn't tell them the accusations Dale had thrown at him before his death, how he'd likened Beck to an average killer whose avarice was extreme violence. That he was every bit the villain in his own story. His silence, though, hinted at what he was leaving out of the conversation.

"What else did he say, Dad?"

"Nothing important."

"I can see it on your face," Millie insisted. "Even in the moonlight and the shadows through this mist, I see it. You're thinking about something, and those demons you talk about are chattering in your ears."

How did she know him so well? Even as his own blood, it had been more than four years since she had seen him. Before that, their visits had been limited to his time ashore or every other holiday. He'd gone to jail when she was too young to understand. By the time he got justice, she was old enough to know he hadn't been around.

Yet here she was, reading him like a book. There really was something magical about a daughter and her father.

Beck never liked that popular hashtag #GirlDad. He thought it was as ridiculous as the #BoyMom trend. Parents were parents. Regardless of whether his child was a girl or a boy, he would love her or him the same. To call attention to the difference, or to make it out that somehow dads who loved their daughters were somehow special was ridiculous. In that moment, though, as they rode through the cool Kentucky humidity in the middle of the night toward an uncertain future, he was as proud a girl dad as he had ever been. His thoughts shifted to the moment she'd embraced him in the middle of the road. All pretense gone. Any hint of anger or resentment evaporated. She was his daughter; he was her father. They were inextricably bound to one another, and there was nothing that could change that. Not now, not ever.

"I'm okay," he said. "But you need to stop putting your voodoo powers to work on me."

Millie giggled. It was a little-girl giggle, and it brought a smile to his face. Chris smiled, too.

"I haven't ever heard you laugh like that," Chris said. "It's almost like you're a woman."

Millie steered her bike toward his and forced Chris through standing water. He almost lost control of his bike but steered back onto the wet pavement.

"Don't you ever forget I'm a woman," she said. "Got it?"

Chris offered a salute. "Yes, sir."

They all laughed. It was good. Beck's smile stuck to his face. He couldn't help it. They had survived another night in the horrible world. He was with his daughter, the most important person on the damaged planet. That he could smile, given the pain that racked his body and the knowledge of the formidable foe they would face that day, was a miracle.

Yet John Beck was a man of miracles.

As he pedaled south and the subject shifted to food they missed from the pre D-Day world, Beck's gut told him they would need their share of divine intervention if they were going to leave Hopkinsville alive, let alone with Regina, Rebecca, and Lucy in tow.

CHAPTER 19

The sun was vengeful as it rose over the horizon. Making up for its absence, it carried with it scorching heat and suffocating humidity. Beck wondered what season this was. It made no sense to him. Cold and rainy giving way to hot and humid was the sort of seismic shift he didn't think happened in this part of the country.

He wondered if a climatic apocalypse was to follow but quickly buried that thought as more pressing matters clawed their way to the surface.

"We're getting close," Beck said. "I remember this part of the trip."

The trees thinned along the shoulders. Civilization appeared closer, with more and more houses dotting the rolling landscape. Despite its oppression, the morning air was scented heavily with dewy grass and pine.

"We're close," Millie said. "We've made this trip before. Two hours tops and we'll have to be on the lookout for militia scouts."

Chris rode ahead of them and pedaled back, making a wide arcing circle to rejoin them. He motioned toward the gravel driveways that marked the shoulders every fifty yards. "I'm already on the lookout. No telling if they've stretched their territory, or tried to. That house back there, the one that almost got us killed, was a surprise."

Millie shuddered. "I don't like surprises."

Beck coasted down a slope in the road, then pedaled as it gave way to a gentle rise. "You never did, not even as a little girl. You wanted your birthday presents unwrapped. You had to open everything Christmas Eve."

Millie smiled. "I remember that. I also hated it when you'd surprise me with unexpected visits in Tuscaloosa or last-second cancellations. It didn't matter whether the surprises were good or bad, I didn't like them."

"Why is that?"

"I don't know," said Millie. "Maybe it's a control thing. Being surprised by something means I wasn't in control."

"Control of what?"

She shrugged and slowed her roll to ride even with him as the incline steepened. "Everything. My emotions. The world around me."

Beck chuckled. "That's mighty introspective of you, Miss Beck."

She smirked. "Keith says the same thing. He says he's thankful he didn't know me when cars were a common thing."

"Why's that?"

"Because if we were driving and I was in the passenger seat, I'd be a backseat driver. You know, telling him where to park, what route to take."

Chris interjected. "How can you be a backseat driver and sit in the passenger seat?"

"Figure of speech," Beck said. "And Keith sounds like a winner."

"Dad," Millie said, "he's a good guy. Really. He treats me like a queen. Right, Chris?"

Chris demurred. He shrugged. "I'm going to ride ahead and scout for scouts."

He stood in the saddle and accelerated. The bike wobbled from side to side as he muscled it up the hill.

"Gee, thanks," Millie called after him. "Appreciate you having my back."

Chris waved and held up a finger. He did not turn around.

Beck motioned to Chris. "Now he's a winner. I *like* him."

"Really? Because yesterday you clocked him in the face and broke his nose."

"I changed my mind. I like him now."

"Why? Because he doesn't support Keith and me?"

"He doesn't?"

"Nobody really does, if I'm being honest. I think they're jealous."

The more Beck heard about Keith, the less he was inclined to ever like him. Nothing he had heard was positive. He also was inclined to hate the kid because his daughter loved him, or said she did. That was a given, so he had trouble reconciling his assessment as it related to objectivity.

Then again, he remembered how much Debbie's parents had disliked him. They were probably right to hate him. Beck knew they were. They'd told him as much, and he'd agreed with them before and after he went to jail. Sometimes he wondered if the demons in his ears were the voices of his ex-in-laws.

"Why don't you tell me why you love him? Give the positive stuff."

Millie rolled her eyes and wiped the sweat from her brow as they crested the hill. She conveyed her annoyance in a whiny response that sounded like the young teen he remembered.

"Daaad," she said, "do we *have* to do this now?"

"You want my blessing?"

This caught her by surprise. Her brow twitched. Then she frowned. "Why would you ask that?"

"If you love the guy, and he loves you, at a certain point you make it official, right? D-Day or no D-Day, commitment is commitment. If you both love each other, at that certain point, the guy asks the girl's father for his blessing."

"Did you ask Pa for his blessing?"

Pa was what Millie called Debbie's father. Her mother was Ma. The nicknames were as uncreative as Debbie's parents. So it fit.

"I did."

"He gave it to you?"

"He did not. He told me he would give me his blessing over his dead body."

Millie's face brightened with the gossip. "Seriously?"

"Seriously."

"Then what happened?"

"Your mom said she was marrying me anyway and didn't need anyone's blessing but God's."

"Then what?"

"Pa said I'd already asked God, as far as he was concerned, and the answer was still no."

"I had no idea."

"It wasn't a favorite family topic."

A moment passed while they pedaled in silence. Chris wove back and forth ahead of them, surveilling their surroundings. Nothing but the cries of blackbirds and the occasional rustle of wind through the evergreens greeted them as they rolled south.

Millie broke the silence. "I guess."

"You guess what?"

"I want your blessing."

"Then start spilling, sister."

Although she rolled her eyes again, she did open up. Like a middle-schooler talking about her first crush, she chattered on about his eyes and his smile, how he made her feel special.

"You are special."

"Daaad, you know what I'm saying."

"Go on."

"He's whip smart. Always has an idea about how to make us better. Protect us. Deal with threats."

"How so?"

Millie hesitated. She checked over her shoulder as if somebody were listening and then edged her bike closer to Beck. When she spoke, she lowered her voice. "Can I trust you with something?"

Beck's reaction must have betrayed his disappointment in the question. Millie immediately backtracked.

"I didn't mean it like that, Dad. Really."

"It's fine."

"No," she said, "it's that Chris doesn't know. Only a few people know, and I don't want it to get out. Plausible deniability."

"Where did you learn that phrase?"

"Keith."

"Of course."

"We have a spy in the militia."

Beck wasn't sure he'd heard her correctly. "A what?"

"A spy. It was Keith's idea. He thought we should try to infiltrate the militia. Learn about them. Kill Leo and then try to free the people living under his dominion."

"Dominion. Another big word."

"Dad, c'mon. This is serious."

"Who's the spy?"

"His name is Carl. If you remember when we left, Keith mentioned his concern that our mission might interfere with our long-term plans."

"I remember. I asked you about it then."

"Right. You did. Well, those plans involve Carl. He's supposed to kill Leo in a public place, make it clear the leader is dead."

Beck considered this new information. He tried to roll it over in his mind, ascertain how it might impact his effort to free Regina, Rebecca, and Lucy. It was too much to process. He had to hope one wouldn't negatively impact the other.

Beck turned from his daughter and looked south. Chris was still far ahead and rode on the western side of the road, checking driveways as he passed them. He couldn't hear their conversation at that distance.

"What do you think?" she asked.

"That's a suicide mission," Beck said. "This Carl guy, he's not coming back."

Millie nodded. "He knows that. I mean, he's resigned to that possibility. But he's smart, and if anyone could pull it off and get out of there alive, it would be him."

"How long has he been there?"

"A couple of months. Three maybe. I heard he was part of the team that brought you to us at Churchill Downs. A couple of my people who helped you saw him outside the gates. So as of then, he was alive and had gotten pretty close to Leo."

"That's good, I guess. But why didn't this Keith fellow do it himself? It's easy to volunteer someone else to die."

"Actually, he did volunteer. He said it was his idea and he would do it. He would sacrifice himself for the cause."

"But you said no."

"Of course I said no. Plus, Carl volunteered. He said he couldn't live free while so many others lived under the thumb of a tyrant. He called his mission a worthy sacrifice."

"You know Leo isn't the only tyrant. They're all over the place. Kentucky is just like everywhere else, minus these damned hills. I've seen it, Millie, and it ain't pretty. These tyrants, as you call them, are a dime a dozen. Big towns, small towns, doesn't matter. Evil finds purchase in places where the good lack will. I've seen it again and again."

Millie's expression soured. "What are you saying? That it's pointless?"

Beck sensed the tension. It was instantly as thick as the humidity. He tried to cut through it with a smile.

"No. I'm not saying that at all. Hell, if it *was* pointless, what in the world have I been doing for the last four years?"

Her tight features softened. "Looking for me."

"True. But you know what I mean. I'm only saying that if you're about stopping the bad guys, this is just a start."

"I'm not saying that's my mission, Dad. Maybe it's still yours. Stopping the bad and rescuing the good. That's why we're climbing these damned hills you love so much. But I've committed to saving as many people as I can. We make trips north, get people to a safe place where they can thrive instead of survive."

"The migration."

"Yes."

"How often do you do it?"

"Whenever we have a big group of people. Word's getting out about a utopia north of the border. It's more dangerous than it was a year ago, but we make it work."

"How long will you keep doing it?"

The conversation had taken a hard left turn. Beck had

more questions about Keith, but he was following her path, and as long as she kept talking, telling him about her life, he would take her direction.

"That's the thing. Like I said, it's getting too dangerous. Too many people found out about what we're doing, and it's made us a target. So part of the plan was to get rid of Leo and free as many of his people as possible. Take one more trip and then stay north of the border."

"In the utopia."

"It's not a utopia, but it is nice, and I look forward to ending up there."

"So it was coincidence that I ended up on your doorstep when I did," Beck said. "Another month or two and you'd be long gone."

"I'd have left you a note. If you'd gotten to Churchill Downs and I was gone, I would have figured out a way to signal to you how to follow. I never gave up on you, Dad."

A sudden flood of tears welled in his eyes. This was the kind of surprise Beck didn't like. Perhaps Millie took after him. He blinked back the tears, and sweat blurred his vision.

Beck cleared his throat. "All right. So we rescue my friends, and if Carl hasn't already done it, we kill Leo. Then we all go back to Churchill Downs and join the migration."

He didn't intend to make it sound like an order or that he was making a decision for them. It was more of a question lobbed as a statement, and thankfully, Millie took it that way.

"I think so," she said. "But we have a lot of roads ahead of us before that happ—"

A gunshot cracked through the air. Beck turned from Millie and faced forward. Up ahead, thirty yards from them, Chris was off his bike and on the ground.

CHAPTER 20

D-DAY + 4 YEARS, 6 MONTHS, 21 DAYS
NORTH OF HOPKINSVILLE, KENTUCKY

Beck dropped his bike and hopped off, stumbling into a run as he unholstered his nine-millimeter. Millie was ahead of him, and they raced toward Chris. Both crouched as they advanced, wary of hidden threats. Beck's pack dug into his shoulders and bounced on his back. His body fought him with every step, but he kept moving and scanned the edges of the road. He held the Glock with both hands and acted as if he were providing cover for his daughter.

Another volley of gunshots lanced through the humid air. They popped like firecrackers, and Beck had no concept of their origin.

Millie reached Chris first. She almost skidded to her knees beside him. Beck's vision blurred from the sweat in his eyes, but he moved as fast as he could. When he reached them, he kept his head up and searched for the source of the gunfire.

Another quick succession of cracks and Beck saw the culprit. Muzzle flashes sparked from the western edge of the road one hundred yards ahead. The weapons sounded like rifles from their reports. Whoever pulled their triggers were too far away for Beck to target them with his Glock. He had to get closer.

"Be right back," he said. "Take cover."

Millie didn't respond to him. Beck heard her voice speaking to Chris, but his focus dulled the words. Beck shrugged off his pack and raced to the west. Having eliminated the extra weight, he felt light on his aching feet and quickly reached a gravel driveway that dipped behind a cluster of red maples. Without looking back, he leapt from the road, and bark from one of the maples exploded. Shards of the tree hit his side. A large splinter knifed across his cheek and drew blood, but he ignored it, taking cover to reassess his surroundings. His eyes shot back to Millie and Chris.

From the dip in the road, which led to the twin snipers, Beck saw their advantage. Anyone standing in the road before the dip was easy prey. But crouched low or prone, the angle was too sharp, and the balance of power shifted to the person on the rise. A flash of movement to their left drew his attention for a split second, but another rifle shot forced his focus toward the snipers ahead of them.

Millie and Chris still had their rifles. They could take out the attackers if they had the chance and stayed low. Beck narrowed his focus. Millie's back was to him, and she blocked most of Chris's body. No blood that he could see, but that didn't necessarily mean anything. Beck guessed, however, that Chris was alive. If he was dead, Millie would know better than to waste time on him when she could be returning fire.

Beck called out to her, "Get low and take aim. They can't get you if you're low."

Millie didn't turn around, and Beck had no sense as to whether she heard him or not. He cursed and punched the tree closest to him. The maple didn't give, and he cursed again, this time at his stupidity. He shook the bolt of pain from his knuckles and made a decision.

Despite his muscles' protest, he started south at a full

sprint through the woods. He ran at full speed, the Glock low in front of him in both hands again, bobbing branches and weaving around the trunks that held them.

The sun filtered through the intermittent canopy and gave him plenty of light to see the obstacles on the ground beneath his boots. His side stitched, and he almost fell over from the sharp, sudden, breath-stealing pain, but pushed through it and made his way closer to the snipers.

When he guessed he was twenty yards from them, at most, he slowed to a jog and then a careful walk. He took slow breaths in through his nose and pushed the air in long exhales through pressed lips. Using the trees for cover, he scanned his field of view for the snipers.

Ahead of him, no more than thirty feet, the trees gave way to a wide clearing. One of the snipers was in the prone position, legs splayed behind him. Both of them—he could spot two in total—had their eyes to scopes and their fingers on the triggers of their NGSW Sig Sauers. These were militia. They were scouts.

Then Beck realized he hadn't heard a shot when he'd raced through the woods. The men were conserving their ammunition. That was smart. After the round that splintered the maple above his head, the volleys had stopped.

Then it hit him. The shot into the tree. There was no way either of the snipers on the western edge of the road could have hit that tree at that angle.

There was a third sniper. Someone on the other side of the road. And Beck had left Millie alone with Chris. Exposed. Unprotected.

For a split second, he considered running back. Instead he cursed himself, told the demons to shut the hell up, and headed for the snipers.

Both men had their attention on the upslope. They didn't

see him coming.

Beck used the thick trunk closest to them as cover and lowered himself to one knee. He extended his arms, one hand cupped under, finger off the trigger. He waited for a bead of sweat to roll past his right eye and took aim. He practiced a quick sweeping motion from one head to the other.

He slid his finger to the trigger, exhaled, and applied even pressure. The first sniper's head snapped to one side, and he went limp. Before the second shooter could react to the Glock's pop, a round drilled him in the neck. He slapped the wound with his hand like one would a mosquito bite. His eyes fluttered and rolled back, his mouth gaping like a fish. Beck emerged into the clearing and grabbed one of the rifles. Lying prone next to a dead sniper, he raised the scope to his eye and focused, his aim at the top edge of the rise in the road. He squinted and looked away from the scope.

Nothing.

He recalled from their prone position, the snipers couldn't get a clear shot at Millie or Chris unless they stood.

Beck pushed himself upright, drew the rifle to his shoulder, and took aim at the spot where Chris had hit the ground. Again, nothing.

Not nothing, exactly. The bike was there. Farther up the road, Millie's bike and his lay askew on the asphalt.

Where were they? Where was the third sniper?

Beck swept the road from side to side. His heartbeat accelerated, and he worked to control his breathing. Something was wrong. Had he taken bait?

His eyes darted back and forth. There was no sign of Chris or Millie.

Beck cursed aloud, then cursed again. Then he grabbed both rifles, pilfered two extra magazines, which he stuffed into his back pockets, and ran back into the woods that flanked the road. He raced along, dodging limbs and roots. The climb back uphill was more arduous, especially given that both of his arms balanced twin Sig Sauer rifles.

He huffed and fought another stitch before he reached the gravel drive where he'd nearly lost his head next to a maple. Breathing hard, he shrugged away sweat from his brow, slung one of the rifles over his shoulder.

Why hadn't he done that before trekking up the hill? This time, the demons cursed him, and rightfully so. He'd lost his daughter. Again. Emotion fogged his thinking.

C'mon, Beck. Settle down. Focus. You'll get yourself killed.

Staying behind the cover of the splintered maple, Beck snuck a peek toward the road. Something struck him as odd. He lifted the scope to his eye and aimed it at the spot where Chris went down. His bike was still in the road. So was Beck's pack.

No blood. Was Chris even shot? Why was he on the ground?

It didn't sit well with him. A thousand possibilities ran through his mind. He considered the things his daughter had revealed about her plans. She had a spy working for her whom she believed had infiltrated Leo's militia. What if Leo had figured it out? What if Leo had a spy?

God bless his daughter. Millie was brilliant. She was a natural leader, no doubt. But could she outsmart Leo? Beck had his doubts. Not because of her weakness, but because of Leo's strength.

Leo ran a mostly well-oiled machine. He was deliberate. And even in the fever-racked conversation Beck had shared with Leo after his capture, Beck could tell the man was smart. He too played a long game.

Beck remembered what the man had said to him when Beck challenged him to a fight and Leo refused. The militia leader's snide grin was vivid in his mind's eye.

"Leaders like me, we have responsibilities, Beck," Leo had said. "I don't expect a renegade like you to understand that. But we do. Real responsibilities. For ourselves, for those in our charge, and I for one take that role very seriously. I have to think of the long game, Beck. The long game is the key to survival. More than survival, really, it's the key to unlocking a new kind of civilization. That's where my head is."

Beck processed all of these thoughts within a split second, as if every synapse fired at once and dumped countless reams of data instantaneously. He removed the magazine and replaced it with a full one from his back pocket. His Glock was firmly on his hip. He didn't remember how many rounds he had remaining.

"I would take a lot of pleasure out of dispatching you, John Beck," Leo had said in that conversation. "Put your head on a spike and leave it on the highway for people to see. Talk about street cred! My name would end up in those pulp comics that made you out to be an unstoppable force. There'd be *The Adventures of Leo*. Or even better *Leo and the Kentucky Militia*. Of course, there would be a final installment of your story, Beck. A denouement, am I right? It would chronicle your demise."

Beck remembered the cool and collected, almost detached, Leo clapping his hands together.

"Yet that cannot be," Leo had said. "I cannot let my own temporary gratification trump the need for that long game. I have to keep you alive, reap the rewards from the Sheriff, and let it go. Onward and upward, as they say. Am I right?"

Chris was a spy. He worked for Leo.

He was a plant. He had to be the one who took the potshot at him where he again stood. The whole thing was a setup. But why now?

It was a reach. A huge leap with the little information he had. Yet as Beck's mind swirled in a wobbling vortex of thoughts, suppositions, rationalizations, and self-doubt, this made as much sense as anything.

He crept back onto the road. As he did, he had the hi-tech rifle pressed against his shoulder. He scanned his surroundings and swept the muzzle with his finger on the trigger.

He worked to keep his attention on the tasks at hand. Finding Millie. Killing Chris.

For the countless time in minutes, he chastised himself. He had been so focused on Keith and his influence over Millie, he'd failed to interrogate Chris. Not once had he asked how long Chris was with her. Never did he delve into Chris's background and motivation. He'd taken the kid's loyalty on blind faith.

He reached the spot in the center of the road where he'd last seen them. Chris's bike was on its side. Beck looked down the slope. The two dead snipers lay there, one rolled onto the other.

A quick spin on his boot heels and he searched behind him. Nothing. Nobody.

Lucy came to mind.

When they had faced the cannibals, the hostiles had snuck up from behind and quietly spirited her into the woods. Had that happened here?

Were there more militia scouts just waiting and watching? Then when Beck made his move, they made theirs?

There was too much to process. He gritted his teeth and flexed his jaw. Beck was exposed, standing in the middle of the road with no cover. He understood that, and a little part of him, the part that listened to the demons and believed every word they hissed, wanted a sniper to take him out then and there. He'd earned that sort of ignominious death. *Ignominious.* Gabe would like that word.

His sweep carried him in a full circle. Seeing nothing, he crouched, and keeping his eyes up, Beck shouldered his pack one arm at a time. His pulse pounded in his neck and at his temples. His breath came in shallow, short puffs. The sweat was drying across his brow and on his cheeks, and Beck wondered if he was on the verge of dehydration. There was nothing to do about it. Not now.

Beck stood, shrugged the pack to a more comfortable position, and shouldered the rifle. Again, he scanned his surroundings. Like a man in the middle of an ocean with no land in sight, the effort seemed useless. The demons suggested it was an exercise in futility, like everything he'd ever done.

He swallowed past the dryness in his mouth and licked his teeth. Then Beck closed his eyes and listened. Not to the demons but to his surroundings. It was impossible that his daughter and Chris were gone without some sort of clue. He played the previous minutes back in his mind.

Chris fell; Beck ran; Millie passed him; the snipers took single shots from their position at the edge of the road at the bottom of the rise.

Beck recalled realizing his advantage on the high ground. Anyone standing in the road before the dip was easy prey, but crouched low or prone, the angle was too sharp, and the balance of power shifted to the person on the rise. A flash of movement to his left had drawn his attention for a split second, but another rifle shot had forced his focus toward the snipers ahead of them.

A flash of movement to his left.

Beck spun back to face that direction, pressed the fully loaded Sig Sauer tight against his shoulder, and marched forward with urgency. He kept his head up and darted his eyes in short sweeps of the area where he remembered seeing the movement.

Somebody had been in the woods. There was a third scout.

It still didn't make sense. It wasn't possible a single scout could take both Millie and Chris without a sound. The scout and Chris working together though…

He pushed the theoretical and paranoia from his mind and worked with facts. He had seen someone or something in the woods. And he was headed straight toward it.

Beck stepped from the road onto the crumbling shoulder. Pieces of it gave way under the push of his boot as he peered into the woods that stretched away from the road. He stopped cold.

He brought his finger to the rifle's trigger. "Get your hands up. Now. Or I end you."

Twenty yards from him, a man sat on the ground, his knees up to his chest and his back against the wide trunk of an oak. His hands were hidden in his lap.

"I said to raise your hands. Slowly. Now."

The man appeared to look at Beck.

Beck adjusted his aim and pulled the trigger. The round drilled a hole into the trunk above the man's head. A spray of bark rained down on his head. He didn't react.

Beck took two more steps from the road. Then another two. He checked his surroundings, then moved forward. He was ten feet from the man when he understood why the target failed to comply.

His dark shirt stuck to his chest, glued there with his own blood. The shirt was drenched. The man's complexion was gray. His lips and eyelids were bluish, almost purple. His tongue lolled in his mouth.

"Who are you? You work for Leo?"

The man's eyes jittered toward Beck and met his gaze. He nodded almost imperceptibly.

"Where's my daughter? What did you do to her?"

The man blinked. He started to laugh. Then he coughed. Blood spurted from between his lips and stained his teeth. His eyes widened, and fear masked his expression. His chest heaved, and his lungs rattled out a final breath. One final involuntary twitch and he was gone. Dead at the base of the tree.

Beck cursed and checked the man for weapons or any indication of who he was. He found nothing of value and studied the ground. The layer of detritus was even and thick all around him except for a thin, disturbed path that led deeper into the woods.

Beck followed the path with his eyes. It wound its way deeper into the woods beyond his line of sight. He checked over his shoulder as if searching for the bikes they'd left in the middle of the road.

Beck considered his options and determined he had none. So he started along the path, the rifle across his body but its butt against his shoulder. He kept his finger against the trigger guard.

The sun, still rising, cast odd shadows against the tangled canopy of dead and dying trees that dotted the thinning woods. As they had on the other side of the road, the trees grew in clusters, which created dense pockets that gave way to narrow clearings.

He moved deliberately along the path, stepping over and around the thick, bulging roots that threatened to trip him. His pulse thumped in his ears, and he worked to maintain his calm.

Beck failed to summon the rage that typically fueled and

informed his violent assaults. Instead, he worked to control his emotions. Anxiety pounded at his thoughts and threatened to overtake him. As experienced and as lucky a survivor John Beck had become since D-Day, Millie was undoubtedly his purpose, his mission. No matter how old she became or what sort of leader into which she evolved, she would always be his little girl. The thought of her in imminent peril was almost too much.

As much as he had suppressed those thoughts during his four-and-a-half-year search for her, it was almost impossible to compartmentalize the rational from the emotional now. Now that he'd found her, the idea of losing her again was almost debilitating. Millie was his kryptonite.

Beck adjusted his grip on the rifle and moved along the path. He alternated checking the path and his surroundings. He watched and listened but saw and heard nothing that gave him hope. Then something struck him as odd. He stopped and leaned against a tree.

He thought he was headed east. But as he looked at the trees around him, he noticed moss creeping up their trunks in the wrong spot. Wrong if he was headed east.

In the northern hemisphere, moss almost always grew on the north side of a tree. All of the trees around him had moss growing on the side of the trunk facing him. He checked over his shoulder and saw his winding path had taken a distinct turn he hadn't noticed until now.

Beck was headed south. He was moving toward Hopkinsville.

This was good and bad. It meant Millie was moving toward their destination. That was good. But she hadn't come back for him. That likely meant she wasn't under her own power or free will. That was bad.

With renewed purpose, Beck marched toward a wider

clearing ahead of him. When he reached it, the trees and shade gave way to the bright sun and a cloudless blue sky. Beck squinted until his eyes adjusted. When they did, he sucked in a deep breath of the humid air.

The town of Hopkinsville lay before him, a mile ahead. He saw the tops of the scattered downtown buildings. He was parallel to the road on which they'd ridden from the north.

His eyes fell from the low skyline, and he saw a horse loping toward the city. Two people rode on the saddle. A third walked beside the horse. Beck tried to gauge the distance. A half mile? Maybe less.

While he couldn't be one hundred percent certain, his gut told him Millie was one of the three. He was almost sure she was on the horse in the front. The figure behind her made it hard to be sure. But whoever it was wore a Stetson just like Millie's.

He wanted to call out but thought better of it. The distance was likely too great to carry his voice. If Millie was the prisoner of the other two, calling attention to himself could only make matters worse.

Beck wiped his brow, realized he was sweating, and pulled a water bottle from his pack. He started after the trio at a quick pace after taking two long pulls from the bottle. His water was almost gone, but the swigs quenched his thirst for the moment.

As long as the horse didn't accelerate into a trot or bolt from view, as long as he kept Millie and her captors in sight, everything would fall into place. At least, he hoped it would. Pounding the earth with his boots, ignoring the aches in his shoulders and lower back, Beck gave chase.

CHAPTER 21

D-DAY + 4 YEARS, 6 MONTHS, 21 DAYS
HOPKINSVILLE, KENTUCKY

Regina stared at Carl. She hadn't really known him, but as the life had drained from his body, so had her hope of escaping this place alive.

He had taken his final breath in her cell. Guards had tossed him to the floor and left him in a heap. She could tell immediately, in the angular shaft of light that filtered through the open door, Carl was hurt. It wasn't until they had closed and locked the door, and she scurried to his side, did she understand how bad his injuries were.

Now she sat next to him, one hand on his still chest, praying he would suddenly awake and his heart would beat again. That wouldn't happen. She knew this. But one without hope wishes for silly things. It made her think of a saying an old teacher of hers used to repeat often.

"It might as well be a million dollars if you can't afford five."

Regina always liked that sentiment, the idea that if something was out of reach, it mattered not how far it was. It could be an inch, it could be a mile.

And if she was stuck dying here, and escaping was out of reach, then so was wishing for Carl's reincarnation. One was as likely as the other.

She ran her fingertips back and forth over the fabric of Carl's shirt. For whatever reason, and she couldn't place it, this made her think of Beck. Was he alive somewhere and coming for her? Or was he more likely dead, his body cold and still like Carl's?

It felt like hours since the guards had left Carl with her. It could have been longer. Keeping track of time was almost impossible in here.

Losing days or even weeks was common on the outside. It took a concerted effort to log sunrises and sunsets in a world without electricity. She wished she had an analog, self-winding wristwatch. That would've helped some. In the dark, with no concept of day or night, it was impossible to distinctly conceive of time.

Although her eyes were heavy and she wanted to sleep, her nerves kept her exhausted body awake. Her thoughts drifted aimlessly from memories to possible futures. None of those futures were long lasting, nor were they pleasant.

Regina wavered between consciousness and the hazy place between it and sleep. The darker the images of life to come, the deeper her desire to dream of something beyond her control.

A click at the door and the creak of its hinges snapped her from the unwanted reverie, and a figure appeared in the doorway. She was certain the dark shape belonged to Leo. His voice confirmed it.

"I can see clearly now the rain is gone," he sang and continued with lyrics that rang vaguely familiar.

Regina scooted from Carl's body as the opening at the door widened and revealed more figures standing at the threshold in the flickering candlelight. She counted three beside Leo. He was the only one to step into the room.

"The arena is still sloppy," he said. "It's not as dry as I'd like. But our situation here has changed, and I think it prudent to move ahead. We've got a lot of gears turning today. The mechanisms are all in harmony."

Regina scooted farther from him as he approached, and tried to maintain her distance.

"Carl, or Casca, or whoever he was, was gumming up the gears," said Leo. "I had to remove him. Nothing personal. He was a fine young man. Dutiful. Whip smart. Loyal. Only problem I had with him was that his loyalty wasn't to me. It wasn't to this, am I right?"

He stretched his arms wide, gesturing to the space around him. The question was rhetorical, but he repeated it again for his henchmen's benefit. "Am I right?"

The men at the door hooted. One of them grunted an affirmation.

Regina's back was pressed against the wall. She had no more room to move.

Leo stopped at Carl's body. He looked down at it and shook his head. "He wasn't who he said he was, but you knew that, right? I saw you make googly eyes at him during our games of chess. Were they googly eyes?"

Regina slid along the wall until she was in the corner. While this was the foulest part of the cell, it gave her the most space from Leo.

He followed her with his shoulders, always twisting his position to face her like the shadow of a sundial chasing the sun. But he did not advance past Carl's body. He folded his arms across his chest.

"He worked for the Sheriff. I don't know if he told you this or not during his little visit to your cell yesterday, but—"

Regina's thoughts drifted for a moment to her conversation with Casca. Or Carl. He was Carl. As much death as she had experienced since D-Day, and it was an inordinate amount, processing the death of someone with whom she had just had an important conversation was difficult. His death in her cell, his final phlegmy gasps for air as blood and fluid filled his lungs, rattled her. It only proved to accentuate the fragility of life, the thin invisible line between health and death.

"—made him believe I trusted him, or would trust him. He was naïve enough to believe his ruse played. Unlike you, who masterfully duped me into losing games through clever subterfuge, Carl failed to employ the same tactics."

Regina heard but didn't understand his last several sentences. Her mind hopped from one disparate thought to another. Finally, they crystallized into what mattered. The only thing that mattered.

"What are you going to do to me?"

Leo smiled. Although Regina couldn't see it, she heard it in the way he spoke. Affability spiked with hubris and condescension.

"I'm going to make you watch. C'mon, enough chatter. I've given my lecture for the day. Time to go. Chop-chop."

Regina didn't move. "You're going to make me watch what?"

Leo clapped his hands together twice. A master calling a dog to heel. "C'mon. Let's go. We can talk along the way."

Regina's pulse accelerated. "Tell me now."

Leo sighed. It was dramatic. His shoulders slumped. "Fine. But you already know the answer to your question. You're going out there with me to watch your friends fight. Rebecca and Lucy. One lives, one dies. Maybe they both die. Either way, it'll be a hoot, as the kids like to say, am I right?"

"I don't think the kids say that," Regina said.

He motioned with his hand, a gesture indicating she

needed to hurry up. "My patience is wearing. Get up on your own now, or I'll have my men assist you. They won't be as kind as your dear Carl was the other day."

Regina glanced at the men in the doorway. They were big. Bigger than Leo. She didn't want them touching her if she could help it.

She pressed her hands against the floor and pushed her back up the wall. When she stood upright, she steadied herself against the wall.

"You okay to follow us under your own power or—"

Regina held up a hand. "I'm fine. Give me a second. I'm coming."

She gathered herself and took in a deep breath of the moldy, fetid air. Hands out at her sides for balance, she crossed the room, passed Leo without looking at him, and moved into the hallway. The guards gave her a wide berth when she walked beyond the threshold.

From behind her, Leo called, "To the left, dear. Go to the left. I'll catch up with you."

In a moment, he was at her side, and they moved along the corridor. Regina traced one hand along the wall, steadying herself as she walked toward the end of the corridor. She noticed that every door they passed was open, the cells inside them empty. She tried counting the number of rooms but lost track. Leo hurried past her to the door at the end of the hallway. The door led outside, and he pushed it open, then gestured for her to proceed.

"Ladies first," he said. "I am nothing if not a gentleman."

Regina walked through the door, chuckles of Leo's men trailing behind her as she ascended a flight of stairs to the outdoors. She tightened and relaxed her fists. It took everything in her not to turn around and gouge out Leo's eyes. Her anger gave way to awe as she reached the top of the steps. At first, the glare from the bright sun and cloudless sky blinded her. Then her eyes adjusted, and she saw the spectacle before her. It was unnerving.

The stands were full, more so than the previous gladiator fights she'd attended. It reminded her of a rock concert or a sporting event pre-apocalypse. People sat shoulder to shoulder, some almost on each other's laps as they sardined themselves into the bleachers. One row after the next teemed with anticipation.

Regina was unaware this kind of audience was possible in Kentucky or anywhere outside the big cities. It reminded her of the denizens inside the pyramid in Memphis. Desperate for something to take their minds off the stressors of their lives, they packed into a communal space for diversion.

As incredible as the crowd was, and it spilled into standing room along the edges of the track, what horrified Regina even more was the collection of gladiators who stood corralled at one end of the field.

She pointed toward the group. "Are those fighters? All of them?"

"Every last one we have," Leo said. "Fifty-eight. Fantastic, isn't it? I'm thinking we'll do a few group challenges before we reach the grand finale with your compadres. I'm thinking this will be an all-day affair. Might last until nightfall. Or even into the dark. We'll have to light torches so we can see it, but, oh, how fantastic would that be?"

He ran his hand in an arc in front of his face as if pantomiming a theater marquee. "Arena under the Stars. Has a ring to it, am I right?"

Regina's stomach turned over, and it twisted uncomfortably in her gut. A wave of nausea threatened to overwhelm her, but she held it together. She had to present a brave face. Any little crack in her armor was an invitation for

Leo to claim victory.

All she could manage was another question "Fifty-eight? All of them were prisoners inside the building?"

"All of them."

"Why make all of them fight today? I don't understand."

"We have guests on their way. Very special guests. It's important they see our power and the lengths to which we will go to maintain our grip on what is ours. Plus, it's expensive feeding fifty-eight—well, fifty-nine—prisoners. This battle royale will help the bottom line."

"Who are your guests?"

Leo's wide smile broadened. He was so smug. So pleased with himself. "You'll see. Now, let's find our seats."

Leo put his hand on the small of her back and nudged her toward the stands. At first, she saw no openings, no place for them to sit. But as he guided her up the steps, she realized they were not sitting in the stands this time. They were going to sit above them, in what had been the press box during the facility's days as the community football stadium.

From this vantage point, the entire field was visible. Leo took a seat at what would have been the fifty-yard line. He pulled out a chair and gestured for Regina to take a seat. She hesitated, then sat. What was the point in picking unwinnable battles?

She was no longer bound at her feet. Regina guessed Leo figured she was too weak to run, and if she did, she couldn't get far. Her wrists were free, too. This made Leo vulnerable to a surprise physical attack. But again, how would she succeed? Even if she managed a quick blow or got her thumbs into his eyes, his men would act quickly to end the threat.

Regina imagined Leo had calculated all of these possibilities ahead of time. He would've determined the odds so in his favor as not to worry about restraining her. She might be more of a problem with her hands and feet bound than free.

The field was muddy. Puddles pocked the low spots in a dozen places across the field. However, it was not the slop pit it had become during the torrential rains. Regina watched soldiers divide the gladiators into groups and lead them from their corner of the arena.

The sky was azure blue, almost tropical in its hue, and the sun was brutal. No clouds mitigated the direct light and heat baking the earth. Regina half-expected to see the puddles boil and pop like geysers.

Sweat beaded on her forehead, and drops of it ran down her back, tracing her spine. Regina licked her lips and tasted the brine. It surprised her she could perspire given her lack of hydration. She shrugged and swiped away a sheen of sweat from her cheek.

One of Leo's henchmen, a man she recognized because of the long scar that ran from his ear to his mouth, climbed the steps away from the field and toward the press box. She might not have noticed him had it not been for the rough way he handled any spectator who got in his way. He shoved and pushed, impatient in his ascent.

Beside her, Leo purred, "Hmmm. I wonder what the little birdie brings me."

"Little birdie" was not a moniker she would've picked for the burly, scar-faced man who looked like he might kill her for looking at him the wrong way. If anything, she might have thought him more of a pterodactyl, as he looked more prehistoric with his hunched posture and heavy brow. He glanced up at Leo and gestured a greeting with his prominent chin. His hard gaze shifted to Regina before his bulk disappeared underneath the press box.

A moment later, he was behind them. His odor announced his arrival even before Leo said hello in a low but welcoming voice.

"What news have you brought me?" he asked the man.

The scar-faced hulk eyed Regina before speaking. Leo assured him it was fine.

Still, he hesitated before he spoke. "We spotted them."

Leo lifted an eyebrow and sat up in his seat. A smirk threatened to curl at one side of his mouth. "Really? Already?"

"Yes. We're missing three. They're missing two. But we have what we need."

"Who are we missing?"

"A pair of scouts and one of the grunts. They were expendable."

"Who are they missing?"

The hulk opened his mouth to speak, but his heavy brow furrowed such that his dark eyes seemed to disappear into his head.

"Never mind," Leo said. "It doesn't matter who's missing. What matters is who isn't missing, am I right?"

"Yes, sir. I have confirmed we have who we want."

Leo clapped his hands together, and the smile fully materialized. "Excellent. Nice work. Tell the others to be ready. This will be epic."

The scar-faced man attempted a smile.

Leo rubbed his hands together and then slapped the hulk on the shoulder. He squeezed the thick muscle of the man's triceps and thanked him again. "Excellent work. Tell the others. Really excellent."

The hulk nodded, his features expressionless, and he stepped from sight. Regina didn't turn around to watch him leave. Her attention was on the two teams of five gladiators, each stepping toward the center of the field.

From her seat in the box, Regina could not definitively tell the men from the women. She imagined the larger fighters were men, but with masks or helmets and ill-fitting clothes, being certain was impossible.

So focused was she on the gladiators that she failed to clarify the conversation between Leo and the hulk. Either that, or subconsciously she believed Leo couldn't help but tell her the unsolicited details. Other than violence and subjugation, talking seemed to be Leo's favorite pastime. He didn't disappoint.

"You haven't asked what that was about," he said. "Aren't you curious? I pegged you as curious."

Regina shifted in her seat but kept her eyes on the field. "I pegged you as someone who would tell me whether I asked or not."

Leo laughed and shook his head. "You are something. I *do* like you. I really do. In another time and another place, who knows what could've happened."

"Is this where I get the 'we're not so different, you and I' trope?"

Leo leaned away from her so he could get a better view. His smile shrank, and he pursed his lips. His eyes appraised her. "We're not. But that's beside the point. I think we could've been friends and—"

"I don't think so," Regina cut in. "It doesn't take an apocalypse for you to become a narcissist. Someone once said that crisis doesn't create character, it reveals it. This is who you always were, Leo. We would've never been friends."

He studied her for a long moment. Even as she watched the fighters stretch and practice with their chosen weapons, Regina was acutely aware of his intense gaze.

"That's a pity," he said after a long moment. "But it's

neither here nor there, am I right? We'll never know what could have been because of what actually was."

Regina didn't reply. Leo sat back in his seat, his shoulder against hers, and touched her hand with his. She considered pulling away but thought better of it. Picking battles…

"Getting back to the question at hand. I told you earlier that your friends were the finale. After all of these other fighters have conquered one another, Lucy and Rebecca will take center stage. That's no longer true."

This got her attention. She pivoted to face him. Hope stretched her features. "Have you changed your mind? Are you doing the decent thing and—"

He shook his head. "Oh, no. It's nothing like that. I see the expectation of good news in the brightness of your expression. You're pretty when you have hope. You know that?"

Regina looked away. Conscious of the blush in her cheeks, she brought her hands to her face to shield them from view.

"Your friends are still fighting. One or both will die today in the arena. That's as certain as the sunset. No, what I wanted to say was that they are no longer the grand finale. We have something much better now to appease the masses. It's a big surprise, but I'll whisper it to you if you want to hear it."

Regina didn't want to hear it. Not at all. If the news didn't involve sparing her friends their gruesome fate, it wasn't worth her time. Yet she understood his offer contained no choice. He would tell her whether she liked it or not. That was exactly what he did.

Leo leaned in even as she leaned away. "Have you ever heard of the Sheriff?"

Regina's body stiffened. Of course she had heard of the Sheriff. That was who she and the others were helping Beck find, even though the unnamed desperado had a bounty on Beck's head. The Sheriff, it seemed, might be the key to Beck's daughter Millie's whereabouts.

She didn't say anything, but Leo must have sensed her reaction. He chuckled.

"Of course you have," he hissed. "That's where you were headed when you trespassed on my land and we intercepted you. Well, the exciting news is that we've found the Sheriff. She's ours now."

She?

Again, the perceptive Leo grinned. "Ahhh, you didn't know. The Sheriff is a woman, Regina. She is a young woman whose name might be familiar to you."

Regina couldn't look away any longer. She faced him. "Spit it out," she said. "I'm tired of the games."

He squeezed her hand. She had almost forgotten he had it there.

"Okay then," Leo said. "The Sheriff is Millie Beck. John Beck's daughter. We have her, and she'll be in that very arena—fighting for her life. And you want to know the best part?"

Regina's mind swam with confusion. The new information was too much to absorb. She almost didn't catch the next thing Leo said. But it sank in, and it made her want to puke.

"The best part, Regina, is that she's fighting you."

CHAPTER 22

D-DAY + 4 YEARS, 6 MONTHS, 21 DAYS
HOPKINSVILLE, KENTUCKY

Leo sat back, pleased with himself. Her expression and the way the color drained from Regina's face was cake enough. Seeing her fight Beck's daughter in the arena would be the icing.

He opened his mouth to speak and, for perhaps the first time in his life, said nothing. It was better to leave his last words buzzing in her ears, making her process them, replay them over and again. This was delicious.

He patted her hand and moved away from her. His attention shifted to the field. The grandeur of it. Sure, this was post-apocalyptic Hopkinsville, Kentucky. He hadn't created what the despots in New York, Miami, or Los Angeles had managed to build. They were on another level, oppressive in a way he could never achieve here. But this society, the one built from guile and cunning, was something of which he could be proud.

And he was. Leo smiled to himself thinking about his ex-wife, Gretchen, and her boy-toy, Darren. If only she could see this. If only he could put the two of *them* in the arena.

"You're a teacher," she had said. *"A teacher who makes less than a fast-food chicken manager. You will never be able to retire. I will never*

237

have the life I deserve."

Leo imagined Gretchen on the field, on her knees, begging forgiveness. In his mind's eye he saw Darren beside her, eyes averted and unable to accept his fate.

Would a blade be the weapon of choice? A rifle? Poison? Force them to drink their own death?

No. None of that. He would pardon them. He would offer them refuge and prove to her every day how he was the superior survivor. How he, the lowly professor, had risen to such heights without money and eighteen-inch biceps.

That was power. That was strength. That was leadership. To pardon the one who had aggrieved him most. He blinked from his daydream and focused again on the moment, the coming glory of the day.

He peered through the box's opening toward the cloudless sky. The winds and rain were gone, and they had given way to a gorgeous, albeit hot and humid, day.

A lone blackbird circled above. It glided on the current, swooped down toward the field, and then ascended. Flapping its wings, it climbed toward the sun and then arced wide around the arena. Leo smiled at the clairvoyant bird, a sign he believed portended the coming violence, and exhaled.

It was time.

Leo stood and applauded the two teams of gladiators who faced each other at the center of the field. The men and women who stood there looked like actors on a stage without any lines. Even from his distance, Leo saw the confusion and feared that masked their faces. That is, he saw it on those whose faces were not covered already.

The crowd joined in the applause. They stood and cheered. Some chanted while others hollered their suggestions as to how the competitors might best their opponents.

On the field, a trio of armed militia stood guard. The referees, as they were, of this group activity, they formed a triangular position around the two teams.

All three settled into their positions, their rifles shouldered and aimed in the general direction of the gladiators within their perimeter. In a coordinated movement, all three shifted and looked toward the press box.

The applause waned, and Leo raised his hands. He eyed the referees and waited, building the anticipation. The crowd noise shrank to a low murmur and then to virtual silence. Everyone who could see Leo looked back and up at him. He had everyone's rapt attention. It was glorious and invigorating. There was nothing like holding people in the palms of his hands.

He counted backward from ten in his head, and when he reached one, he dropped his hands to his sides.

The referees shouted, breaking the silence, and the battle commenced. The crowd roared.

Leo folded his arms across his chest and watched the drama unfold before him. A smile stretched his cheeks, and he grinned like a Cheshire cat. He even giggled.

The team left of center was the aggressor. They wore red strips of torn fabric on their arms. They advanced on the five gladiators to the right, who wore blue and seemed overwhelmed from the start.

The two smallest red fighters attacked together. They chose the largest of the blue team members and had him on the defensive immediately.

Both small reds carried nail-embedded sticks. The gruesome weapons looked like spiked bats ripped from the Middle Ages. The large blue fighter carried a staff with curved blades at either end. He parried and blocked the barrage of swings from the two reds. When the red fighters adjusted their tactics and one went high while the other dropped low, the large blue could not react fast enough. He took a heavy swing to his calf and another to the back of his knee. It hobbled the blue fighter, and he lost his balance. That was all it took.

The twin red fighters pounced and knocked the large blue to the ground. He lost hold of his staff, and Leo turned away when the amount of blood told him that part of the battle was over.

The crowd roared its approval. The twin reds relished the adulation for the briefest moment, and this pleased Leo. There was something psychological about the arena he enjoyed observing.

It did not matter how much of a pacifist someone might be when they entered. If they survived and managed a kill, their savage instincts took over. It was something akin to bloodlust but more primeval. Against the backdrop of a world gone mad, the idea of concentrated violence was something particularly transformative. Leo scanned the field, soaking in the totality of the violence, and cheered with the others. He balled his fists and shook them at the white-hot sun above.

The other three red fighters took on their opponents individually. While one was down and on the verge of losing, the other two had the upper hand. When the twin reds, fresh from their kill, joined a heavyset gladiator in his knife fight, they again triumphed with little effort.

Now the three reds joined the fourth, and they swarmed the single blue gladiator. A slight woman, she'd held her own against a red fighter of similar size and skill. Against four, however, she was no match. She tried running but tripped in a divot, tumbled head over heels, and landed facedown in a puddle. She died facedown in the water.

Now the four turned their attention to the lone remaining blue fighter. A muscular woman carrying a club in one hand and a short spear in the other stood her ground. Her muscles tensed as she flexed and roared. It was a guttural call, a warning to the others.

Blood streaked her face, and a spray decorated her oversized shirt, which hung almost to her knees. The four red fighters took their time. They encircled the blue warrior and orbited her with slow, catlike movements.

The crowd was on its feet. They stomped in rhythm, and the structure vibrated underneath Leo. He felt the box sway and the beat pound in his chest. A single chant began low and reached a crescendo as seemingly everyone in the audience, the hundreds who had come to watch others fight to the death on command, called out the same words.

"Kill her now! Kill her now! Kill her now!"

The blue fighter had to hear this. She had to know she was alone, on an island, and the only one within fifty miles who wanted her to live. Leo's chest swelled with anticipation. His heart thumped with excitement.

Kill her now. Kill her now.

The four red fighters appeared to measure one another. None advanced, though they tightened their orbit and probed with random jabs into the center, testing the defense.

The blue gladiator spread her stance. She returned the jabs with short lunges and quick swings. All of them landed short of her opponents, doing just enough to keep them at bay.

But she was a cornered animal. Surrounded, with nowhere to go.

Leo flexed his jaw.

Kill her now. Kill her now.

This was the world he'd created. An imperfect place with desperate people willing to do anything to survive.

The blue fighter cried out. An inhuman shriek that sounded more like a banshee than a woman, and she attacked. Not a parry or a stab, a full-on, go-for-broke attack.

She caught the smallest red fighter off guard and slashed across his middle as she dropped to her knees and slid across the wet ground. The shocking move did three things that suddenly changed the complexion of the fight.

First, it dropped the small red gladiator, whose life gushed onto the field. The odds were now three to one.

Second, it moved the blue fighter outside the circle. Her momentum and the wet earth carried her several feet on her knees before she slid to a stop, spun, and got back to her feet. Now she faced the other three head-on.

Third, it silenced the crowd. A collective "whoa" followed by low murmurs replaced the chant. A sure kill for the red team and a righteous end to the battle was no longer a guarantee.

The blue gladiator gathered herself and faced her opponents. Both hands holding weapons, she held them out at her sides and screamed again. Covered in blood and mud, she was a magnificent sight. A monster whose stature seemed to grow with every passing second. The excitement of what she might do next instantly replaced the pang of disappointment in Leo's gut after he watched her survive the circle of four in a masterful stroke.

Who was this woman? She was magnificent. Absolutely magnificent.

Leo realized he was pacing back and forth in front of his seat. He stood still, folded his arms across his chest, and focused all of his attention on the blue warrior.

The crowd still didn't know how to react. They remained relatively silent until the blue warrior instigated another bloody confrontation.

She pointed the club directly at the largest remaining red fighter and ran straight at him. She closed the distance in the blink of an eye and leapt into the air. She spread her legs and arms and tackled the big man to the ground, clinging to him for a moment before she rolled off him, swung the club at his head with a backhand, and knocked him senseless.

The other two red fighters responded fast. One swung a blade at her that sliced across her arm and forced her to drop the club. The blue fighter cried out in pain but rolled away onto a knee and lunged upward with the blade in her other hand. It drove into the red attacker's thigh. She tore the blade free, and the red fighter collapsed to the ground, rolling in pain.

The crowd cheered at this. They were on her side. All that remained was one of the small red fighters, whose jittery, unsure movements betrayed the gladiator's fear.

"Kill him now! Kill him now! Kill him now!"

Feet stomped in unison, and the stadium rocked. Like thunder, the pounding boomed again and again underneath, the cries for blood.

Kill him now. Kill him now.

The tide had turned.

Both fighters measured one another, keeping their distance as they stalked their opponent. The longer they did this, the softer the chant. The crowd stopped stomping. They stood in near silence. Waiting. Watching.

Two of the downed red fighters were alive but on the ground. The clubbed one was unconscious and unmoving. The other was bleeding out and moaning in pain. The cries were modulating groans and sounded like a wounded animal. They were hard to hear, and Leo winced at the noise.

He motioned to one of the three referees, who walked over to the downed red fighter. A short burst from his Sig

Sauer NGSW stopped the cry. The soldier looked at the unconscious fighter and then at Leo. Leo nodded. The soldier repeated the mercy with the unconscious red gladiator.

The cracks of gunfire startled some in the crowd, but nobody moved from the stadium. This was too good. It was better, even, than the fights before the rain. This was bloodier and more entertaining. The blue gladiator knew how to put on a show.

The soldier returned to his position in the triangular formation. He shouldered his weapon and aimed it at the combatants.

The blue fighter shook her head, and sweat and blood flew in all directions. It reminded Leo of a dog drying itself. He smiled as the fighter stopped moving and held her ground. She dug a toe into the mud and flexed. One arm bled profusely, and she balled her hand into a fist. The other was in front of her, holding up the blade.

The red fighter held the two spiked bats, which dripped blood as he extended them. He was smaller than the blue fighter, though not by much, and he was heavier. He carried more weight in his shoulders and hips. If they grappled, and he managed to gain leverage, he would have the advantage. Yet he did not advance. He moved from side to side, not content to plant himself in the earth as had his opponent. He stalked her, looking for the right opening. The blue fighter did not offer one, but she did growl an inviting taunt.

"Come and get it," she snarled. "Or I'll come and take it."

The red fighter's eyes were wide with fear. The stalking was as much hesitation as it was strategic. It appeared the fighter was looking for an opening. There was none.

The blue warrior shifted her body without moving her feet and showed the red fighter as slim a profile as she could. The woman was simultaneously patient and ready to pounce. She really did remind Leo of a big cat. Her intensity zeroed in on her opponent, and she was unwavering in her expression. Her body tensed. It was a coiled spring ready to explode.

Without warning, as if he grew tired of waiting for the right opportunity, the red warrior bounced on his feet and charged. His heft bounded the short distance to the blue gladiator; his knuckles blanched from his tight hold on the twin spiked clubs. He never got a chance to swing them.

As he reached back to unload a wide swipe at the red fighter, she moved to one side. That was all she did, a side step. That was enough.

The combination of the wide swing, the red warrior's momentum, and the slick, wet ground meant he couldn't shift his angle of attack. When she moved, he twisted his body to adjust, but lost his footing and tumbled to the ground. He lost his hold on one of the clubs and landed on the other.

He cried out in pain, and when he slid to a stop, the club was embedded along one side of his torso. His face contorted in anguish as he tried to free the spikes from his body. He could not. They were too deep.

The hushed crowd began to chant, "Kill him now! Kill him now!"

The blue fighter, who had taken only that one side step, shifted to face the crowd. She watched them with detached interest for a moment before she lifted her free hand and put a finger to her lips. Blood ran down the heel of her hand as she held the pose long enough for the assembled to quiet. When they did, she bowed. Then she took slow, deliberate strides toward the struggling opponent.

He was on his back, flailing against the embedded club, and appeared oblivious to her approach. When she stood over him, he stopped moving and lifted an open hand toward her.

Leo couldn't hear what the man said to her. He tried to read his lips and thought the downed warrior asked for mercy. He said please. Leo could read that.

The blue fighter batted away the red warrior's extended hand and stood over him. She planted her feet outside his hips and studied him for a long moment, prolonging the man's agony and building the anticipation.

She turned her head toward the crowd, and without looking at the red fighter beneath her, she slowly lowered the blade to his chest. The man tried to stop her, but he could not. He wailed as she carefully pushed the blade downward. Inch by inch, she drove it through the man until he stopped crying, stopped moving. Then she lifted a boot, her eyes still searching the silent crowd, and used his body as leverage to pull out the blade.

The blue warrior then stabbed the blade toward the bright hot sun overhead and screamed in victory. Blood drained from the soaked blade and ran down her arm. She was bathed in blood now, some of it her own and much of it from her vanquished enemies.

Leo clapped. Others followed. The audience stood and gave the victorious blue warrior an ovation that lasted more than a minute. It only stopped when Leo signaled the trio of the militia guards to escort the winner from the field. They kept their distance and used the muzzles of their rifles to direct her toward the building at the end of the stadium. She dropped her blade, followed their commands, and disappeared from view.

"If I'd known she would be that good, I might have put her against ten gladiators instead of five," said Leo. "It's almost an unfair fight, am I right?"

He eased back into his seat and turned to his guest. Regina was tense. Every muscle seemed taut with nerves, anger, or something he couldn't read on her face as she turned to him.

Leo smiled at her and crossed one leg over the other, pretending to pick lint from his pants. "Your name," he said. "It's Regina. As in queen."

He punctuated the consonants, letting the sounds hang in the short space between them for emphasis.

"Most nobility, at least the ones of consequence, have a nickname. You know, something to characterize them in the history books."

Regina's gaze met his. Still, she remained silent.

"There was Alexander the Great, Bloody Mary, Olaf the Brash, Louis the Cruel. The list goes on ad infinitum. I wonder what yours will be."

Her brow creased. "My what?" she said through clenched teeth. "My nickname?"

Leo nodded and gestured to the field below them. "Of course. Out there. What will you do that earns you a nickname?"

Her eyes flitted to the field and back to him. Her expression shifted and revealed fear. The defiance was gone.

He smirked and pressed. "Regina the Brave? Regina the Wicked? Regina the Strong? Regina the—"

"I get it," she said and shook her head. "I'm not royalty. I never ascribed to the idea I'm worthy of power over others."

"Your parents must have thought so," Leo said. "Otherwise, why give you a regal name? They had big plans for you, right? First woman president? Astronaut? Brain surgeon? Nobody names their child Regina and thinks she'll be average. They considered you extraordinary or, at the very least, hoped you would become extraordinary."

"My name has nothing to do with who I—"

Leo wagged a finger. "Stop there. It absolutely does matter. I read a study, and this was long before the power went out. It made the rounds on the internet. I'm sure you heard about it. Everybody did. Well, anybody who was anybody did, and with a name like Regina, you had to be somebody."

Her face reddened. So did her neck, which took on a blotchy appearance, which betrayed the nerves she obviously tried to suppress.

"A father in New York named one son Winner. He named the other Loser. He had other children too, but Winner and Loser had the most unique names. What do you think became of the boys?"

Regina didn't bite.

"C'mon," Leo prompted her. "Play along. You've got nothing better to do, am I right? The next fight won't start for a few minutes. What do you think happened?"

Regina shook her head. "No idea."

"Winner went on to become a criminal. Loser became a highly decorated police officer. This was after he went to college and played football. He was a success. Loser was the winner, and Winner was the loser. So, see? Names do matter."

Regina narrowed her gaze. "By that logic, I am anything but regal. I'm the opposite of aristocracy."

"Not necessarily. Do you think Winner and Loser's father expected them to be the opposite of their names? Of course not. Neither did your parents."

"You didn't know my parents."

Leo was about to speak when Regina's eyes glanced over his shoulder. He pivoted and saw his hulk of a soldier standing behind him. Leo clapped his hands together.

"Perfect timing," he said. "It's your turn, Regina."

The red in her cheeks drained. "My turn?"

"The arena. It's your turn to head down to the field and

prepare. Remember to choose your weapon carefully. It could make all the difference."

He sensed the spike in her anxiety and half expected she might run. She did not. Instead, Regina pursed her lips and stood. She crossed in front of Leo and walked from the press box with the hulk.

Leo sucked in a deep breath of the humid air and glanced up at the sun. It was bright and hot and unobstructed. This was a beautiful day and held more promise now than it had when that same sun was low on the horizon.

CHAPTER 23

Millie's eyes burned. She was out of tears, but the lingering effect of crying left her exhausted and barely able to focus. Her body swayed with the movement of the horse that carried her closer to the stadium. She heard the roar of the crowd and understood what that meant. People were fighting and dying for the entertainment of a madman.

Millie swallowed hard against the thick knot in her throat. She blinked against the wetness in her eyes.

She hadn't wanted to cry and did her best to suppress the urge. For more than four years, she'd succeeded in building an almost impenetrable emotional wall. She'd had to do that. A woman leader in an apocalyptic landscape had no choice but to be more hardened and more of a badass than the man next to her. It was the only way to survive.

But that emotional wall had a fissure wide enough for her to fall in love. Keith had found his way through her weakness. He'd courted her in such a way she couldn't help but open herself to him.

Millie had trusted him. She'd sought his guidance. She'd loved him. There was a time not long ago when his touch

250

thrilled her. Goosebumps raced across her skin when he stood close or whispered in her ear. The mere thought of being with him made her heart race and turned her stomach in knots.

Now, with one arm around her waist and the inside of his thighs pressed against the outside of hers, she wanted to vomit. Keith was never the man he'd pretended to be. And while Millie's tears were in part about his betrayal, they were more plentiful and stung more acutely because she hated herself for being so naïve.

The crowd roared again, and Keith nudged her from behind. "They're going to cheer like that for you. Or maybe the person you're fighting. Who's to say?"

Even the sound of his voice made her skin crawl. She glanced at Chris. His march was more of a succession of stumbles. Exhaustion threatened to topple him, and if that happened, the ropes tied to his wrists could kill him.

"Give him some water," Millie said. "You don't want him dying out here. Especially if your boss wants us to fight in the arena."

Keith bristled. "He's not my boss."

"Then what is he? He sent you to spy on me; then he told you to come kidnap me. If he's the one giving the orders and you're following them, he's your boss, Keith."

"You'd better shut your pretty mouth if you know what's good for you," he hissed in her ear, his hot breath rank. "I work for myself. I don't work for Leo. Got it?"

The argument was futile. From the moment Keith had overpowered her in the woods and knocked her unconscious, he was unwilling to negotiate.

Sure, he was more than happy to tell her about how clever he'd been. How he had seduced her and gained her trust, all while reporting back to Leo and the militia. Those trips he took? They were little more than opportunities to report back his findings. He was the one who told Leo about Carl the spy, who told Leo the vaunted Sheriff was actually a woman, and he was the one who uncovered that the woman Sheriff was John Beck's daughter.

With his help, Leo had played them. He'd seized an opportunity to expand his growing empire. While at first Leo might've been satisfied with his hamlet, Keith claimed he was the voice in Leo's ear who pushed him to want more.

Keith told Millie he was Leo's equal and that when they expanded, taking over her territory and shifting the underground railroad from an evacuation route to a black-market path between the US and Canada, Keith would have his own militia.

Keith nudged her when she failed to respond. This time, he put a blade to her neck. It was her blade, the one with the pink handle her father had given her before D-Day.

He pressed the edge of it to her skin. "Did you hear what I said? When I ask you a question, you answer me."

"I heard you."

Millie had never understood the demons that spoke to her father until now. Because now, in the awful wake of Keith's betrayal, Millie heard those demons. Or she heard her own demons telling her over and again how stupid she'd been.

With his other hand, Keith pulled on the reins. The horse slowed and stopped. It shook its head and nickered. Keith pulled a bottle from a saddlebag on his right and shook it at Chris.

"Take a sip, then give it back. We're almost there."

Chris shuffled over to the horse and took the bottle with both hands. He tipped it back and chugged. Half of the water spilled down the sides of his face.

"That's enough," Keith said.

Chris took another swig and handed back the bottle. He glanced at Millie, disappointment as much as fatigue masking his features. The demons hissed as he turned his back and shuffled away from the horse.

You're no better than your father. An arrogant know-it-all who allowed emotion to cloud your judgment. You deserve what you get.

Millie shook the thoughts from her mind and tried ignoring the masochistic taunts. She wondered if, like intelligence or alcoholism, self-loathing was an inherited trait. Her father was like this. No matter the good he did, it was the bad that resonated. The drop of red wine on the white tablecloth scenario. Millie envisioned her father looking for her, blaming himself for losing her a second time. This gave her hope. His own demons might push him toward a successful rescue. His self-doubt might propel him into overcoming the odds that were clearly stacked in Leo's favor. She forced a smile.

"You know my father's coming for me," she said. "And when he does, he's going to kill you."

Keith snorted. "Really? I doubt it. The legend of John Beck is overplayed. He's an over-the-hill gunslinger with a misguided code of justice. The more I think about it, the more you resemble him. At least the misguided part."

"I'm all that matters to him. That should matter to *you*. If you let us go, he might let you live. If you don't, you'll wish you had."

Keith laughed. His trim belly shook against her back. "You're ridiculous and naïve. There's no going back, Millie. You're done, your people are done, and soon enough John Beck will be done. This is a banner day. That's why the sun is shining so bright."

The sun *was* bright. Too bright. Against the cloudless blue sky, the almost white-hot appearance smudged at the edges and gave the star an amorphous shape where its curves were almost unseeable.

Millie sucked in the humid air and wondered if it really felt like a sauna. That was what old people would say when the heat and moisture combined to make the day miserable. She had never been in a sauna, though. There was a lot she had never had the chance to do before the power went out. While most of it was something she would never experience, and as a result never really know what she was missing, there was one thing she wished she'd never experienced.

Love.

It was soul crushing. *He* was soul crushing. Having his hand around her waist as they loped toward the arena made it all the worse. Rather than challenge Keith or goad him, she decided a question was the best course of action, even if she was unsure whether she truly wanted him to answer. The answer wouldn't make things better. It would probably make them worse. It would make the demons chatter.

"Why did you do it?" she asked.

"Do what? Kidnap you?"

"No. Yes. Why did you do any of it? Why did you make me fall in love with you?"

Keith chuckled. "That was never the plan. We didn't know the Sheriff was a girl. Everyone, everywhere, who thought they knew anything about the Sheriff believed you were a dude. It just made sense. When I figured out you were the Sheriff, it made the job easier."

She tried to turn, but with her hands bound to the saddle horn, it made it almost impossible to do any more than twist. The line that affixed her wrists to the leather rubbed against her skin, adding a stinging pain to the bruises already there.

Millie winced and clenched her jaw.

"What?" Keith asked. "What's got you so hot and

bothered? Well, in a different way than when I got you hot and bothered."

Millie squeezed her eyes closed. She had never wanted to kill anyone so much in her life. Not even the man nicknamed Goose, the one who took her from her home and killed her mother, had made her blood boil in the way Keith now did. Then again, she hadn't given herself to Goose.

Even now, he seemed to read her mind.

"Never mind," he said, "I get it. You wonder why it was easier. Yeah, well, I wouldn't be able to use my good looks and charms on a man. Well, I guess I could, but like I said, it was easier with you."

He moved his hand from her waist and slid it up toward her chest. She squeezed her arm against her side to stop him. He chuckled and moved his hand back down.

"Can't blame me for wanting to go somewhere I've already been," he said.

They were close to the arena now. The cheering was so loud she could almost make out the undercurrent of a chant. The rumble of the stadium bleachers rolled like thunder.

Keith persisted, echoing the voices of the demons who whispered to her. "You wanted to be in love so bad, I hardly had to try. The moment I figured out you were the one in charge, I put all my effort into bagging you. When I got word to Leo that you were the Sheriff, I thought he might give me my own army. I mean, I guess he *is* giving me my own army. So there's that."

While Millie thought he was only vaguely coherent, Chris had apparently paid close attention to their conversation.

"I thought he wasn't your boss," said Chris.

Keith's body tensed behind hers. He sat up a little straighter and tightened his one-handed grip on the reins. The leather squeaked in his hand. "He's not."

Chris pulled back his shoulders and lifted his chin. Maybe the water had given him some energy. He blinked past the sweat that rolled into his eyes. "If he's not your boss, then why would he need to give you anything? If you're equals, why wouldn't you take what's yours?"

"I don't have to explain myself to you," Keith growled. "Shut your trap, or I'll put this horse into a gallop and leave parts of you all over the road."

Chris started to speak, but Millie shook her head. He faced forward, focused again on the path ahead.

None of them spoke until they reached the exterior wall of the stadium. It was a large structure for such a small town, and its size surprised Millie. She studied the architecture, looking for exits should she find a way to escape.

A pair of uniformed militia approached them, and Keith motioned for one of them to handle Chris. He told the other to watch Millie while he dismounted. Watching her meant aiming a high-powered rifle at her face.

When Keith hit the ground, he put his hands on the rope that tied Millie to the saddle. He winked at her. "You gonna be a good girl?"

She didn't respond. The demons cackled.

"You know, I usually like it a little rough," Keith said, "but today's different. Take it slow and easy, and nobody gets hurt. You gonna take it slow and easy?"

She remained silent, and he put a hand on her wrist. He squeezed. "I wanna hear you say it."

Millie swallowed. "I'll be good."

Keith grinned. The same grin that had melted her heart days earlier now burned like acid in her gut.

He loosened the binds and put a hand on her elbow to help her from the horse. Millie started to acquiesce, but as she pivoted, she kicked up her leg and drove the toe of her boot into Keith's jaw. She heard the crunch of bone as his head snapped back. His eyes fluttered, rolled, and Keith dropped to the ground like a sack of wet cement.

She hopped down and straddled him. Planted her hands on the ground beside him before pulling them to her side. She spat on his face and pushed herself to her feet.

Chris used the distraction to plow his elbows into the chest of the guard beside him. The guard doubled over and dropped his weapon. Chris raised his hands above his head and hammered them into the guard's back. The guard landed hard on his chest, the air audibly forced from his lungs.

For a split second, it seemed they might escape. But before Millie could attack the second soldier, he had the barrel of his weapon at her chest. She froze and raised her hands above her head.

"If you weren't set for the arena," the soldier growled, "I'd plug you right now."

Chris started to move for the rifle on the ground, but the standing soldier took two steps back and covered both of them.

"You too," he said. "Stay where you are. Both of you."

A moment later, three soldiers appeared from nowhere. They surrounded Millie and Chris.

"Get on your knees," the first one said. "Now. Hands behind your heads."

Chris immediately complied. The downed guard next to him gasped for air. He clawed at the ground and roiled in pain.

Millie hesitated. She eyed Keith unconscious on the ground. Blood drained from his mouth and nose and pooled around his head. His jaw was askew, and her spit bubbled on his cheek. Was he breathing? Did she care?

Another pair of militia soldiers marched toward them.

One of them carried a backpack slung over one shoulder. He crouched beside Keith, then looked up at the others.

"Get them inside," he said in a deep, resonant voice. The man was older than she'd first thought. "They're ready for them. I'll take care of Keith."

As two soldiers took her by her arms and yanked her toward the stadium entrance closest to them, she glanced back at the soldier with the backpack. Keith was important enough that the man knew him by name. He wasn't some nameless, faceless cog in Leo's machine. Maybe he *was* an equal.

The soldier dropped the pack to the ground and unzipped it. Before she could see what was inside the pack, her guards turned a corner, and she lost sight of him.

Chris's boot steps crunched behind her. He was breathing hard. She tried twisting to get another look at him, but the men escorting her gripped tight under her arms and kept pressing forward.

They dipped inside an opening, and the roar of the crowd enveloped her. It bounced off the concrete walls that served as a ground-level concourse that wrapped the stadium.

"Where are we going?" she demanded.

Neither guard spoke. They only tightened their hold and accelerated their pace. Another crescendo from the crowd washed a deafening roar through the concourse. Her pulse accelerated as her mind imagined the horrors unfolding on the field beyond the concrete walls.

Another trio of soldiers marched past them in the opposite direction. They slowed, all of them following Millie with the slightest turns of their heads. Quizzical expressions squeezed their faces. It was obvious she was someone important, someone who required an armed escort.

She asked again, "Where are we going?"

No response. The guards gave her an answer when they reached a large door flanked by another pair of militia soldiers.

The one holding her right arm motioned to the sentries, and they swung open the door. A dank odor, a mix of sweat, urine, and mold, hit her nostrils, and she flinched. The guards let go of her and shoved her forward into the dark.

Millie stumbled but caught herself. Chris was right behind her and tripped into her. They held each other for a moment to regain their balance. When their eyes adjusted, dark forms appeared around them, materializing like apparitions at the edges of the dim shaft of light that speared its way through the narrow space between the door and its frame. A dozen or more people shared the space, whatever the space was. All of them appeared worn and weary. None spoke. What was this? A holding tank? A cell?

She blinked and tried to better adjust her vision. Millie shuffled her feet on the hard floor and pivoted to better gauge the size of the room. When she faced the door, a guard snarled.

"This is where you're going."

The door slammed shut, and they were plunged into darkness.

CHAPTER 24

D-DAY + 4 YEARS, 6 MONTHS, 21 DAYS
HOPKINSVILLE, KENTUCKY

Beck crouched beside the soldier with the dying man's collar gripped in his fist. "Where did they go?" he growled. "I know you saw them."

The soldier coughed. His eyes fluttered. Beck jerked him closer until their noses almost touched. "Tell me where they went, and I'll take away the pain. Keep quiet, and I'll make it worse."

Although Beck was not a sadist, he loved his daughter more than his own soul. And while he cursed himself for having gotten into this untenable situation, he reminded himself of who he was and of what he was capable.

His flexible, selfish morality served him well in circumstances like this. The young soldier in his grasp was no more than twenty, perhaps as young as fifteen. The kid was only doing his job, standing watch at the edge of town.

Beck had snuck up on him and drove a blade into his side. He'd jabbed it into the upper part of the soldier's abdomen and aimed for either his liver or spleen. Both large organs could produce heavy internal bleeding. Perhaps he'd done too good a job. The kid was reluctant to talk, or unable to from the pain that squeezed his sallow expression.

"Where did they go?"

This time, the soldier blinked but managed to focus on Beck. His mouth parted, and he whispered in a raspy voice that sounded more like a series of weak grunts than enunciated words. "The arena. They took them to the arena."

Beck should've known. Where else would Leo want them? Where else would Chris, that conniving piece of crap, take his daughter? Of course it would be the arena. That way, Leo and Chris could put her in her place in front of a large audience. Payback for what Millie herself had planned for Leo.

"Can I have water?"

The question surprised Beck. If he were dying from a stab wound, water wouldn't be what he wanted. Something stronger. Moonshine perhaps.

Beck was low on water. His bottle was almost empty, and he was on the verge of dehydration. Having lived much of the past four and a half years on the edge of virtual desiccation, he recognized the symptoms: the headache, the dry mouth, the lack of sweat. He suffered all of them in that moment. No need to waste a drop of water on a dead man. Still, he wasn't cruel.

"Sure," he said. He let go of the soldier's shirt and scooted back to his pack. He pulled out his bottle and shook it. Remnants sloshed in the bottom of the container. He uncapped it and offered it to the soldier.

The kid lifted his trembling hand and took the bottle. Beck eased closer to him. As the kid raised the bottle to his lips and tipped back his head, Beck drew the blade across his exposed neck.

It was a lightning-quick move the kid never saw coming. His eyes went wide with shock, and before he dropped the bottle, Beck caught it.

In less than five seconds, the kid was gone. His head slumped; his body exsanguinated.

It was as painless a death as Beck could offer. A pang of guilt poked at his gut, but he suppressed it.

"I'm sorry, kid," Beck said. "You got in the way."

He closed the soldier's eyes with his fingertips and stood. This was an unforgiving world, and had Beck not gotten the drop on the soldier, the young guard would've just as soon killed him. That was what Beck told himself as he marched toward the roar of the crowd. It was distant, but he could peg the general vicinity, and the closer he got, the easier it would be to pinpoint the arena's location.

He was on the northern edge of town, where the density of buildings began to increase. Beck walked a half block before he heard a voice behind him. He swung around and leveled the Sig Sauer NGSW he'd taken from the kid.

When he turned, there was nobody there, only the soldier's slumped body leaning against an electrical pole. Beck swept the street twice. He spun back and took another few steps before he heard the voice again. It called his name.

This time when he pivoted, he immediately squeezed off a trio of shots. They cracked in quick succession and echoed in the heavy air.

Nobody was there but the dead man. The man Beck had killed.

"You didn't have to be a killer," the voice said. "You could've learned what you wanted to know without violence."

It was then Beck realized the voice was in his head. A demon.

Beck cursed the demon and then himself. He shook his head, tried to clear his mind, and started his march again toward the arena.

The voice was not silent. Beck tried to ignore it and did

not turn around, though he kept his finger on the Sig Sauer's trigger. For what reason, he couldn't say, but it felt like the right thing to do.

"You've always justified your killing," the demon said, "by telling yourself you were doing it for the right reasons."

Beck clung to the buildings that lined the streets, keeping a low profile and providing himself cover from more militia sentries. He spotted a pair a block ahead and ducked into a narrow alley to avoid them.

"The right reasons were always selfish," the demon persisted. "They suited your agenda. Think of how many people whose lives you ended but could have saved. Dozens? Hundreds? All under the guise of some misguided purpose. Nobody appointed you judge, jury, and executioner. You did that yourself, and it makes you no better than Leo. It makes you no better than the squatters who killed me in Memphis."

Beck stopped in his tracks and pressed himself flat against the brick façade of an aged building. His breath caught, and he closed his eyes.

The demon voice was not the kid he'd just killed. The demon was Lucas. Poor Lucas, who always asked too many questions, who treated Beck like a father, and whom Beck considered a son. Lucas, who warned Beck about shooting first and always taking the offensive. A Quaker by upbringing, the kid wanted to think the best of people no matter how dark it got. And despite his brutally unleashed skill in the midst of a gunfight, Lucas was as kind a person as Beck had ever met.

The realization struck him like a punch to the gut. More than anyone else since his ex-wife, Debbie, Lucas's death clung to Beck's psyche. The guilt he carried was heavy and sometimes threatened to paralyze him. As if he needed more guilt to carry.

Beck steadied himself and tried to clear his mind, tried to silence the voice.

"I'll deal with you later," he said under his breath. He cursed the demon and prayed for strength. More than ever, he needed to focus. He adjusted his grip on the rifle.

"You're as evil as Leo," the demon told him. "Two sides of the same coin."

Beck decided to stop trying to quiet the demon. As he peered around the alley's corner, he spied the two militia sentries. They appeared to have heard the shots but seemed confused by echoes. Both had their Back's turned to Beck.

He listened to the stinging words meant to hurt him. They were true, and they did hurt. He funneled that pain into anger-fueled adrenaline. His muscles tensed, and he flexed his forearms.

Beck stepped from the alley and shouldered the rifle. Before the sentries could react, he aimed and fired two quick bursts into the twin sentries. Both men dropped like sacks. Beck hurried over to them. As they bled, he pocketed their extra magazines. One of the men was bigger than the other. He was roughly Beck's size, even a little bigger. An idea popped into his head.

He dragged the larger man back to the alley and quickly undressed him. Beck traded his clothing for the dead soldier's. The pants were a little big at the waist, but he cinched the tactical belt tighter, and the bunched pants held above his hips. The shirt was a little short in the arms. The blood at the collar glistened. It would have to do.

Beck kept his own boots. They were not exact matches to the militia's, but they were close enough. If someone had enough time to ask about his footwear, Beck figured he was already a dead man.

He shouldered the rifle and emerged from the alley. This

time, he strode along the middle of the streets, moving with purpose and following the roar of the crowd. He was getting closer.

The voice in his head persisted. "You're just dumb enough to get caught, old man. You'll be the death of everyone you ever loved."

This powered him forward, and he picked up his pace, jogging toward his destination. He passed four militiamen marching up a cross street perpendicular to him. They eyed him with suspicion, but sensing it, Beck played to them. He eased to a walk, stopped several feet from them at a wide intersection, and nodded his head toward the direction of the crowd noise.

"Are the fights still going on? I don't want to miss it."

One of the soldiers' tight expression eased. "We wondered why you were in such a hurry."

A second one added, "I think they'll be going on a while. We heard a rumor they got some big fights coming up."

Beck smiled. "Good. I live for these things. They had me posted on the outskirts. My relief was late. You think this is the fastest way there?"

The first soldier nodded. "Yeah, you're going the fastest way. Straight up here and then a left. It'll take you to the closest entrance."

"Thanks." Beck turned, leaned into his first step, and was about to accelerate when the soldier called out. He stopped and lowered his finger to the Sig Sauer's trigger.

"Hey," the soldier said. "Is that blood on your shirt? My partner here says he—"

Beck sighed. He faced the quartet but kept the muzzle aimed toward the ground. "Yeah, it's blood."

The soldier took a step forward, and the others tensed and adjusted their rifles. None shouldered their weapons though, and none took aim.

"I got into a fight," Beck said. "No big deal. You know how the people here don't like taking orders. Sometimes they get a little too much moonshine in them, and stuff happens."

The lead soldier held his ground. His eyes flitted between Beck's collar and his face. Beck sensed doubt when the soldier narrowed his eyes and took another slow, deliberate step toward him. He glanced at Beck's collar.

"Is that a bullet hole in your—"

Beck didn't let him finish the sentence. He took a giant step toward the soldier and fired a single shot into the man's face. The soldier stood motionless, mouth agape, long enough for Beck to use his body as a shield while he moved to the side and unloaded on the other three soldiers. Only one returned fire, but his errant volley missed Beck completely. Within two seconds, all four were down, and Beck tallied another foursome to his gruesome collection of killings.

Without taking the time to pilfer from the dead men, Beck raced toward the arena. He was running out of time. Any minute, he imagined his daughter could be in the arena or on a firing line.

Beck ignored the hitch in his side as the stadium came into view. He ran past other soldiers, who ignored him, and reached the venue's expansive parking lot without any other confrontations.

He slowed when he hit the cracked and weed-infested asphalt lot. Catching his breath and keeping a steady pace, Beck released the partially used magazine from the Sig Sauer rifle and replaced it with one fully loaded.

He pocketed the used mag and scanned the surroundings. The structure was surprisingly large. The roar and chants coming from inside its walls were remarkably loud. He imagined nearly everyone in the region was inside watching the show and expected it was why he'd encountered so little resistance on his way through the town.

Beck reached a wide, gated opening and started to enter the stadium proper when two armed guards stepped in front of him. Both wore frowns and dubious expressions. Beck tried to step around them, but they blocked his progress. The bulkier of the two, who looked barely old enough to piss standing up, put a hand on Beck's chest.

"Hold up there, boss," he said with a thick Kentucky twang that elongated the vowels. "Where do you think you're going?"

Beck nodded toward the underside of the bleachers. "I'm here to watch the fights in the arena."

"Aren't you a little old to be militia? I mean, you must be—"

"I'm not too old."

"Then where's your pass?"

Beck studied the soldier's expression. He was serious. "My pass?"

"If you don't have a pass, you're not getting through. That's how it works. Everyone needs a pass to get into the fights. You should know that."

The guard lowered his hand, then looked at his fingers and rubbed them together. They were red and slick.

The soldier raised his rifle. It was six inches from Beck's chest. The second guard did the same.

"What's with the blood, soldier?"

The second guard jabbed his weapon at Beck. "And what's with the boots? Those aren't regulation boots."

"Put down your weapon," said the first.

Beck considered his options and concluded he had none. Two more soldiers approached. They lifted their weapons and aimed them at Beck. He'd taken down four of them at once minutes earlier. That was luck. Doing it again would be a miracle. Beck figured he needed to save his miracles. Better to go along for the moment.

The first soldier scowled. "Do it, or I'll drill a hole right through you."

Silently cursing himself, Beck crouched and set his rifle on the ground in front of him.

Chapter 25

The sun was somehow brighter on the arena floor. The heat rose from the muddy earth beneath Rebecca's boots and threatened to suffocate her.

She sucked in deep breaths of the damp air, inhaling the aroma of death that surrounded her as she tried to calm herself. Maybe it wasn't the heat that suffocated. It was the idea of fighting Lucy, who stood facing her twenty yards away.

Rebecca looked to her left at the bloodthirsty crowd. They'd already witnessed a dozen or more killings, and the sun had barely begun its descent, as it hung almost directly overhead.

She could see their mouths moving, their fists pumping, their fingers pointing. They couldn't get enough. She shifted her weight from her bad leg to her good one. It did little to dampen the pain that pulsed with each accelerated beat of her heart.

Rebecca wondered if the crowd's desire stemmed from its need to see others suffer so it lessened their own anxiety. This was the modern-day version of reality television, a voyeuristic window into the dysfunction of others. It was an opportunity to see how low others had sunk and, in the process, make one's predicament somewhat more tenable. She had never watched any of those reality shows, but she remembered her mother calling them her guilty pleasures.

Guilty pleasure or not, none of it mattered. The reason was irrelevant to what she had to do. Reason itself, she thought, was irrelevant to the way of life in places like Hopkinsville. It was not the first dystopian hamlet in which she'd found herself since D-Day, but she imagined it might be her last.

She would die at Lucy's vicious hand. On her back, staring up at the sun, hearing the applause and stomps beat faster than her own heart as the life seeped from her tired body. Then she could join Lucas. They could be together forever. But did she want that just yet? Forever could wait, couldn't it?

Rebecca shook the thought from her head and urged herself to concentrate on the here and now. She had to formulate a plan, stay alive as long as possible. With every passing second she survived on the arena floor, there was a chance, however slim, she might survive.

She looked down at the weapon in her hand. It was a flail. A medieval-looking torture instrument with a long wooden handle at one end and a spiked metal ball at the other. Connecting the two was an iron chain. The weapon was heavy in her grip, but it was either that or a spear, and Lucy had taken the spear. Rebecca had let her choose first.

The guards moved into position around them. Three soldiers stood in a triangular formation with their rifles shouldered. All of them looked away when she tried to make eye contact.

Everything appeared different on the field. From the stands, she had a sweeping view of the arena. It was a sterilized vantage point. With the mud sucking at her boots, and the odors of filth, blood, and spilled guts, her position now stripped the glamour from being a gladiator.

A soldier stepped from the running track and onto the field. He was a hulk of a man, and he strode with swaying confidence to what would have been the fifty-yard line had this still been an amateur gridiron. He glanced at Rebecca. The scar that stretched the length of his face twitched like he was trying to suppress a smile. The hulk looked at Lucy for a moment and then turned his back to both of them and faced the crowd. He raised his arms, and the audience fell silent. From atop the stadium, standing in the press box, Leo opened his arms wide with welcome.

His voice boomed. "Ladies and gentlemen, I give to you what was to be the grand finale today. I am an impatient man, and I know, like me, you also cannot wait to see two friends fight to the death as honorable gladiators."

The crowd erupted. They cheered, chanting Leo's name. He calmed them with a shushing motion and cleared his throat. They fell silent, hanging on his words.

"Believe me when I tell you, this is not the biggest surprise today. I have another that might trump this one. Also, my good friends, this battle is delicious."

The crowd cheered, though the applause was more subdued. They seemed restless and anxious. Leo was delaying the start of their match, and the audience was impatient.

"Suffice it to say, these are two women who have tried to kill each other before," said Leo. "Then they became friends, or at least allies. No longer. Now they fight one another to the death. Let the match begin!"

Leo extended his arms and stretched his fingers. Then he balled his hands into fists and pumped them in the air above his head as the crowd erupted again. Their feet stomped in rhythm against the metal bleachers, and Rebecca felt it in her chest.

She looked away from the crowd and faced Lucy. Her ally was stone-faced. She held the spear in one hand like a staff, the butt of its shaft resting in the viscous mud.

Rebecca adjusted her grip on the flail. She closed her eyes for a split second and saw Lucas. He smiled at her. His cheeks flushed, and his pupils widened. Her heart fluttered when he told her she could do this. She could succeed and survive. He would wait for her no matter how long it took, and he wanted her to have a long, fruitful life.

All of this he told her in that single blink. It gave her strength, and she pulled back her shoulders. Rebecca dug a toe into the muck and leaned forward, bracing herself for Lucy's approach.

Lucy did not move. She stood still with the spear vertical, its point aimed toward the cloudless sky.

The crowd chanted, "Fight. Fight. Fight."

Rebecca twisted and faced the crowd. They were red-faced either from the heat, their bloodlust, or both. Atop the stadium and standing with his arms folded over his chest, Leo stared down at her. His face was expressionless.

"We don't have to fight," Lucy called out to her above the din. "What are they going to do?"

Rebecca considered this. There were a thousand things they could do if both of them refused to engage. Each possibility was likely worse than the one before it. Death was likely the most desirable.

Yet, perhaps Lucy was onto something. They could fight but not kill each other. How long could they go, how much time could they buy themselves, if they playacted?

Rebecca rotated the flail's grip in her hand. The chain swung slowly, but as its momentum increased, the spiked ball at the other end of the weapon spun faster and faster. It cut through the air beside her with a whooshing sound.

She took two steps forward, and the crowd responded with a roar. Another step and they pounded the bleachers in a sick drumbeat.

Lucy's expression tightened, and she lifted the staff from the mud. She spun the spear in her hand, twirling it end over end, and then caught it with her other hand so that she held it out in front of her body.

Rebecca advanced another cautious step. She swung the flail in front of her, and the shift made the weapon heavy in her hand. Her forearm felt the weight of the effort as she kept the flail moving.

Lucy swung the spear's tip forward and set her feet. She bent her knees and leaned forward to balance her weapon.

The crowd, perhaps sensing violence, was on its feet. The rhythmic chanting and pounding against the metal bleachers was almost deafening. It surprised her how loud it was in the open-air stadium, but it provided cover, too.

"We can pretend," she called out as she took an exaggerated swipe from feet away.

Lucy either didn't hear, or she didn't understand. Her features twisted with confusion, and she took two quick steps forward and jabbed the spear at Rebecca. It didn't come close.

Rebecca feinted to one side, as if stalking her prey, and swung the flail in a wide arc in front of her body. The movement was a pantomime of a lemniscate, the lazy eight curve that represented infinity. Lucy moved in the opposite direction as they circled one another.

"Did you hear me?" Rebecca asked. "Did you hear what I said?"

Lucy took a big step toward Rebecca, shifting her

movement and catching Rebecca off guard. Lucy swung the spear backhanded, like a racquet, and the staff caught Rebecca on the leg. It stung and knocked her off balance, but she recovered as the crowd erupted.

Clearly, Lucy hadn't heard her suggestion. She was the one who'd proposed not fighting at all.

Rebecca glanced at the nearest soldier. He stood a good fifteen yards or more behind Lucy. Rebecca doubted he could hear either of them, so she took a chance.

Swinging the flail wide, her arm extended almost straight, she charged Lucy. Rebecca ran straight at her as best she could on her injured leg. Adrenaline fueled, it almost didn't hurt as she accelerated. Lucy's eyes widened. She pulled back her spear to use it defensively. As she brought it up, holding it horizontal to the ground, Rebecca used the maneuver as an excuse to plant her boot and cut to the right. This brought her close to Lucy but just out of the reach of the spear. As she passed it, she wrapped the flail's chain around the pole and yanked hard.

Lucy tried to hold onto the weapon, and in the effort, she fell to one side and lost her grip. When the spear flew from her hand, it also took with it Rebecca's flail. Rebecca stumbled forward and landed beside Lucy. The crowd cheered.

Rebecca scrambled to her knees and pressed the struggling Lucy to the ground with her weight. Her ankle and foot throbbing with pain, Rebecca gritted her teeth.

"Let's not fight," she said between sucks of air. "Let's pretend."

Lucy glared at her. Then she twisted her legs, angled her hips, and flipped on top of Rebecca. The lightning-fast move pushed the air from Rebecca's lungs, and she gasped when she hit the ground hard with Lucy on top of her. Hands gripped her throat, and her frenemy leaned close. Her hot breath puffed with each enunciated word.

"This *is* pretending," she said. "If I weren't pretending, you'd be dead."

Rebecca wanted to respond, but she couldn't speak. She felt like she might suffocate, and the sensation flooded her with panic.

Lying there, watching Lucy's face contort with rage, she realized the grip around her throat was loose. Lucy was acting. This was for show.

Lucy threw back her head and cried out. She shook her hands at Rebecca's throat. The bright sun above them cast a dark shadow over Lucy's face.

Then, as quickly as she'd lost her breath, she gained it back. A deep gasp returned the air to her lungs, and Rebecca lifted her arms, shoving Lucy in the chest and knocking her grip from her throat.

Rebecca was vaguely aware of the crowd, but now, the sounds of their chants and jeers was muted. She was so focused on the task in front of her, of making Leo believe they were actually trying to kill one another, she could not truly hear the audience and their calls for death.

Lucy punched a fist into the earth next to Rebecca's head, and Rebecca rolled away, able to free herself from Lucy's pin. She scrambled to her feet and scoured the ground for her weapon. Through blurred vision from beads of sweat that fell into her eyes, she spotted the flail and dove for it.

Lucy reached the weapons at the same time, and they struggled for control. Neither could retrieve their weapon. As one would almost have it in her grasp, the other would knock it free. It amazed Rebecca the two could move with such coordination despite a lack of planning. How long could they keep it up before Leo spotted the ruse?

The answer came less than a minute later. Lucy finally secured her spear and spun away from Rebecca's hold. That left Rebecca to regain her weapon without any fight from Lucy.

Before she knew what had happened, the triangle of guards closed in around them and raised their weapons.

"Hands up!" one of them shouted above the crowd. "Drop your weapons and return to your starting positions."

Rebecca didn't obey at first. She began swinging the flail more forcefully, and the whoosh it made became a low hum.

Lucy also ignored the order and held the spear with both hands. She stood in an aggressive position, her shoulders forward over her feet and her head up.

The guard came closer. "Hands up. Drop your weapons. Return to your starting positions."

The crowd's cheers devolved into a chorus of boos. Some hissed their disapproval.

Rebecca and Lucy locked eyes. An unspoken, almost telekinetic language connected them, and at the same time they acted.

Both dropped their weapons and raised their hands. Neither moved, however. They stood their respective ground. The crowd grew silent.

Lucy took the opportunity to call out to Leo, "What is this?" She pointed at him and spat. "You bring us here to fight, to kill one another, and then you stop us and take our weapons?"

The crowd reacted with a low rumble, a combination of agreement, dissent, and disbelief that a gladiator would speak to their leader in such a way. Lucy pulled her shoulders back in defiance.

Rebecca took the cue. "Are you afraid, Leo? Are you frightened that one of us will so impress the audience, they will like us more than you?"

It was a stretch, but it was the only thing she could think of to say. If her hope was to buy more time, this worked. Or perhaps it did not. At any second, Leo could order the guards to gun them down, and it would be over.

Leo grinned. Even from this distance, his toothy white smile was visible.

The crowd craned their necks to get a glimpse of their malevolent dictator. He, possibly sensing their interest, exaggerated his movements. He spread his arms wide, as if offering an embrace of a long-lost loved one. But he had no love for anything but power and control.

"Bring out the others," he said. "That will force these two actresses to fight for real."

The others? What did that mean?

Rebecca scanned her surroundings. The three guards widened their triangular formation as a group of men and women marched into the arena from the end closest to the fieldhouse.

They carried various weapons and appeared as disinterested in being here as Rebecca was in having them. Her gaze swept across the entrants and counted six people. She pivoted back to face the crowd and lifted her head to look at Leo.

His grin was wider, if that was possible. He rubbed his hands together in front of him. It was a cleansing motion that made Rebecca think of all the blood about to spill on the field and drain into the mud and weeds.

She had killed plenty since leaving her home in New Mexico. Traveling with John Beck came with its challenges. But she was always of the impression that the people whose lives she took deserved it. Or at the very least, would have killed her had she not acted first. While she lacked Lucas's pure skill in battle, she was capable when not hobbled. Right now she was hurt, and despite the adrenaline, the injury was painful. She shifted her weight and tried to relieve the pressure on her ankle and foot. Rebecca would have to ignore the pain if she was to survive this.

A wave of noise rolled across the crowd. They mumbled and muttered, perhaps trying to make sense of the game change. Leo's voice boomed above the low buzz from the stands.

"Since our two gladiators are not willing to fight themselves, these new warriors will take them on," he clarified. "Whoever among them kills our hesitant fighters gains freedom."

The murmurs grew louder. Leo gestured to Rebecca and to Lucy.

"If our two gentle souls should decide to play by the rules, whoever among them survives shall also gain her freedom. But if they are the last two standing and refuse to fight again, I will kill both myself."

He shifted his hands, and with them he replicated handguns, pointing twin index fingers at Rebecca and Lucy. He moved his thumbs as if they were the hammers. "Bang, bang."

The crowd understood before Rebecca did. They cheered and chanted. Rebecca was in her own head and didn't process what the crowd shouted in unison. Her mind reeled as she worked to process the new rules. Leo was empowering all six of the new fighters to kill Lucy and herself. If they should survive their attackers, then either one of them killed the other or they both died. This was not good. She shook herself from her daze in the instant before a large man charged at her with a long curved blade. Screaming, he ran at her, strings of spit stretching across his open mouth, leading the pack of would-be killers. Mud splashed and spattered across his body, but he ignored it. His focus was on one thing and one thing alone. Killing her and winning his freedom.

Rebecca sucked in a breath, tightened her grip on the flail, and began swinging it to gain momentum. This was do or die. There was no choice. Yet as he grew closer, when she heard his battle cry crescendo into an earsplitting whoop, Rebecca slowed the spin.

Dying now at the end of a blade might be better than the alternative. Lucas was waiting. She was ready to join him.

CHAPTER 26

D-DAY + 4 YEARS, 6 MONTHS, 21 DAYS
HOPKINSVILLE, KENTUCKY

"We're not dying today," said Millie.

The others in the holding cell gathered close. Only seven others remained, not including Chris. Moments earlier, the guards had taken six of their cellmates and forced them into the daylight.

Millie tried to ask questions. The guards ignored her and slammed shut the door.

Her eyes adjusted to the darkness, and she made out the figures who stood near her. Though she couldn't see the expressions on their faces, she heard the worry in their weak voices and the chatter of their teeth.

These people were not warriors. They were victims. Slaves. One of them, a young woman by the sound of her voice, challenged Millie's assertion.

"How can you say that?" she asked. "We're all prisoners. We're all going to be forced to fight to the death. That's what happens here."

"We're not fighting in the arena," she said. "Not if I can help it. We're going to kill the next guard who steps in here."

Another voice, carried on hot breath, questioned her. This

one was deeper. An older woman, a young man? Millie couldn't be sure.

"They don't give us the weapons until we're at the field," the voice said. "They're armed with rifles. How are we supposed to kill them without getting killed ourselves?"

A chorus of voices joined in the skepticism. They talked over one another, the volume of their discussion getting louder.

Chris stood next to Millie, his shoulder brushing hers. "Be quiet," he said. "We can't let them hear us out there. I'm telling you, if the Sheriff says we can get out of this, we can get out of this. She's never let me down."

Millie bumped her hip against his. "Thanks, Chris. Though getting us caught outside town wasn't my finest moment."

"Wait," said the first voice, the young woman, "the Sheriff? What Sheriff? Not the one who runs the migration? That can't be."

"Why not?" asked Chris.

"Because the Sheriff is a man," she said.

Outside the room, the crowd roared. The muffled chants were indecipherable, but it was clear the action in the arena was entertaining.

"Who says the Sheriff is a man?" Millie asked.

The others said nothing.

"Millie Beck is the Sheriff," Chris said, breaking the silence. "She's the one who runs the migration. I owe my life to her many times over."

The ambiguous voice asked, "You're Millie Beck?"

"That would be me. Now, are you up for getting out of here? Or would you rather wallow in self-pity and go along with Leo's plans for us?"

They all agreed to follow her lead. She stepped into the center of the small group.

"Leave it to me," Millie said. "When they open the door, one guard always steps into the room. The others wait outside. Right?"

"Yes," said the young woman. "I don't think I've ever seen more than one guard come into the room."

"Right," Millie said. "That's what I thought. So I want everybody against the wall, behind the door."

Millie then explained her plan. She gave everyone a job, a role to play in what would determine whether or not they lived or died. If her idea failed, there was a good chance the guards would gun them down in the room, and they would never even see the arena. If they succeeded, however, they might get out of Hopkinsville alive, and she could lead them to salvation north of the border.

When Millie finished her explanation, the half-dozen cellmates did as she instructed. They worked their way along the cell walls to the door and huddled against it. While they readied themselves, Chris pulled her aside and whispered so the others wouldn't hear.

"This is great and all," he said, "but what about your father? What about his friends? Are we going to leave without any of them? With all due respect, we're here so we can save his friends. That's the whole reason we're in this mess."

"My father can take care of himself. I don't have any doubt about that. In fact, he's probably figuring out a way to rescue us. And those friends are *his* friends, they're not ours. We bear no responsibility for them."

Chris was silent for a long second. Then he exhaled. "That's harsh. But okay. I'm with you, whatever you choose to do."

Millie considered his response. It carried an unspoken judgment. She bit the inside of her cheek. "Look," she whispered, "if we run across his friends, if we can figure out who in the hell they are among all of these other people, we'll help them. But we don't even know what they look like. I can't remember their names. How are we supposed to rescue them without my dad?"

"Regina, Rebecca, and Lucy," Chris whispered.

Millie nodded, although she doubted he could see her face in the dark. Maybe her head movement was enough to convey her understanding of his concern.

If they could find the women on their way out of Hopkinsville, she would help them. But damned if she was going to start asking the name of every woman she saw.

"C'mon," she said to Chris. "Let's get ready. They could open those doors any moment."

Chris followed her to the other side of the door. They waited there for what felt like hours but might only have been minutes. Time had a way of sliding and stretching in the dark confines of a dank cell.

She tensed when the click of the door lock signaled a guard's entry. Chris moved away from the wall to face the opening. Millie readied herself to pounce.

The door swung into the room, and an armed guard stepped across the threshold past Millie. Daylight from outside the room cast a shadow across the soldier's profile.

He stood inside the room and stared at Chris. "Hey," he said, "where is—"

That was when Millie made her move. She shoved the guard from behind as Chris pulled on the soldier's rifle. When the guard stumbled forward and lost his grip, the others who crowded the other side of the door heaved it shut.

The door banged closed and cloaked the room in darkness. While the half dozen men and women tried to hold the door closed, Millie jumped on the guard and held him down, finding her way to his neck, against which she pressed the blade of her pink knife. The knife she'd taken back from an unconscious Keith after kicking him to the curb.

The stupid guards had never thought to search her after taking her into their custody. They must have assumed Keith had disarmed her, which he had.

"I'll slice this across your throat if you so much as move," she hissed. "And if you try anything, my friend has your gun aimed at your head."

The soldier stopped struggling. He was on his stomach. Millie felt his muscles relax, and he laid the side of his face on the floor. She kept the knife at his neck. Chris flipped on a tactical light mounted on the Sig Sauer rifle. The fan of white light almost blinded Millie, and she looked away from it. The guard froze, clearly aware of his predicament.

Outside, the guards banged on the door. They tried forcing it open. Cracks of light shone at the edges, but the half-dozen prisoners held their own. The guards outside shouted angry threats of prolonged, tortuous violence if they did not open the door.

"You're going to help us get out of here," Millie told the guard. "You understand?"

"I can't," the guard protested. "No way."

Millie pushed the edge of the blade against his soft flesh. Warm blood ran onto her fingers. "You can't, or you won't?"

"I can't. They'll kill me and then kill you. I'm no good as a hostage."

"We can't hold it much longer!" called one of the other prisoners. "They're too strong."

Millie stole a glance over her shoulder. The door opened and closed. Each time it opened, the gap was a little wider than the time before. Shouts from the other side ordered them to give up, to let them inside the room.

"Hang on another minute. You can do it."

The others groaned and grunted, pushing against the door. Their boots scraped the floor as they worked for purchase and leverage.

"You got him, Chris?" Millie asked.

"I got him."

Millie released her grip and rolled away from the soldier and got to her feet. He stayed on the ground, whimpering. She backed away and stood next to Chris.

"All right," Chris said. "What now?"

"We use him as a hostage."

"That won't work," the guard said. "They'll kill me and then you. I'm telling you."

"You believe him?" Chris asked.

"No."

Millie thought about their options. What would her father do? How many times had he found himself in situations in which there was no obvious escape? She closed her eyes.

One of the half dozen prisoners cleared her throat. "Excuse me."

The woman came closer. Chris stepped back to give her room to move but kept the rifle trained on the soldier on the ground.

"I have an idea," the woman said. "What if we—"

Millie silenced her. "Don't say it."

The woman's voice quavered as if scolded. "I just—"

Millie softened her sharp tone. "Sorry, I didn't mean to snap. Just hang on a moment."

Chris shrugged. "What is it?"

"Do we have anything to use as a gag? I don't want our prisoner listening to our plan and then shouting it through the door."

"Good idea," Chris said.

Another of the half dozen prisoners came forward with a

grimy rag in her hand. She offered it. "Would this work?"

Millie nodded. "Perfect. Shove it in his mouth."

The guard protested. "Please don't. Don't put that in my mouth. I won't say anything. I promise. I'll keep my mouth shut. I—"

Millie squatted in front of him. "It's either a muzzle or a bullet. Your choice. What's it going to be?"

The guard closed his mouth.

Millie stood. "That's what I thought." She gestured for the woman to stuff the gag in the soldier's mouth.

A moment later, the gag in place, Millie told the woman with the idea to speak.

The woman talked through her plan. Her voice was soft, but she spoke with keen intelligence. Millie and Chris agreed her plan could work. It wasn't as if they had a better idea, regardless. So they got ready, and everybody took their spots.

"What's your name?" Millie asked the idea woman.

"Clara."

"Clara," Millie repeated. "I'll remember that."

Chris shouldered the rifle. "I'm ready. Let's do this."

They moved the guard into position.

Millie motioned to the others. "Be ready. All at the same time, let go of the door and back away. On my count."

She glanced back at Chris. He was close enough she could see him nod.

"Three," Millie said, pausing for a moment. "Two."

She walked to the door and took the same position where she had stood before trapping the guard they now held hostage.

"One."

The others let go of the door, and it swung open, banged against the opposite wall, and two soldiers stumbled into the room. The sudden shift of force made them lose their balance, and they fell onto one another, both of their rifles skittering across the floor. Clara and one of the other prisoners were smart enough to snatch them and train them on the fallen soldiers.

Millie kept her spot until a third person entered the room. She had her hands raised above her head and was not in uniform.

"Don't shoot," she said. "Please don't shoot."

Millie held her ground a moment longer, eyes on the ground. A shadow behind the woman told her another guard was coming. From his shadow, he looked big. Huge even.

The woman took another two hesitant steps into the room. Chris kept his rifle leveled at her, but he didn't pull the trigger.

Four of the other prisoners huddled in a dark corner of the room, out of the fan of light that spread across much of the cell. The two with weapons held their ground at the edge of the light and kept aim on the two soldiers who had fallen on the floor.

"Don't take another step," Chris warned. "I will shoot both of you."

That confirmed what she already knew. Another guard was with the woman. Who was she? A prisoner? Part of Leo's entourage?

"Please," the woman said. "Don't shoot—"

"All of you, drop your weapons!" the soldier boomed. "You cannot escape. It's pointless. Better to give up now."

Millie tensed and waited for her chance. She held the knife tight in her hand, at shoulder level, her thumb pressed against the slide of the blade.

The woman took two more steps, pushed in by the soldier. His profile moved past Millie, and she pounced. She jumped him and jabbed the knife into the side of his neck. He dropped his rifle but somehow managed to grab Millie's wrist. He squeezed until she lost her hold on the knife and then grabbed her around the throat. His hand was like a collapsing meat hook, and he squeezed. Millie's feet lifted from the ground as he choked her.

Stars broke across her vision and blurred the image of the hulking soldier whose face bore a long, nasty scar. The knife still stuck from his neck.

Millie heard muffled voices and the pop of gunfire. She focused on her consciousness and grabbed with both hands at the man's grip. Each of his fingers was like a bicep as they flexed against her neck. All of this happened within seconds, though time slowed as Millie struggled to stay lucid.

How had he managed to swing her from the ground and lift her from it with a knife buried in his neck? Who was he?

Darkness crowded the edge of her vision, and the stars faded. She sensed she was about to lose the fight. Then, instead of keeping her hands on his, she reached out and grabbed the hilt. She yanked it out and dragged it toward her.

Warm blood sprayed her face, and the grip loosened. She fell to the ground, gasping for air. Beside her, the behemoth choked and gagged before he fell back against the door, his body slumping. A woman in the dark screamed with shock. Millie was on her knees. She swallowed against the throbbing ache in her throat. She was okay. She was alive. He was not. His eyes fixed on her, but there was nothing there except the vacant gaze of someone whose soul was elsewhere. Millie crawled to him and picked up the knife. She wiped it on his shirt and faced the woman. Chris still had his weapon trained on her. The guards on the floor were motionless. One was dead. Blood pooled from underneath his body and leached across the floor. The other was wounded but alive. He whimpered for mercy.

Millie wiped the blood from her face with the back of her arm and crossed to the woman, pointing the blade at her. "Who are you?"

The woman twisted but kept her hands in the air. She studied Millie for a moment and smiled. Then her eyes moistened, and tears rolled down her cheeks.

"You're Millie Beck, aren't you?" she said. "You're John Beck's daughter."

Millie glanced at Chris, then back to the woman. She took a cautious step toward her but kept the knife raised. "I'm Millie," she said. "Who the hell are you?"

"Thank the heavens," the woman said. "I am *so* happy to see you."

Millie quirked a brow. "Who are you?"

"It's the eyes," the woman said. "I recognize you from your eyes. You look just like him."

"Lady," Millie said, "you'd better tell me who you are and how you think you know me, or I'll—"

"I'm Regina," she said. "I am...I *was*...your father's friend."

Millie lowered the blade. "You're Regina? As in Regina, Lucy, and..." She searched her memory for the third name. It did not come to her.

Chris helped. "Rebecca."

"Yeah," Millie said, "Rebecca."

Regina nodded. Tears rolled down her cheeks. "They're out there fighting right now. Lucy and Rebecca. He made them fight."

"Each other?"

Regina nodded again. "You and I are next."

"Next what?" Millie asked.

"Next in the arena. He wants us to fight one another to the death."

Millie laughed. "That's not happening. I'm not stepping into that arena to fight anyone."

Regina blinked and lowered her trembling hands. Then Millie recalled something Regina had said moments earlier.

"Hey," she said, "you just told me you *were* my father's friend. Why did you use the past tense?"

Regina's expression tightened. She tilted her head. "You don't know?"

"Know what?"

"John Beck is dead."

CHAPTER 27

D-DAY + 4 YEARS, 6 MONTHS, 21 DAYS
HOPKINSVILLE, KENTUCKY

John Beck was not a dead man. Not yet. As long as he had breath left in his lungs, he had a chance to survive almost anything. While being captive of the militia at their arena was not ideal, it was far better than the alternative.

He held his hands above his head. The muzzle of a Sig Sauer rifle pressed into the small of his back. He climbed the steps with his eyes on the prize.

Not that Leo was really a prize. But he was gift enough if Beck could get close to him, and he figured from the way the soldiers nudged him closer to the press box atop the bleachers, that was about to happen.

His and Leo's eyes met before Beck disappeared into the stairwell that led from the bottom of the press box to its second floor. Beck smirked, having caught the slightest flash of recognition on Leo's face. Beck imagined the militia leader had a hard time reconciling him in a soldier's uniform.

The soldier with the rifle at Beck's back jabbed him. "Move."

Beck quickened his pace up the steps. When they reached the second floor, two of the guards escorted him to Leo.

Beck wasn't sure what to expect from the dictator, but being offered a seat next to him was not on the list.

Leo smiled and motioned to the empty chair beside him. "I was getting lonely. So glad to have some company. It's nice to share the afternoon's entertainment with someone who appreciates it."

Beck studied Leo for a moment. Leo smiled. It was close to a grin, and he motioned his head toward the field below. It took a moment for Beck to process the scene.

He counted three armed soldiers spaced in a triangular pattern. They wore the same black uniform as Beck. Inside the triangle, four attackers surrounded two women who stood back-to-back. Two bodies were at the women's feet.

One woman swung a medieval-looking torture device, and the other held a long spear. Initially, he didn't recognize them, but the way the women moved was familiar, especially the one with the flail. She was favoring one leg.

"Is that—?"

"It is," Leo said. "Two of your friends. Lucy and Rebecca."

Leo's answer surprised him. Beck thought he had muttered the question to himself, in his head, and didn't realize he'd actually said it aloud. Rage began to boil. He gripped the arms of his chair and growled.

"You put them in the arena to fight for their lives? Two against six?"

The four attackers circled Beck's friends like sharks in the water. Their movements tightened as they probed for weakness. Each of them carried a different weapon, but none held guns. Only the guards had those.

"No." Leo shook his head. "I put them in the arena against one another, but they're stubborn, like you. They refused to fight. They played at it for a few minutes until I'd had enough. So I brought in the others to liven it up. Make it interesting, am I right?"

Beck moved to get up, but the soldiers behind him pressed on his shoulders and kept him in his seat. He relaxed, and the men released their hold.

Leo grinned. His teeth were too white. They needed punching.

Beck flexed his hands and tried to focus on the fight while trying to figure out some way to help his friends. He had come all this way, lost his daughter for a second time, and would not sit idle to watch any of his people die useless deaths.

His eyes scanned the crowd. They appeared restless. Despite their cheering and chanting, there was something about them that gave Beck the impression they were uncomfortable in their seats. They did not like the gladiator games as much as their applause might suggest. Beck didn't know these people. He could be reading them wrong, but he didn't think he was. His attention shifted back to the field.

Lucy twirled the spear in her hands like a propeller as the four hostiles tightened their circle. Rebecca was hobbling, but she appeared to swing the flail like an expert. She crossed it back and forth in front of her body. The women were shielding themselves from any quick advance.

Beck expected them to hold their positions, back-to-back. That way, they protected themselves from any unseen attack. Lucy's skill did not surprise him. Woodland bandits, self-proclaimed Robin Hoods, had raised her to be the warrior she clearly had become.

Rebecca was different.

In many ways, he still saw her as the young Quaker woman whose life he'd saved on Coaster Road in the middle of a battle for her village. She had come so far in the short time between then and now. Beck wanted nothing more than to be on the field with them, fighting alongside the brave women who refused to kill one another despite what it meant.

"You wish you were there with them," Leo stated. "In the arena."

Beck glanced at Leo. "It's not right, what you're doing. Forcing these people to kill one another for sport, for entertainment."

The first of the four attackers made a move. He had a pair of short swords and tried a quick maneuver to separate the women. Rebecca repelled his attack and caught him on the back of the head with the spiked ball at the end of her flail. The contact made a sickening thud, and the crowd groaned collectively when the ball stuck to the man's head and dragged him to the ground. Rebecca yanked back the weapon, and the man's body jerked before going still.

Leo chuckled. "I thought you were smarter than that, John Beck. This isn't about entertainment. Except maybe for me. This is about control."

Beck stared at him. "How so?"

Leo waved a hand at the crowd. "These people in the audience. They don't love me, they fear me. They know that if they don't do what's required of them as citizens of my realm, they'll end up on the arena floor, fighting for their lives. I mean, I'm smart enough to understand that my hold on them is tenuous. All it takes is a spark and, poof, everything for which I've worked goes up in smoke. That's why I put threats into the arena. One by one, I have my enemies kill one another. I don't do it. Not directly. They do it to themselves. Do you play chess?"

Beck shook his head. "Not much for board games."

Leo smirked. "I didn't think you were the type. Not much for real strategy, am I right? More of a 'fly by the seat of your pants' kind of guy?"

Leo glanced at Beck and then pointed at the field below. "Those gladiators, aside from your lady friends, are just like the people in the stands. They're their neighbors and friends. Sometimes, they're even family."

Beck shook his head. Disgust soaked his voice. "And they cheer?"

"Of course they do. If they don't, that's suspicious. They don't want to be suspicious. Sometimes I think it takes everything in them not to throw me into the arena. If they were smarter, they would realize they have the numbers. Sure, I have a nice-sized militia and they're armed, but under the right circumstances, the proletariat would easily make me eat cake."

"You're a sick man."

Leo laughed and slapped a hand on Beck's leg. "And you're funny. The last time I saw you, you were at death's door. I did not think you would live. Yet you did. And instead of counting your blessings and playing house with your long-lost daughter, you come back here, into the proverbial lion's den. For what purpose?"

Beck was unsure he had heard Leo correctly. How did he know about his daughter? Chris? He really was a traitor. Something must have flashed in his eyes. Leo's features lit up with interest.

"Oh," he said. "That's right. You had no idea I was spying on your little tin-star Sheriff, did you? That my birdie told me that Millie Beck and the Sheriff were one and the same? Classic. Almost Shakespearean, am I right?"

Beck had never read Shakespeare, but he knew enough about the English playwright to understand the bard dealt in tragedy. That was enough for him to get the reference, even if it was wrong. It was wrong, wasn't it? Nothing tragic had happened yet. Had it?

The anger boiling in his gut shot through his body. Adrenaline mixed with pure hatred made him want to strangle Leo right then and there.

"Where's Millie?"

Leo shook his head. "I was waiting for that question. Actually, I'm disappointed it wasn't the first thing out of your mouth. I mean, you know she's here. Otherwise, why would you have come? It wasn't just for the dead women walking, was it?"

On the field, two of the three remaining gladiators made their run at Lucy and Rebecca. They both attacked Lucy. One went high and the other low. Lucy jabbed one of them in the face with the butt end of the spear. It knocked him off balance, and she sliced the business end across the other man's face. He grabbed at the deep gash and dropped his weapon. Lucy used the moment to drive the spear up and into his chest. She withdrew it as fast as she'd stabbed and swiped it across the first attacker's arm. He too lost his weapon. Rebecca swung around as the women stood back-to-back, and she finished him off with a crunching blow to the side of his head. The crowd went silent for a split second and then roared.

Beck pumped his fists in the air. He cursed under his breath and cheered on his friends. Now it was two to one, and they had the advantage. Beck looked away from the fight for a moment and focused on Leo. He didn't like the insinuation that he had somehow minimized his daughter in favor of his friends. Beck had thought about Millie every second of every day. Before D-Day and most certainly in its aftermath.

This day was no different. But the sight of Rebecca and Lucy in the arena had thrown him off his game. It distracted him. Now he thought of another woman.

"Regina? Where is she?"

Leo regarded him with renewed interest. He clucked his tongue against the roof of his mouth. "And therein lies the rub. You have too many women in your life, John Beck. Too many people you love. That's a problem. It's a handicap. Can I say that? Is it politically correct? Or am I better saying it's an Achilles' heel? Either way, you were far more effective as a legendary killing machine when you were alone. When nobody loved you and all you had to keep yourself going was the mythical quest for your daughter, am I right?"

"It wasn't mythical. I found her."

Leo narrowed his eyes. "But did you? I mean, first of all, friend, I took you *to* her. You did not find her. Secondly, perhaps more critically, she was no longer your daughter, she was the Sheriff. Those are two different people, even if they share the same name and same father."

Beck looked back to the field and saw the last of the gladiators was dead. Lucy had her foot on his shoulder so she could pry the spear from his throat. The crowd gasped when she did, and blood fountained into the air like a geyser. Perhaps the last gladiator was not dead yet.

"You don't know me," Beck said, "and you sure as hell don't know my daughter."

"Oh, but I do," Leo crowed. "I know people. Look at this place. If I didn't have a unique understanding of the human condition, an almost Godlike ability to manipulate and influence, do you think I would be sitting here right now about to enjoy your daughter fight your lover in the arena?"

"What do you mean?"

Leo shrugged. His eyebrows lifted. "I mean, as soon as these two down here are done fighting, I'm putting Millie Bo Billie into the arena with Regina the Self-Righteous."

Beck clenched his jaw. The demons hissed, and his blood pumped. He felt it in his chest and his neck and the tips of his fingers, which he balled into tight fists.

"There's nothing you can do but sit back and watch the show. So I suggest—"

Beck punched Leo twice. Once in the nose. A second time in the mouth. They were quick, short jabs. His knuckles caught the militia leader just right. The pop of cartilage and crack of teeth preceded a grunt and groan.

Beck did not have a chance to see his handiwork. Leo's hands covered the damage, and the guards knocked Beck to the floor with a rifle butt to his back between his shoulder blades. A volley of punches knocked the air from his lungs, and he sank to the floor between his chair and the open wall of the press box.

As he gasped and winced in pain, Leo stood over him. The dictator kicked Beck in the gut hard with his boot. Then he kicked him again.

Beck tried to breathe but couldn't inhale. He felt as if he were drowning. His vision blurred, and a sharp pain lanced behind his eyes.

With a curse, Leo left Beck on the floor and disappeared from view. Beck fought to stay conscious. Only after an agonizing thirty seconds, he sucked in a breath of air. Then another. An inhuman groan forced chills along his spine. It wasn't until he took his third breath that he realized he was the one making the noise.

His chest burned, and he hitched when he breathed. His ribs were bruised or broken. Beck rolled onto his knees and spat onto the floor. Behind him, Leo's heavy boot steps pounded the floor as the dictator paced across the narrow space.

Beck spotted two bloody teeth on the floor in front of him. He reached out and scooped them into his hand. It felt good to have exorcised his anger on Leo's smug face, but the sensation waned fast as the demons reminded him of his dilemma. His daughter was somewhere on the property. So was Regina.

To make matters worse, Lucy and Rebecca faced each other on the battlefield below. Fresh out of opposition, they must fight one another to the death.

There were too many angles. Too much to overcome. The demons assured him they would all die because of his foolishness and his inability to control his rage. All of these, all of the bloodshed and pain, and Beck had not changed at all. He was still a vengeful man ruled by emotion and petulance.

Or was he?

Had he not overcome every challenge in his way? Despite losing loved ones and friends, was he not the man who freed countless oppressed people all across the former United States? Most of all, wasn't the man who killed his ex-wife and stolen his daughter in the hours after D-Day in the ground? Yes, he was. Beck had put him there. Through relentless pursuit, dogged determination, and guile, he was a man of action. John Beck was a freaking legend. If this was the end, what did it matter if he went out in a blaze of glorious retribution? At the very least, what he did in the moments that followed might give the four women in his life a fighting chance.

He wrapped his hands tight around the teeth and steadied himself. This was his moment. He might not get another.

Beck silenced the demons, controlled his heart rate and his breathing, and focused on the task at hand.

You're John Beck.

You're John Beck.

You are John Beck.

CHAPTER 28

Rebecca stared at the bodies around her. Her flail was soaked in blood. So were her hands. It was on her face and her shirt and her boots. She backed away from Lucy, unsure of how her compatriot might behave now that the others were dead. This was the moment they were to attack one another. Rebecca resisted that urge.

She had overcome a fleeting fatalism that had threatened to end her life when the man with the curved blade came at her, wielding steel and an unbridled fury. In the final instant, her survival instinct took hold. She'd feinted to one side but cut to the other and threw the man off balance enough that he missed her with a wide swing of his blade. As he tried to stop, his feet slid in the soft earth. Rebecca backhanded the flail and delivered a near-fatal blow. The man crumpled toward the ground, his body folding onto the blade and impaling him before he hit the mud. It seemed a gladiator's own weapon was often his own worst enemy.

After the brush with death, Rebecca regained her poise. She summoned her strength, ignored the pain and weakness in her ankle and foot, and survived the calculated but ill-

301

timed onslaught from the remaining fighters. Now she and Lucy again faced one another, surrounded by armed soldiers who demanded one or both of them die on the field with the others.

Rebecca leaned on her good leg and adjusted her slimy grip on the flail's handle. It was heavy in her hand. Heavier than before. Exhaustion threatened to overwhelm her as she tried to rally the adrenaline for a second wind. Or was it a third wind?

She checked with the crowd and noticed they were distracted. Almost none of them faced the field. Instead, they had their attention turned toward the enclosed section atop the stands.

"What are they looking at?" Lucy called out to her.

Rebecca searched the box for answers. Leo was no longer in his seat. There was movement in the box beyond the opening and in the shadows where the sunlight did not reach. Someone paced; others stood at attention. She imagined the agitated man was Leo, the others his guards.

Someone in the crowd shouted, "Now's the time!"

Another cried out, "This is it! This is what we've waited for!"

The crowd cheered and started moving from their seats.

Rebecca took cautious steps forward, closer to the stands. She lifted her empty hand and held it at her brow, shielding her eyes from the sun in hopes of a better view.

"Get back to the fight!" a soldier shouted from the field. "If you don't, we have orders to execute you. Right here, right now."

Rebecca glanced over her shoulder toward the voice. She shrugged with one shoulder and shot a side eye at Lucy.

"Do it, then," she told the soldier.

What did she have to lose? She was already in the throes

of a death match. There was nothing anyone could do to her that would worsen her predicament.

She half expected a bullet in her spine as she turned back to the crowd. None came. Instead, boot steps sucked at the mud as the soldier approached her. She tightened her grip on the flail and spun it. When she felt him get close, she turned, dropped to a knee, and swung the flail up.

It caught the guard on his chin and snapped back his head. Bone cracked, and he lost his hold on the rifle. Rebecca dropped the flail and yanked the weapon from the soldier as he collapsed.

She flipped the rifle and shouldered it, taking aim at a stunned guard who was slow to open fire. Rebecca dropped him with a pair of shots that caught him in the chest, and swept her aim toward the third guard. He was already on his back. Lucy towered over him with her spear buried in his gut.

The quick bursts of gunfire from Rebecca's rifle caught the crowd's attention. Some screamed while others ran from their seats. Surprisingly, none came for her. Instead, she saw groups of people attacking the soldiers. They mobbed them. The soldiers appeared frozen with surprise as they disappeared beneath the mobs.

Gunfire popped across the stadium. That did nothing to deter the revolt.

Lucy was at her side, rifle in hand. "What just happened?"

"I have no idea," said Rebecca. "But I think I don't have to kill you anymore."

Lucy laughed. "You're funny. I didn't know you had a sense of humor."

Rebecca gestured toward the violence in the stands. "What do we do now?"

"I say we find Regina and get out of here."

"Then what?"

Lucy shrugged. "No clue. Let's worry about things one step at a time."

They raced off toward the fieldhouse. It was the building in which they had been housed before their fight. They slopped through the mud and danced around the bodies in their way. To their left, more gunfire cracked. It echoed amidst the cries and shouts from those taking back their power.

They crossed the field, ran over the track, and reached the fence that separated the arena from the fieldhouse. A pair of soldiers emerged from behind the building, but their attention was on the riot in the stands. Neither saw Lucy and Rebecca as both women took aim and dropped the soldiers where they stood. Lucy stopped at their bodies and took their extra magazines. She handed one to Rebecca.

Rebecca pocketed the magazine and winced. "I don't know how much longer I can stay on my feet. My foot and ankle are killing me."

"You don't have a choice," Lucy said. "If you don't keep running, you're gonna die. After all this, I'm not going to let that happen."

They exchanged smiles and nods, and Lucy gestured toward the fieldhouse entrance. It was fifty feet ahead. "You lead."

Rebecca sucked in a breath. She kept the rifle pressed against her shoulder and had her finger on the trigger. *Lucas would be proud,* she thought as the fieldhouse door slammed open in front of them. Rebecca tensed. Lucy took a position beside her. A pair armed with rifles emerged from the dark opening, and Rebecca took aim.

In the millisecond before she applied pressure to the rifle's trigger, she recognized one of the soldiers, who was not a soldier at all.

"Regina?" Rebecca called out. "Regina! How did you get here?"

Regina lowered her weapon and ran toward her friends. "Oh my goodness. Rebecca, Lucy, how did you—what are—where—"

She approached with the other woman. A group trailed behind them. Rebecca counted six women and a man.

"We can talk about everything later," said Lucy. "Right now, we need to move. There's a revolt. Everything's gone to hell. We need to get out of here, now."

Rebecca motioned toward the field over her shoulder. "We were in the arena. But we got out and came looking for you. We have to go. C'mon, Regina. Let's move."

"I can't leave without these other people," Regina said. "They're coming, too."

"Whatever," Lucy said. "But let's move. Anybody know the fastest way out of here?"

The woman next to Regina raised a hand from her rifle. "I do."

Rebecca saw something familiar in the woman. "Who are you?"

"I'm Millie Beck."

"Millie Beck? John's—"

"Yes," Millie said. "That's Chris. We came with my dad to rescue you."

Rebecca searched the other faces in case she had missed something. "Your dad? Where is he?"

"He's dead," Regina said. "Let's go."

"Dead?" Rebecca said. "What do you mean *dead*?"

"We can talk about it later," Regina said. "Let's get to safety first."

Rebecca's mind whirled. How could John Beck be dead?

Nobody argued, and Millie led them away back toward the arena.

"We just came from there," Lucy called out behind her. "Is that the smartest move?"

Millie kept moving. "It's the fastest way. Across the field and south. Otherwise, we have to go the long way around and face the threat of more soldiers."

Nobody argued, and they moved back onto the field. To their right, the stadium was a free-for-all. The militia was on the losing end despite more soldiers entering the fray. It was every bit the violent bloodsport that had played out on the arena floor minutes earlier.

They were halfway across the field when Rebecca spotted something in the press box. Leo was fighting someone. No, not just someone. Was that John Beck? Did she see a ghost? Was it wishful thinking?

"Hey!" she shouted. "Everybody stop." Rebecca pointed toward the box at the top of the stadium. The others followed her gaze. "Isn't that Beck?"

"I don't think so," Millie said.

Regina blinked. "It could be."

"I can't tell," said Chris.

"Does it matter?" Millie asked. "It's not like we're going to run into the middle of that just to find out it's not him. If it is my dad, he would want us to get out of here."

A new voice turned everyone's attention toward the fieldhouse. "You're not going anywhere, Sheriff."

Standing feet from them, breathless but armed, were four men. The one in the middle looked like he'd taken a beating. Dark circles ringed his deep-set eyes, dried blood caked his crooked nose, and sick yellow bruises colored his cheeks and jaw. He might have been a good-looking man if not for the injuries. It was hard to tell.

Millie stepped toward him. "Keith? I thought I killed you."

His wounds altered his voice, softened the edges. "Not yet, but I'm about to return the favor."

"Keith," Millie said, "if you shoot me, my people will shoot you. Nobody wins. We all die here for nothing. Let us go. You go your way; we go ours. Live to fight another day."

He threw down his weapon. "Oh, no. That's not how this will work."

Keith pushed his sleeves up, crowding the fabric above his elbows. He squared his shoulders and spread his feet. "We're not shooting each other. We're fighting. Here in the arena. Hand to hand, with no weapons."

Rebecca studied Millie's features. The woman looked so much like her father it was uncanny. She had his dark, brooding eyes. Her jaw was a more feminine version of Beck's. And her posture, her aura, was identical. There was something else too. There was pain. She wore it like a cloak.

"You want to fight like gladiators?" Millie asked.

"Absolutely. It's poetic, don't you think? One last battle in the arena while the kingdom collapses? You and me, one on one. Like old times."

A sly grin stretched his battered face. He winced as he tried to play off how ridiculous he knew he must look. It was possible he'd failed an attempt at a wink.

Millie was unamused. She shook her head. "I don't think so."

Keith raised his hands, palms out. "Why not? You used to love wrestling with me. Don't you remember? I do. Rolling around in the dark. Just you and me, the dirtier, the better. The—"

Millie drilled a single shot between his eyes. His expression froze, and he blinked once before his tongue wagged, and he slumped to the ground.

Without hesitation, she shot the man next to him. Chris took down the third soldier, Lucy pegged the fourth, and just like that, it was over.

"Who was he?" Regina asked.

"Nobody," Millie said. "He was nobody."

CHAPTER 29

Beck leveled a punch that landed hard on Leo's jaw. It knocked the militia leader off balance and into the wall. He caught himself, his battered hands painting the wall with blood.

"This is how it ends," Beck said. "Right here in the arena."

Leo wiped his mouth with the back of his hand, then balled his fist. Strings of blood and spit stretched from the side of his face.

Both men had fought for several minutes. It felt like hours. They measured one another, fatigue beginning to best both of them. Sweat dripped into Beck's eyes. He tasted it on his lips. His head hurt, as did most of his body. He couldn't distinguish one ache from another.

Beck braced himself for another barrage. Leo was a good fighter despite his age. He was incredibly strong, his sinewy muscles packing power with each swing. Though Beck noticed the man was tiring. He too was drenched in sweat. He took long, labored breaths, and his nostrils flared in the attempt to bring in more oxygen.

The two men were alone in the box. The soldiers who protected Leo were gone. They'd left to fight the crowd when Beck was on the floor, Leo's teeth in his hand. Leo sent them to deal with the insurrection before any of the ingrates found their way into the press box. The move backfired on Leo when Beck got back to his feet, buried his shoulder into Leo's gut, and drove him into the wall.

Leo threw a pair of swings at Beck's head. The first missed, but the second glanced off Beck's ear. While it was not a direct hit, it hurt, and Beck's ear rang, and stars blurred his vision for a moment. He shook it off in time to avoid an uppercut that whizzed past his nose.

The men danced around each other in the small space. It was appropriate, perhaps, they fought without guns. That was how they did it in the arena. It was old school. Beck liked his chances despite Leo's surprising endurance and strength.

Beck searched for an opening. His chest pounded, and it hurt to breathe. Each fast movement sparked bolts of pain across his midsection. If it weren't for that, he'd have probably bested Leo already.

Leo backed away, stole a glance to his right, and grabbed a chair. He swung it forward and threw it. Beck blocked the chair with his arms and deflected it, but the instant he repelled the chair, Leo was on him. He kicked at Beck's leg and barely missed his knee. Still, it forced Beck to the ground, and Leo was on him. When they fell, Beck hit the side of his head on the floor. It dazed him, and he lost focus long enough that Leo wrapped an arm around his neck and pulled. Beck grabbed at the chokehold but couldn't escape it. He kicked and tried to flip Leo, but the older man maintained his leverage and kept Beck on the ground.

Pressure tightened around his neck, and Beck felt the lack of oxygen to his brain. His head hurt. The ringing in his ears grew louder. The world grew dim as if someone had pulled a shade over everything. He was losing the fight.

He summoned the demons to help him, to anger him, and give him that one last surge of adrenaline. In his mind's eye, Beck saw himself wrongly imprisoned for a murder he did not commit. He saw his wife leaving him outside the courthouse after their divorce was finalized. A vision of Millie hugging him goodbye when she left with her mother for a new home in another city. He saw his ex-wife, Debbie, dead in his arms and heard himself promise to keep their daughter safe.

Flashcards of memories flipped across his darkening vision. He was in search of Millie, looking for her. Gabe was beside him as they fought off an ambush in Oklahoma City and in Colorado. He was in New Mexico with Rebecca and Lucas. Poor Lucas, dead in Memphis. And Regina. He saw Regina reaching out to him, calling his name and pushing him to fight back.

Anger welled in his gut, and rage built in his chest. Beck knew he was on the verge of passing out. He managed to twist his hips enough that he was able to ram his knee into the small of Leo's back. It was just enough to loosen the grip for Beck to suck in a desperate gasp of air. Pain shot through his chest, and he seized for a split second before jamming his fingers into Leo's face. He hit either a nostril or an eye because it stunned Leo. He cried out in pain and lost his grip.

Beck flipped. His neck throbbed. As he tried to crawl away and get space from Leo, a gunshot exploded so close to him he felt it shake his bones.

He waited for the heat that came with a gunshot wound. Then the searing, radiating pain. He felt nothing. Nothing at all.

Was he hit in the back? Was he already dead? Where had

Leo gotten the gun? How had he—

"Beck?" a voice called. "Beck, is that you?"

Beck blinked. His throat hurt so much he was now sure he wasn't dead. He tried to move but couldn't. His body was too weak.

A hand touched his back, and he flinched. Then it moved to the back of his neck.

"John Beck," the woman's voice said. "It's really you. You did come for me."

The voice was so familiar. It was as if he'd always heard it and known to whom it belonged. But in that moment, he was too confused to place it.

The hands reached his shoulders and rolled him over. He was on his back and gasped for air. Breathing hurt so much. The light was so bright he couldn't make out the face so close to his.

When she kissed him on the lips, he immediately recognized her scent. She held him for a moment; a tear dripped from her face to his. She pulled away.

Beck whispered, "Regina?"

He blinked, and her face came into focus. She was more beautiful than he remembered. "How did you—"

She put a finger to his lips to quiet him. "Not now. We have to get you out of here. There's a revolt. The king is dead, and his pawns have taken over."

"The king?"

"Leo. I shot him in the back. Then in the face. I owed him that much."

Others appeared in the space behind and above Regina. There was Rebecca and Lucy and Millie. There was Millie. Thank heavens, there was Millie.

Millie reached out her hand. She smiled. It was a weak, sad smile. "C'mon, Dad. Let's go home."

With Regina's help, Millie got Beck to his feet. When he wobbled and nearly fell, they held him up. The four women, the four people, the four survivors, the four warriors, who meant the most to him in this world, led him from the box and along a back exit out of the stadium.

Behind them, crowds chanted. They no longer called for blood. Now they cheered for peace, for self-determination.

By the time they were outside the stadium gates, Beck had regained most of his equilibrium. He pushed away his help and insisted he walk on his own. The four said very little to each other. They focused on the task at hand, getting out of the city alive.

As they rounded the northern side of the stadium and reached the western edge, Beck stopped in his tracks. He pointed at a group of people clustered together. They were armed and stood in a circle, protecting one another's backs as Lucy and Rebecca had done in the arena. Beck counted twenty-five. He glared at one of them, the only one he recognized, and reached for Millie's rifle. She pulled back.

"Give me that," he said.

"What for?"

He pointed at the man closest to them. "Chris. He's the spy. He's the one who betrayed you and nearly cost us our lives."

Millie shook her head. "No, Dad. It wasn't Chris."

"But I saw him with you. And the horse. And the dead guy in the woods and—"

Millie put a hand on his shoulder and squeezed gently. "Dad, it wasn't Chris, I promise. Chris tried to help me. He *did* help me. If it weren't for him, I'm not sure we'd be here right now."

"How do you know that? Did you know there was a spy? Leo told me—"

"I know who the spy was. It wasn't Chris."

"Who was it?"

Millie looked away. She tucked her chin.

"Millie? Who was it?"

She looked up at him; tears welled in her eyes. She blinked, and they rolled down her cheeks. Millie looked like the little girl who once idolized him. She was twelve again and leaning into him at a scary movie.

"Who was it?"

"It was Keith. He was the spy. He used me. He used all of us."

Beck looked at the ground, unable to face his daughter.

"I screwed up, Dad. I let someone in, let him get close. That won't happen again, okay? I won't let it happen again. It's you and me. It's us."

Beck shook his head. He wrapped his arms around his daughter.

Lucy cleared her throat. "We really should get going. It's getting dark soon and—"

Beck glared at her, and she closed her mouth. Her eyes widened, and she held her hands up in surrender.

"I screwed up, Dad," Millie sobbed into his chest. "You were right. I was wrong."

"Shhh," he said.

His throat hurt, and his voice was hoarse, but what he had to say needed to be spoken.

"You weren't wrong. You made a mistake. Besides, Keith was a major ass, but that's not your fault. Remember, I was a pretty bad guy, and that wasn't your mom's fault."

Millie pulled back and sniffed. With the back of her sleeve, she wiped the snot from her face. It made her look all the more like the child he missed so much. But he reminded himself of how much there was to love about this young woman.

"So you screwed up," he said. "Big deal. We all do. The key is not to make the same mistake more than once. That's how you learn."

"That's what I'm saying, Dad," Millie said. "I won't fall for a guy again. That solves the problem."

"That's not what I mean. You can't stop yourself from falling in love with the right person just because you did with the wrong one, okay? Don't harden your heart. That's the worst thing you can do."

Millie wiped her face again, then smiled. "You're trying to be all parental and stuff, aren't you?"

"I'm trying."

She shook her head and took his arm. Together, they joined the others and began their march north toward Churchill Downs.

They were thirty all together. Beck, Millie, Regina, Lucy, Rebecca, Chris, and a group of men and women who'd escaped with them. Some had shared a cell with Millie. The others clung to them as they escaped the chaos.

"Assuming Keith didn't screw things up too bad," Millie said as they walked, weapons drawn, "we'll be back in time for the last migration."

"The last one?" Beck asked.

"It's time to put this world behind us, Dad. Start a new one. We've got a start in Canada. If we can manage the trip one more time, we'll be in a good place."

"That's why we've got these stragglers with us?"

The sun was low in the sky. The heat from the day was dissipating, and a cool breeze brought with it the promise of a more temperate night. The clear skies were a sign it might get chilly after dark.

"Yes," Millie said. "I was hoping we could take more. But given that Leo is dead and the people revolted against the militia, I think Hopkinsville will be okay."

"I guess I found you just in time," said Beck.

"Or I found you just in time, Dad. Though I never would've stopped looking."

"Me either."

"I know, Dad."

Although Beck struggled to move with any speed, this was as good as he'd felt in a long time. Maybe he would like Canada.

Regina eased up on his other side. Millie noticed and seemed to take an unspoken hint.

"I'm going to check on the others," she said, "make sure we find a safe place to camp once it gets dark. I'd like to avoid another massacre."

She nodded at Regina, then doubled her pace to catch up with Chris. Once she was several strides ahead, Regina nudged Beck's shoulder with hers.

"*Another* massacre?" she asked. "That's sounds like an interesting story. Then again, it could be any of your stories."

Beck chuckled, then hitched. "Don't make me laugh. It hurts to laugh."

"Sorry. Didn't mean to hurt you."

They walked in silence for a minute before Beck put his hand in hers. He felt heat rush from his chest into his cheeks. It was a sensation he wasn't sure he'd ever feel again.

"Thanks for back there," he said. "You saved me."

"I thought you were dead."

"Really?"

"Leo told me you were dead. He told all of us that. Then when I saw Millie, I told her you were dead. She was confused but thought I had learned something she didn't know. A big lack of communication."

"I'm not that easy to kill."

"Especially with me around," she said. "Am I right?"

Beck laughed again and caught his breath. He grabbed his side and grunted.

Regina put her hand on his back. "I'm sorry. I made you laugh again."

"It's okay. Like I said, you saved me. You can do whatever you want."

He took her hand, and they started walking again. The fading sunlight hit her in such a way that she appeared to glow. Her eyes twinkled. A dimple pocked her cheek when she smiled. Had he noticed a dimple there before? He didn't remember a dimple.

"You saved *me*," she said. "More than once."

"True," he said. "I did."

"What's next, Beck? For us?"

Beck sighed. "I guess we're going to Canada together."

Regina smiled again. "I guess so." She glanced over at him and squeezed his hand. "Are you going to be okay?"

"Yeah. My ribs will heal soon enough. I'll be back to new."

She shook her head. "That's not what I meant."

He glanced at her, confused. "I don't understand."

"You don't have a quest. No grand adventure in front of you. Are you okay with that?"

Beck looked ahead and paid attention to the groups of people marching ahead of him. They were all headed north. Uncertainty awaited them at Churchill Downs. The road beyond would be treacherous. And Canada, oh Canada. That was an unknown. Plus, the biggest adventure of all was holding his hand.

He brought her hand to his lips and kissed it. "Yes. I'm okay with it."

"Good," she said.

It was good. Everything was good. Beck almost smiled.

Then a demon whispered in his ear.

Acknowledgements

To my wife and children, I am endlessly grateful for their support and patience.

Thanks also to the pros who make these books better than when they found them. Editors Felicia Sullivan and Sabrina Jean, copy editor Pauline Nolet, cover creator Hristo Kovatliev, and formatting wizard Stef McDaid are wonderful collaborators.

Kevin Pierce is the voice of this series and brings it to life.

Also, much appreciation my beta readers, Steve Kremer and Bob Chamness. And always, to you readers for your loyalty and honest feedback, many thanks.